DEAD

Jan Edwards is the UK author of the award-winning Bunch Courtney Investigations, a series of crime novels set during the Second World War.

She has published over fifty short stories in crime, horror, fantasy and mainstream anthologies including *The Mammoth Book of Folk Horror*, *Criminal Shorts*, *The Book of Extraordinary New Sherlock Holmes Stories*, volumes 1 and 2, and appears in multiple volumes of the *MX Books of New Sherlock Holmes Stories*. She is a member of the Crime Writers' Association.

The Bunch Courtney Investigations

Winter Downs
In Her Defence
Listed Dead
In Cases of Murder
Deadly Plot

Other Titles by Jan Edwards

Sussex Tales
Fables and Fabrications
Leinster Gardens and Other Subtleties
A Small Thing for Yolanda

https://janedwardsblog.wordpress.com/

https://www.facebook.com/Janedwardsbooks

DEADLY PLOT

A Bunch Courtney Investigation

Jan Edwards

The Penkhull Press

Published by The Penkhull Press
Staffordshire, UK
www.penkhullpress.co.uk

Acknowledgements

Writing is a lonely pastime but never as insular as you might think. I have always had massive support from the Renegade Writers Group's regulars with their honest opinions, suggestions and corrections, which are always appreciated.

Thanks to Misha Herwin for hammering out the kinks at our many coffee klatches and for her patience in reading and red-penning all of those early drafts; to Barry Lillie and Mike Chinn for research pointers; to Paul and Kath Finch for their encouragement and advice; to Kerry Parsons, Kath Middleton, Jill Doyle and all of the other reviewers and bloggers who put the word around; and most of all my thanks to Peter Coleborn, best friend and best of editors whose eagle eyes make my manuscripts fit to be read, and fabulous design skills that make my books pleasing to the eye!

Deadly Plot has been a long time in the plotting but it's here at all last – and Bunch Courtney will return again with her sixth Investigation.

Dedication

For Carolyn Caughey's "Weirdos Workshop",
where it all began. You know who you are!

Thursday 18th December 1941

The chattering lines of tin lids and seashells strung across Wyncombe's Victory Gardens were designed to scare off the crows, and the rotting corpse beneath them should have deterred most people in much the same way. To Rose "Bunch" Courtney, threading her way through the crowd gathering by the village hall, neither theory appeared to be holding water.

The police team excavating the far side of the playing field had attracted the usual crowd of onlookers. Bunch's focus, as she picked her way across the mud, was fixed on three familiar figures standing a little apart from the rest, with their backs turned towards her, their shoulders hunched against a December wind.

"We don't want to be standing out here for too long. That wind is bitter." DCI William Wright tugged his collar a little closer. "All right, Carter. You'd better tell me what we have."

"Doc Letham's still examining the remains," DS Carter replied. "He hasn't said much except to confirm that the deceased is a human male and has been dead for several months."

"I was first on the scene, Sir," PC Botting added. "It looks as if the body was scavenged by foxes. Or disturbed by our parsnip thief."

"Parsnip thievery?" Wright turned a laugh into a cough as he realised Botting was quite serious. "That's a new one on me. Is it worth your time, Botting?"

"You wouldn't think so, Sir, but we've had a spate of produce being stolen these past months and tempers are running hot," Botting replied. "Vegetables may not be on ration but prices 'ave bin rising sharpish."

"My missus was telling me a decent onion'll cost you more than a good steak," said Carter. "Not that there's onions to rustle this late in the year."

"Cattle rustling I'd understand, but onions and parsnips? That's common theft at best." Wright rumbled. "And I think it's fair to assume vegetables of any kind were not directly involved here."

Bunch stumbled on a grass tussock and muttered a choice word or two, loud enough for Botting to glance behind him. "Mornin' Miss Rose," he called.

The three men turned to face her and she half-expected to be waved back but they merely watched as she tramped the final few paces, and she could feel the waves of disapproval rolling towards her as she came to halt at Wright's side. "Good morning, William. Found yourself a body, I hear. Anyone I'm likely to know?" she said. "That I can identify for you, I mean."

"Morning to you, Rose. I wondered how long it would be before you arrived," Wright growled. "I was going to call you when we knew more."

"No need for that. The Wyncombe grapevine is terribly efficient. I would've been here sooner but I have other duties." Wright topped the regulation five feet ten inches but she was tall enough to view him almost eye-to-eye. She stepped closer, waiting for him to comment. He looked away and she berated herself for giving in to a triumphant smirk. Her movie-mad Land Army girls had dubbed him Leslie Howard to her Margaret Lockwood. *Simply because she and I are both brunettes*, she thought. *But he's looking thinner than Howard ever did.* Bunch found both the actor and the detective attractive and never quite knew why she and Wright indulged in this same bristling dance at each new meeting, walking around each other in wary circles like a pair of grumpy cats. *Too alike?* she thought. *Or not nearly enough in common? Whichever it is, one of us needs to call Pax, for heaven's sake.* "Gossip aside…" she said aloud, "obviously a murder's taken place. But what's this about thefts? I couldn't help overhearing."

"Seems somebody was nicking veg, Miss, and dug up a body instead." Carter looked at the brassica stalks and parsnip greens strewn next to the path and grunted. "Can't abide sprouts meself, but that's a waste. My missus says Christmas dinner ain't the same without 'em – and they'd have grown well with all that blood and bone."

Carter was an old hand with a gallows humour that could appear insensitive to some. Bunch thought the quip amusing and wondered whether being a consultant for Sussex Constabulary, however artificial that post was, had hardened her outlook on life. *Perhaps,* she thought, *it's what happens in war. One doesn't allow oneself to care so much.* A shout from the diggers caught their attention. Somebody was waving them closer.

"How long ago was he buried here; do you think?" Bunch asked as they picked their way between two allotment plots to the newly dug Sussex clay.

"Doctor Letham reckons a few months at least. The plot holder is…" Carter squinted at his notebook "…Miss Marion Cawston. We haven't been able to contact her. Some kind of journalist, according to Botting." He rolled his eyes at Wright. "Just what we need, Sir. It'll be front page before we know it." He looked back to his notes with a sigh. "The lady on the next plot found the body and reckons this Cawston woman planted a few things when she first took possession in late summer and has hardly been near it since. I gather Cawston's been slipping some Scouts a few bob every month to keep it weeded since then."

"And nobody saw anything unusual when she was planting whatever it was she put in?"

Carter shook his head. "Plots were all rotavated by the groundskeeper to mark 'em out. That was to start people off an' stop any rows about borders an' that. It was just a case of her makin' some holes and plonking the seedlings in. The body was far enough down for her not to disturb it, even with a decent dibber."

"Would they grow in that?" asked Bunch.

Carter shrugged and looked a little sheepish. "Not well. I mean … joking aside, blood and bonemeal's a good fertiliser but not when it's that fresh. And he was a bit further down than dibber's depth."

"Carter has a point," said Wright. "With a body any closer to the surface, would the smell have been noticed? By the foxes if nobody else."

"Depends," Carter replied. "It was buried fresh and that delays the rot, so it wasn't noticed till now."

Bunch gave the sergeant an approving stare. "You seem to know a lot about bodies and gardens."

"Bodies I know a lot more about than I'd like. Gardens? I've had a plot down Barber Way for a couple of years. I had to let it go. Not enough daylight hours to keep it going."

"Hidden talents." Bunch nodded at the grave. "Any idea who he is? Or how he died?"

"Nary a clue," Wright admitted. "Letham won't commit himself until the postmortem. You know what he's like." He removed his homburg and rubbed the top of his head as he regarded the village worthies gathered a little way off. "You know the drill, Carter. Start by taking statements from anyone that's breathed hard near this place."

"Which basically means the entire village," Bunch added. "The village hall is used by everyone."

"Then yes. Everyone. Nobody missing locally, I suppose?"

"We've been losing familiar faces every week. You've heard about the changes in conscription regs coming up next year?"

"Same here," said Carter. "We've been losing many more officers since they raised the conscription age. Now it's the girls."

"Everyone trying to get in with their enlistment choice before the call up papers arrive," Wright added. "One of ours went for basic ATS training last month. She thought she could get WRNS because she belongs to a yacht club, but was turned down."

"Only need a pulse for the army," Carter muttered.

Bunch snorted. Her stint with the British Expeditionary Force had ended after a horrific crash saw her invalided out of the ATS; a dismissal that still rankled. "They all want to get into the WAAF or WRNS," she snapped. "They think it's all glamorous uniforms and officers. I've heard most don't have a snowball's chance without the right contacts or a special skill that's required. Most will get ATS or even WLA. Anything to avoid the factory jobs."

"I can see why not many would choose munitions."

"Too dammed dangerous. Engineering might be better, I suppose. Most won't get a choice now, any more than the chaps do. But they try."

"None of which answers the question," said Wright. "Are there any instances of people going missing in the late summer? Call-ups aside."

"I don't think so though I may not be the best person to ask. Frankly, I've hardly been into the village of late." Bunch looked around at what was left of the playing field and sighed. "Our parish council was adamant that the square and some of the outfield was to be left uncultivated. Summer cricket was good for morale, you see. If you want my opinion, they'll have a job putting any sort of team together next summer. Meanwhile we're trying to feed ourselves with a village full of pensioners and children. They only dug up this much of the outfield because Granny left them without a choice."

"I wondered why the plots were all around the edges like that. I shouldn't wanna be the one fielding a six and crashing across somebody's prize onions." Carter chuckled.

"The plots on this side only went in after the last season ended," Bunch replied. "I think most people might be chary about working this one now, after it's had a body buried in it." She waved a hand at the team still digging among the brassicas. "God alone knows I'm not squeamish but not sure I would fancy eating something grown on top of a corpse, no matter how short we are on sprouts for Christmas lunch."

"Any help you could give would be appreciated. If you are able?"

"I will do what I can." *Is he now asking me to get involved in the case? He should make up his mind.* Bunch couldn't deny a macabre thrill in having this fresh investigation appearing on her doorstep. She had turned down a consulting detective job back in the late summer; it had come mid-harvest and yes, even with the aid of a *Harvest Camp* they had been hard pushed to get every available grain into store. Her mother's death had been a far more pressing motivation. She would be lying, however, if she said she hadn't missed the challenge in pitting her wits against very human problems. The more grisly aspects of crime she was less keen on, and she moved closer to the crime scene with certain reservations.

Dr Letham, the county pathologist, got to his feet as she came within a few paces and pulled the green woollen balaclava away from his mouth. "Miss Courtney, hello my dear. Excuse me for not shaking hands." He waved his gloved fingers at her and grinned. "Not much to see as yet."

"Then tell me what there is." She pulled the plaid scarf tied over her short dark hair a little further across her face, against the smell.

Letham sniffed and wrinkled his nose. "I suppose he is a little ripe. It takes a while for a body to decompose when it's buried but it will, given enough time. Probably why the foxes dug this chap out now, of course."

"Do you often get foxes digging chaps up?" Bunch asked.

"If they are hungry enough and usually when the body is closer to the surface. This one was approximately four feet down, which is about the maximum depth our little wild canids can detect decay. The top eighteen inches or so had been loosened by the cultivation and that allowed the odours to creep out. The plot holder was obviously not a fan of that double digging the gardening chap on the BBC has been advising, or it would have come to light much sooner." He paused, waiting to see if anyone commented, and smiled. "The nub of which is that while it may not be the sexton's full six feet in the graveyard it's quite deep enough and doubtless why it took a while to detect him."

"You can be sure it's male?" Wright asked.

"Perfectly. Decomposition is in fact not that advanced. Male, aged between twenty and forty." He grimaced. "I'll try to narrow it down further when I've cleaned him up. Approximately five foot eight inches in height. Dark hair. Unidentified military styled clothing – extensively damaged. Old Reynard may have ripped it apart in his efforts to get at the flesh but I imagine all insignia was removed at time of death, so there's no means of identification that we've found yet. Our little *vulpes-vulpes* had a high old time overnight and the crows had their share when the sun came up, so our chap is a bit of a mess. When I get him on my slab I'll know more. As luck would have it, he landed face down in solid clay when he was rolled into his grave, which stopped the crows making too many inroads. They go for the eyes, you know. Eye sockets are the easiest way to get at the brains." He cocked his head at Bunch and smiled an apology. "Too much? Sorry. My point is that we may still have what passes for an identifiable face."

Letham's well-meant solicitude gave Bunch a need to prove her murder scene credentials and she edged forward to peer into the hole. Beside Letham's booted feet the mangled body lay half on its side. Its face – *It,* she thought, *don't attach identifying pronouns. This is just a body, all right. The person it belonged to has long gone.* She swallowed hard and bent to look a little closer. The corpse was pressed into the water pooling beneath it. The right arm was missing below the elbow, presumably scavenged by the fox. The left arm was curled up beneath the head. Exposed left leg and buttock were also badly mauled so that the colours of dead flesh and mud were marled together. The knees were bent up so that in life it must have made an untidy ball. *So casual,* she thought. *This wasn't a burial. It was a dump. Disposed of like some diseased animal carcass.*

She wondered why this cadaver affected her more than previous cases. Of all the bodies she had been asked to deal with, this was the least body-like, up to and including the headless corpse of Kitty Shenton on her and Wright's last case together in May: a young woman's body had been crammed into a steamer trunk and left on a railway platform, and Bunch had come very close to throwing up at the sight, despite her nursing training. She was aware now of Letham watching her, and recalled the stories of his vomit chart, recording all the coppers who had lost their last meal at a scene or in his Brighton mortuary. She swallowed a few more times before stepping back to meet Letham's eyes. "Not much to see," she said. "You'll still be able to find a cause of death?"

"Patience, my dear. You will have to wait for my report, the same as Wright, here. Let me get this chap back to the mortuary and then I can begin to determine any facts."

"You must have some thoughts," Wright said.

Letham looked down at the body for a long moment and then back at Wright. "Given that somebody took advantage of, I gather, newly dug earth to dispose of him, I would hazard a guess that his death wasn't planned. And we've both seen enough bodies buried in a hurry to know they are seldom poisoned. That type of killing takes time and planning. I suspect he'll have been strangled or stabbed or shot, or…" Letham made a hammering gesture in the air "…our old pal, blunt force." He grinned and flapped his rubber gloved hands at the trio. "Now off you all trot. Quicker I get on with this the quicker you will have your answers."

"Let me know when you have him ready."

"Tomorrow afternoon, all being well. Shall we say three o'clock?"

"Three." Wright agreed and turned to look at Bunch. "Shall we see you there?"

"Sorry. I would but it's the livestock market in Storrington. We've steers going in for auction and the last of our capons for Christmas have just gone to the Ministry of Food. Not that we get much of a price from them but I like to keep an eye on it, all the same… I would like to be involved with this case, if I may. With it being on my doorstep."

"Understood. I shall keep you posted. Meanwhile perhaps you'd like to help us with the plot owner?"

"I shall try, though the name isn't familiar. Marion Cawston, you say?"

Wright nodded. "Botting tells me she has a flat over the chemist shop in Wyncombe High Street."

"Then she'll be easy to find."

Saturday 20th

"I gather you've become embroiled in this brouhaha at the Victory Gardens." Beatrice Courtney eased back into her favourite chair and propped her walking cane against its arm. "Please do take care. Village politics have no mercy."

"Hard to ignore a murder when it's on our doorstep. And it's not a popularity contest, Granny. Some poor soul was murdered."

"Indeed. But some people have a habit of taking these things quite personally, if you start questioning them right and left."

"We don't know who the victim is as yet. Botting is certain he's not local but he'll be going door to door to verify that. I have no intention of helping him, have no fear on that score."

"Well, just take care. And do remember that Daphne will be here for lunch. Other than Sunday Service it must be two weeks since you last saw your sister. Or your niece. You should take an interest, given that Georgi is currently your heir."

Bunch rolled her eyes. Beatrice's pointed digs at her lack of husband, and by inference her own heir, were becoming tiresome. "Yes, it will be lovely to see Dodo and the sprog. I shan't be down in the village for long. Wright and I are going to interview the woman who was cultivating that particular plot."

"Marion Cawston, isn't it? Theadora used to read her column in some American magazine she had sent over. All manner of tattle about the great and the good. I am positive Cawston was the name."

And I bet you read the magazine cover to cover when mummy had finished with it, thought Bunch. Beatrice was always a font of knowledge in matters of local gossip and country politics, and Bunch had often speculated on her grandmother keeping a copy of Debrett's by her bedside in order to memorise pedigrees before she went to sleep. "You know more about her than I do," she said. "I don't suppose you kept any of those magazines?"

"I doubt it, but ask Cook. She loves to hoard that kind of thing." Beatrice peered at her granddaughter, eyes glittering with mischief. "Speaking of gossip, Daphne telephoned while you were out. She was Maurice this and Maurice that. Those two are rapidly becoming quite inseparable."

Bunch wasn't sure how to reply without causing offence. "He's a nice chap," she said at last. "If slightly boring."

"Perhaps. Nice to see someone in the family has a social life."

"Stop it, Granny." Bunch avoided Beatrice's eye as she steered the subject away from romances for the second time. "What else have you heard about Miss Cawston? Any snippets that might be useful?"

"She's proving to be something of a talking point." The frustration was clear in Beatrice's tone. "You know how I hate to interfere with village matters but there had been complaints about poorly tended allotment sites, and the committee chair has been reluctant to do anything about it."

"Of course." Bunch didn't bother to hide her grin. Beatrice controlled almost every committee in Wyncombe, like the skilled marionettist she was, and little went on without her knowledge or approval. *She simply takes it for granted that the village will agree, because she's always right, in her mind.* "I assume there was some anger over one of those plots being given to Cawston because she was an incomer?"

Beatrice waved her hand. "There were some objections, I believe, from those who felt outsiders should have been ineligible. It gave rise to a belief from the same few that outsiders are behind the vegetable thefts."

"On what evidence?"

"None at all, I'm afraid. Why on earth would they think a woman like Marion Cawston would bother stealing a few cabbages I cannot imagine. The gossip, however, has prompted a rise of 'us against them'. This corpse turning up is hardly going to help matters. Tongues…" Beatrice intoned "…will wag."

"Along with wringing of hands and cries of 'we'll all be murdered in our beds'."

"Precisely."

"What else do they say about Marion Cawston?" Bunch asked. "And have you inspected her patch yourself?"

"I haven't gone down to see it for myself. I'm a little past tottering around the playing fields in the middle of the winter."

"Of course you're not, Granny."

Beatrice let out an unladylike sniff. "Very sweet of you, child, but you know perfectly well that I can barely manage the length of my own garden these days."

"Lewis tells me your hip will improve with rest."

"My joints perhaps, but this old ticker won't." Beatrice tapped her chest lightly. "Rose, dearest girl, I have been prodded and pulled by the best and they tell me that my heart is damaged beyond their ability to repair, and that one day it will simply cease. Lewis, on the other hand, is an old quack who tells me what he thinks I'm paying him to hear. Charles always said that he couldn't cure bacon."

Bunch didn't know how to respond. Beatrice liked to give the impression of indestructibility despite her health being poor for some years. So what had changed? *She's a creaky gate, as Cook often said, when she had thought the family were elsewhere. And everyone knows that creaky gates hold on the longest.* Rising to the challenges of running the WVS, and all of the many village emergencies that war had raised, had given Beatrice a new lease of life – until Theadora had died earlier in the year. Beatrice had not been close to her daughter-in-law yet the loss seemed to have hit the older woman hardest of all the family. These frequent references to her long-deceased husband in recent months had Bunch wondering if her grandmother was dwelling too much on her own mortality. Bunch did not like to think about how she herself would cope if the unthinkable were to happen and she were to lose her grandmother in the near future. "Perhaps we should take a trip up to Harley Street to see Dr Ephrin?"

"I don't think so. It would mean staying at Thurloe Square and ever since poor Theadora passed away Edward has turned the town house into a Whitehall annex. Daphne went up to town for a little shopping last week and some military oik at the door decided that as her ID card said Tinsley she could not be a Courtney. Fortunately, Henry Marsham turned up and vouched for her." The older woman arched an eyebrow. "I gather he asked after you. Gilsworth tells me he's there quite often with Edward on WD business. Such a charming young man."

And we're back to match making. Bunch wondered if Beatrice's obsessional attempts at galloping her eldest grandchild up the aisle was all a part of this sense of her time left on earth being finite. Or that the family line should not rest on Georgi alone, a fatherless babe in arms. She examined her cigarette and studiously tapped ash into the glass tray and pondered on what else the housekeeper at Thurloe Square had divulged about her relationship with Henry Marsham. Gilsworth was the soul of discretion where the family was concerned, but if asked, Bunch seriously doubted she would be able to keep anything hidden from its matriarch. *Granny trumps the heir every time,* she thought. *Or as the vicar would say, be sure your sins will find you out.* "Henry's nice enough." She leaned forward to put out the cigarette. "I thought Daddy was supposed to be here today to help sort out the Christmas boxes."

"Ah. I was coming to that." Beatrice pursed her lips. "Sutton was here earlier to pack a steamer trunk. Your father, it would seem, has been called away for Christmas. Trust Edward to leave delivering that bombshell to the ever-loyal valet instead of picking up the telephone and telling me himself."

"What? Why?"

"One word…"

"Winnie?"

Beatrice nodded. "Isn't it always?"

"That has to be all about the Americans. Having their fleet attacked in their own harbour has stirred the anthill rather, and dragged them into the war too. We should assume he will be away for the New Year."

"He'll be gone for a few weeks I imagine. I did try to elicit a little more detail. Sutton assured me that Edward will try to call later but has nose to tail meetings for the whole of today and into the night."

"All very hush-hush. I can understand why he wouldn't trust word of his trip to the telephone system." Bunch toyed with her cup, sipping at the rapidly cooling contents more for want of something to occupy her hands than any liking for tepid coffee. This would be the first Christmas without Theadora, and she was taken aback that her father would also be spending it away from them. *I know going away is not his choice,* she thought. *At least I sincerely hope not. There must be others who could go. Unless he wants to be away from here.* "It won't be the first time," she said, her tone as bright as she could muster. "When he and Mummy where in the FO we had some jolly old Christmases without them." She pushed her cup away, an abrupt motion that slopped the half-drunk contents into the saucer. "I've already got Charman plucking the capons and the gifts boxed up for me to take around. It's rather fun visiting everyone, though I do rather miss the servant's ball."

"As do I my dear."

"Yes. Anyway… I have it all set for Christmas Eve." Bunch smiled brightly. "A new tradition in the making."

"Eminently more practical than Boxing Day. It goes without saying there should not be any mention of the capons to William. I am certain handing them out as gifts contravenes all kinds of rationing board regulations."

"It does. Though I shan't say anything if you don't." Bunch sat back to gaze out of the window. "You've heard there isn't to be a Boxing Day Hunt this year? I thought perhaps a shoot to make up for it might be a good plan. We haven't raised any chicks but there are still enough pheasants and partridges up near Hascombe Wood to make it worthwhile for a one-day shoot. And if nothing else we can bag some rabbits and pigeons. Few less to eat our spring barley. Invite perhaps a dozen guns?"

"It may be a little short notice for some."

"I shall put the word around. Better warn Cook and Knapp. Now I need to go and get ready before Wright gets here. Have fun in Harvey Nick's if you decide to go." She went to drop a kiss on her grandmother's forehead and beat a rapid retreat before conversation returned to the town house and Henry Marsham.

Beatrice had been conniving with the Marshams to match up Bunch with their son since her coming-out year, despite her involvement with the late and much-lamented Jonathan Frampton. She had nothing against Henry. Far from it, she was fond of him and felt he had grown in character over the past few years. They had indulged in occasional nights of mutually consoling sex, but she had never viewed him as husband material. With the Perringham estate to run, marriage was not her priory though she knew her family thought otherwise, and she could not help wondering, as she dashed up to her room to fetch her coat, how she could deflect this latest "marry off Bunch" campaign.

When she reappeared in the hall, pulling on her reefer jacket, Bella scampered up and down the hall leaving marks on the floor that Bunch knew Knapp was bound to comment on. "Bella, sit," she told the over-excited dog. "You can't come this morning. Sit." The dog sat, head canted to one side, quivering with excitement. *She's Henry's dog*, she thought, *bequeathed to me because he'd been stationed somewhere that precludes dogs? Or because it creates a link between us? Damn the man.* "Not now, Bella." She bent to ruffle the springer's silky ears and pat her ample rump. "I shall take you out later to run off some podge. You've been hanging around Granny and Alice far too much cadging titbits!" She glanced up at the sound of a car pulling up at the front door. "There's Wright. Off you go to Granny." Shooing the dog away, she crammed her felted fedora onto her head and scooted out of the front door before Wright had a chance to ring the bell.

"You're late," she said as Glossop, Wright's ATS driver, opened the Wolseley's door.

"Am I?" Wright eyed her curiously. "You seem rather eager to get away."

"Don't ask."

"Then I won't." Wright waited for Glossop to start the engine and told her, "Wyncombe High Street. The flat we're looking for is above the pharmacy."

"Yes Sir."

Bunch settled back in the seat, adjusting her scarf and tugging her gloves a little further onto her hands. "What do we know about our absent gardener?" she asked.

"We're not any wiser than we were on Thursday. She had a flat down on the coast until Easter of last year."

"Granny said something similar. What about our victim?"

"Letham confirmed a male, early twenties. He also found the bullet lodged in the victim's left side, which has gone for testing. A flesh wound at the time of death, which I gather would have slowed him down, but was not fatal. Death came from that perennial favourite, the blunt instrument. Possibly a pipe or metal bar of some kind. That's all Letham would tell me at this point. I gather he's still looking into other aspects."

"The victim wasn't liked by at least one person, or possibly more than one, obviously. Do we know the deceased's nationality?"

"Italian. His outer garments were badly damaged but once we had pieced them together they are clearly a uniform. Interestingly, Letham thinks much of the damage was done by a sharp knife and not animals as he'd first thought. The fox predation on the remains came after the burial had been disturbed. We're looking for POWs or internees who may have gone missing in the late summer."

"Is there any reason to believe Miss Cawston was involved in this Italian soldier's death?"

"Other than being buried in her allotment? None whatsoever. She just hasn't been easy to pin down for interview, however, and that always gives us cause for thought."

"Has she been evasive? Or simply absent?"

"That is what we're here to find out."

Bunch emerged from the car outside of Brice's pharmacy and peered into the shopfront as she waited for Wright to join her. The Brices had always prided themselves on their Christmas display and she thought that there was no doubt, it was far less colourful than previous years, but they could hardly be blamed for that. Since the Ministry of Supply had declared a paper shortage gift wrapping had become a distant memory, and what paper decorations there were had been confined to what had been saved from the years before. *And they do at least have a window*, she thought. *Which is more than Selfridges or Bourne & Hollingsworth have in Oxford Street right now.*

Daffyd Brice and his wife Nancy had made a valiant effort. Their shop windows were decked with boughs of holly and any other evergreens they could lay hands on, all of which was arranged around what Bunch realised was probably Brice's own family Nativity set. A range of twelve-inch plaster figures, which had been carefully repainted by Mrs Brice in primary colours, were arranged around a sturdy wooden stable and crib of the pharmacist's own making. Bunch had rarely found time to shop in the village in the previous weeks, and she gazed in awe, mixed with a certain bemusement, at the merchandise that Brice had thought suitable, or more probably whatever he had available. *The vanity sets I understand*, she thought. *Excellent gifts. But Epsom salts? And Beechams Liver Pills? In anticipation of Christmas blow-out lunches no doubt, but I can't imagine many people will have saved enough rations to over-indulge.*

"Where's the door?" Wright startled her from her musings. "Do we need to go through the shop?"

"No, sorry, I was just admiring Mr Brice's window. This way." She plunged down the narrow twitten between Brice's and Wyncombe Stores and paused at a solid ledge and brace gate on the pharmacy's side of the passage. Thumbing the latch on the gate Bunch stepped into the small yard. To the left was another yard door, heavily padlocked and labelled "Brice's Pharmacy – Private". Straight ahead was a house door bearing a discreet sign declaring "20A High Street".

Wright reached forward and pressed the bell for the flat, then pressed again when there was no response. "She's supposed to be expecting us," he muttered and peered through the single diamond pane in the door.

"Do you think she's gone out?"

"I sincerely hope not." He rang a third time.

They heard footsteps on the stair beyond, the rattle of keys, sliding of bolts, before the door opened slowly. "Yes?" The woman's tone was cautious and just a whisker away from belligerent.

"Miss Cawston?"

"Yes."

"Chief Inspector Wright and Miss Rose Courtney. I believe PC Botting told you to expect us?" We're here to ask you a few questions."

Marion Cawston opened the door as far as the stair behind her permitted. "Chief Inspector. Sorry to keep you waiting. You would not believe how many neighbours – who've barely spoken to me before this week – have come calling." Her smile became rueful. "Being on this side of things is a lesson in door-stepping any hack should try. Quite a revelation. Did you have many questions? Only I'm not sure I can be much help. I've given a statement to the constable with everything I know. Which isn't a great deal, I can tell you. It was a terrible thing to happen." She clutched her cardigan close around her neck, giving her visitors a quizzical look, and gave what seemed to Bunch a brief roll of her eyes. "I guess you didn't come to stand around here all morning. Come on up. I don't mean to be rude but I can only give you a half-hour. I have a meeting in Storrington at midday that I simply can't cancel. Taken me weeks to set things up and it'll take weeks more to pin him down again. You know how it is." She flashed a vivid grin and walked back up the steep staircase without waiting for a reply.

Bunch had seen how people's demeanour generally varied between gruff and comically polite in Wright's presence. There was something in this woman's manner that felt different. A confidence that had little connection with guilt or innocence and everything to do with utter self-assurance. This was a woman not easily intimidated.

As they followed Cawston upstairs Bunch could not help but notice that the well-muscled legs of an athlete were encased in expensive hosiery without a single snag or ladder repair.

Since the summer, when a pair of stockings had come to require two precious clothing coupons, even Bunch had taken to wearing slacks a great deal more often. She wondered why Cawston's meeting on her day off warranted such profligacy. *Not worried about rationed hosiery like the rest of us, it would seem. A well-connected beau perhaps? Or an illicit supply? No, that's being rather judgemental; shame on me. With her US connections I'll bet she has them shipped over.*

Cawston had reached the top stair and opened the only door off the tiny landing into the flat's main room. "Can I offer you tea?"

"Yes, thank you," Wright said.

Her face tightened momentarily, as if she had hoped he would say no, but the smile dutifully returned as she vanished into the kitchen.

Presumably because she wants us to be away. Looking around, Bunch imagined that the furnishings came with the accommodation because none of it matched the trim chic Miss Cawston. A heavy horse-hair sofa and carved-oak sideboard, complete with mirrored top, dominated the space and she considered briefly how both could have been squeezed up the staircase. Two mismatched cottage armchairs flanked a surprisingly modern hearth tiled in shiny beige squares. Between two of three other doors in the room was a drop-leaf table with a kitchen chair at each end.

The room was spotlessly clean but somehow depressing. It took Bunch a moment to pinpoint why that should be, and then it struck her. There was not a single photograph or ornament on display, just a few magazines on the dresser. *Soulless as a hotel suite. Not so much as a library book on show. She may sleep in this flat but she doesn't live here.*

Cawston reappeared with a tea tray and set it on the occasional table. "Do sit down." She poured tea into plain china cups. "Milk? I can't offer you sugar, I'm afraid. I've only just got home. Not had time to collect my ration." She perched herself on the sofa, offering another of her film-star smiles, and Bunch suddenly realised what was off about her. She had seen similar on the faces of politicians and hotel dance instructors. *A neutral smile, worn from habit to put people at their ease, and not an ounce of conviction.*

"No, thank you. I gave up simply ages ago," Bunch replied. "Everybody seems to have these days." She sat carefully and accepted the cup. "Thank you."

Cawston handed one to Wright. "It's a terrible business. I don't believe I shall ever be able to eat anything I planted there. Quite makes me shiver to think I have been growing food over a body."

"There's nothing left of the victim now," Wright said. "The pathologist was very careful to remove all of the remains."

"Nevertheless… Have you identified the poor chap yet?"

"Sadly no. Beyond that he was not local we have very little information."

Bunch took a sip of tea to hide her surprise. She would take bets that the locals would have known the nationality of the victim almost as soon as the police, in that unerring way that they did, seemingly snatching facts from the ether. And Cawston lived above the commercial premises of Wyncombe's gossip-in-chief.

"How did the victim die? I'm guessing not suicide. Was he shot?"

"We are waiting for the pathologist's report," he lied. "Why would you leap to guns?"

"No reason." Cawston shrugged. "A guess. We're in the middle of a war … and that's the way a journalist tends to think. Or they do where I come from."

"I see." Wright leaned forward. "We understand that you took over the plot in July or August?"

"I had the go ahead at the end of August. I'm away a great deal with my work so it was late in September before I was able to get anything done. I'll be honest and say I was surprised to get allocated one at all. I only put my name down on the list because Reggie Tallboys persuaded me. I wanted to interview him for my column. Sports in the time of war, that kind of thing."

"There was quite a queue for plots. Why you?"

"I figured it might help me get in with the locals if they

thought I was making an effort to do my bit, as they say around here." She grinned at Bunch. "I don't want to sound critical, but it's been hard to get any sort of acceptance here. It was much easier in Worthing."

"Small village circles are very tight knit," Bunch replied. "What made you choose Wyncombe? Nothing ever goes on here."

"My editor wanted to hear from civilians still living on the south coast. It's the closest thing there is to a front line. Problem is, the military have snapped up almost every bed between Dover and Brighton. What hotels are there with rooms left? As a policeman, I'm sure you know the kind of places that are hired by the night. Or even by the hour." She winked at Bunch's surprise and turned to Wright with a knowing smirk. "I'm sorry Chief Inspector, you were saying?"

Wright lowered his chin to stare at Cawston, holding her gaze for a count of three. "We understood you had enough time to do some work when you took possession of your plot," he said. "And then you stopped tending it altogether. Why didn't you just hand it back?" His change of tack seemed to confuse Cawston for a moment.

"Well … not exactly. Okay, yes, Tallboys said I needed to have something in the ground or I'd lose the plot. Said it was a good place to get to know the real people of Wyncombe and I thought perhaps he had a point. Rejecting the plot so soon was never going to endear me to the neighbourhood. He gave me a tray of plants. Some kind of cabbage? And a packet of seeds. I have to admit I cheated and paid a couple of Boy Scouts to plant them and keep the garden tidy. I fully intended to give it up in the New Year."

"What keeps you here?" Wright leafed through his notebook. "We don't seem to have much information on you."

"No? Well, there's not that much to know. I'm a journalist, which is why I'm travelling around so much."

"What paper do you write for?" Wright asked.

"I have one main American editor who commissions my column." She gestured at the small stack of magazine on dresser. "Though I'll write for whomever will buy a story. I've been here in England since last fall. Sent in a few pieces on the London bombings. As a follow up to Ed Morrow, in a manner of speaking."

"Do you know Mr Morrow?" Bunch asked. "My father has met him a few times and we all heard at least some of his broadcasts from London on the Blitz. Rather emotional, but frightfully good."

"Do I know him? Not really." Cawston bent to pour more tea, hiding a sudden flush of her cheeks. "I mean we've crossed paths, but I don't move in his exalted circles. I'm just a common old hack writer." Cawston flashed another of her dazzling smiles. "It would be exciting though, wouldn't it? Foreign correspondent. Except that I'm not entirely foreign." She looked from one to the other, wide-eyed and nervous now. "My usual editor wants stories of cheery farmers and stoic housewives. Murdered men among the cabbages won't sit well with the American public."

"I can imagine," Wright replied. "I understand you have dual nationality?"

Cawston gave a small chuckle. "You've been checking up on me. In point of fact I have three passports. British and American and also one for South Africa. I assume it's still valid. My husband was a South African national, you see."

"Was?"

"His plane went down under fire somewhere along the Egyptian coast. That was a little over a year ago now, so I don't suppose he's coming back."

"Oh. I'm terribly sorry," Bunch said.

"Thank you."

Bunch smiled. She was surprised that this woman all but admitted so readily that her husband flew for King Farouk when Egypt's position was on a knife edge. *But then there was no telling what an Allied pilot would be doing there.* "I'm sorry," she murmured again. "It must be very hard for you."

Cawston's shoulders raised minimally. "We're at war. One can't expect a great deal else."

"You have no family here in this country?"

"I'm the only child of two only children and we led a rather nomadic lifestyle. My father is an architect. You may have heard of Gabriel Cawston? He was drafting plans for the city of Cairo when war was declared. I somehow doubt that will ever happen now. Or perhaps it will? I rather suppose it depends on whether the fighting reaches that far. I met my husband out there. Married for a whole eight months. I reverted to my maiden name when I came back to England."

"Have you lived here in Britain before … before now?" Wright asked.

"As a child, for a short while. Father had a contract in Wales. It rained a lot as I recall." She pulled her thick cardigan close around her. "We came to Britain for short breaks, until my grandparents passed away. We had a preference for warmer climates and these islands are so damned cold. I swear my toes have not been warm in months. As for the rain? England may be the renowned green and pleasant land, but at least you don't get chilblains in the desert. I don't know how people survive it at all."

"We all have our methods." Bunch smiled brightly. "I was at school with two Cyrenaician sisters. They claimed to be royalty," she chortled. "Probably were. The head was completely gaga over them. Anyway, I remember them being just the same. Always complaining they were so ruddy cold, even in August. Daddy was surprised when I told him because he said the nights got very cold in the desert."

"They really do." Cawston made a show of looking at her watch. "I'm very sorry but is there anything else you want to ask? I do need to get off shortly. A girl has to earn her crust, you know."

"Only to ask if you'd remembered anything odd while you were working the plot," Wright said.

"Odd in what way?"

"We need your impressions of being there. For instance, did you ever feel you were being watched? Did you notice anybody there, a stranger, someone you didn't recognise?"

"Really, Chief Inspector. I am new to this backwater and I had the temerity to claim a piece of the gardens. People here resented that. On the very few occasions I set foot in that field

I can honestly say yes, I was being watched – by everyone that was ever there. I doubt I know the names of even three of them."

"You say Tallboys was frightfully keen for you to apply for a plot," Bunch added. "Fortunate that your name came up in the draw."

She pulled a face. "From my end it was sheer fluke. I keep telling you, I only made nice to get the Victory Garden story and thought it might give me several more articles. I was wrong as it turns out."

"Made nice?"

Cawston looked at Wright critically, her head tilted. "Not nearly as nice as he would have liked. I'll do many things for a scoop but there's a line to be drawn."

"I heard names were drawn from a hat," Bunch said.

Cawston shrugged. "I've been told. I wasn't there for the draw."

"Are you saying he cheated somehow?"

"I don't see how he could. I just figured he was trying to impress me. Is that all you wanted to know, because I do have to go. I'm sure you appreciate that being late for an interview is never a good start."

"Indeed. Thank you for your help, Miss Cawston." Wright took out his wallet and extracted a card. "If you can recall anything more, please do telephone me." He laid the card on the table, carefully, emphatically. "We'll see ourselves out."

Bunch was still buttoning her coat as she hurried to follow Wright. The two of them clattered down the uncarpeted stairs and emerged into the cold of mid-morning before they spoke again. "Well?" she asked as she wriggled on her gloves and tugged the brim of her hat against the keen breeze.

"She wasn't telling us anything we didn't already know."

"Perhaps she doesn't know any more."

"Perhaps. Except she's a journalist. Why would she stay here of all places? The amount of news she could get would run out in a month."

"Her columns are real enough," Bunch replied.

"Carter is still checking on her history. Especially the

deceased husband."

"You really don't like journalists, do you." Bunch glanced up at a clouded sky and frowned. "What else did you have in mind for today? More interviews?"

"I'd quite like to know a bit more about how these plots were allocated."

"Then you'll want to speak with Reg Tallboys."

"He's a market gardener, I understand?"

"Good God, no. Well yes, he inherited his grandfather's horticultural business. Quite a large one, as it happens, but Reggie's brother manages it all – after the old man died. Reggie has no interest in getting his hands grubby himself. He owns the golf club and captains the local cricket team. Thinks that's far more up his street. We were all surprised when he volunteered to organise the Victory Gardens. Granny thinks it was to save the cricket pitch from the spade, and she may well be right."

"He is a man of means?"

"All means to his ends."

"I take it he isn't popular?"

"Until recently he had always made himself useful."

"Not anymore?"

"The fact that he hadn't joined up didn't go down well in some quarters, even after he made it known the RAMC gave him a category D. Medically unfit." Bunch shook her head. "He's still popular enough with some people, though."

"Just not with you."

"Perhaps I'm being unfair. He does a lot around the village." She looked quickly at Wright and arched a brow as she tugged her scarf close around her neck. "It may explain why Wyncombe CC lost quite so often over the summer. Is that where you want to go now?"

"We do need a word with this Mr Tallboys."

"He can invariably be found at the golf club on a Saturday or Sunday morning, hitting small balls into a hole so far away you can't see it without a flag."

"I thought you went in for all of the sporty stuff."

"Never been a golfer, even if Westmere allowed lady

members." She shrugged at Wright's raised brows. "As I don't play I've never seen it as a windmill worth the tilting. Tennis, yes, just socially. I'm not that good at it if I'm honest. Horses, naturally. Oh, and croquet."

"Croquet? Isn't that a little tame for you?"

"Absolutely not a game for the faint hearted. It's so deliciously funny trying to thwart Granny's cheating."

"How can you cheat at croquet?"

"There are many and various ways and Granny is expert in them all. She's straight as a die in most things but put that mallet in her hand and she'd keep the Borgias on their toes. She would have made an excellent polo player but my grandfather never kept a string. He was a hunting and racing man."

"Not a golfer?"

"Not really."

"Shame. Might have been useful when visiting Mr Tallboys."

"'Alas, alack, and well-a-day.'" Bunch cocked her head at Wright's blank expression. "'What though we wish the cats at play'. *Ballade Of the Optimist* by Lang. He was a favourite of my grandfather. Truth is, with all the best intentions, I'll need to be back at the farm in the next hour or two. The girls have all trotted off to Worthing to do their Christmas shopping. Can't imagine what they will find to buy but I suspect it's more about the trip than buying trinkets. Meanwhile, I have cows to milk."

"You milk cows?" Wright asked. "In the sheds?"

"Yes, in the sheds. You're surprised?" said Bunch. "I am not sure why you should be, and I am rather hurt. It's a basic Land Army skill."

"I thought you'd given up that WLA post."

"I did, but I was asked to take at least some of it back on because the compulsory female conscription will be at full throttle this month, and they need me to oversee the new girls under Perringham's sphere, at the very least."

"Is that a lot of work?"

"Fair to middling." Bunch spread her hands. "The estate covers a little over twenty-five hundred acres when you include all of the tenant farms. When Dodo heard, she asked me to include the Banyards estate, which is another fifteen hundred acres and several tenanted properties. So it could be up to fifty women."

"Sounds like a lot of work."

"We all have to do our bit. I would do it with a little more enthusiasm if it wasn't for all of the damnable paperwork. Nothing the ministries love more than churning out forms."

They turned out of the alleyway and saw PC Botting standing beside the Wolseley talking with Glossop. "Sir." Botting came to attention when he spotted Wright. "And Miss Courtney," he added. "Your sergeant phoned the Police House, Sir. It seems your car radio was out of range."

"Invariably it is out here in the sticks," Wright replied. "Did he say what the flap is about?"

"No Sir. Just to say that it was a very urgent order from the Commissioner."

"Orders from on high. That seldom ends well. All right, Botting. I'll come down to the Police House now and return Carter's call, if I may."

"Yes Sir."

Wright glanced at Bunch. "Do you mind waiting? Or I can get Glossop to take you back to Perringham now?"

"I need to get a few things from Brices first. Perhaps I can wander down to join you afterwards?"

He nodded. "Glossop, if you can take time to check the fuel, there's a garage at the southern end of the village."

"Sir."

"Join me at the Police House when you're done."

Wright strode away with Botting bobbing in his wake, while Glossop eased the car into gear and headed for Watson's Garage, leaving Bunch alone on the pavement. She gave the window display another cursory inspection before pushing the door open.

The shop bell had not finished jangling before Daffyd Brice appeared like a short bespeckled genie. "Oh, Miss Courtney. Good morning to you!"

"Good morning, Brice."

"I was going to send the shop lad up to the Dower house with an order for Lady Chiltcombe. Dr Lewis left the usual prescriptions to be filled. Enough to cover the holidays. Her sleeping powders and medication for her joint pain." The little Welshman tilted his head and smiled." Would it be an imposition if I gave them to you?"

"Not at all. Of course, I can take them."

"He's only a lad, see. Still at school." Brice rummaged under the counter and brought out a small package wrapped in brown parcel paper that had plainly been used previously and carefully ironed. "I worry he'd lose these and they'd be dangerous if a little kiddie found them. Do you need a bag? Only what with the paper shortage…"

"I quite understand. Rules are rules." She took the packet and thrust it deep in her coat pocket. "If you're anything like us at the farm, the only paper we're not short of are infernal ministry forms."

Brice chuckled quietly. "That's about the size of it, Miss. Drowning in 'em, we are. Now then…" he placed both hands on the counter and gazed into her face, beaming expectantly "…is there anything else I can fetch for you?"

"Beechams Powders, if you have them. And some aspirin if there are any."

"That's the Beechams." Brice pulled a box from the shelf behind him. "I have three very small bottles of aspirin. Getting hard to come by now."

"I shall take one. Granny does have the most appalling headaches sometimes and she'd hate to run out."

"Yes, Miss. Will there be anything else?"

"There's a box of men's handkerchiefs in the window."

"For your father, is it?"

"Heavens no. Daddy has enough pocket squares to stretch around Chanctonbury Ring, even if he was here over Christmas."

"Going away?"

"That would be telling more than I know." Bunch winced, realising she had said far too much to an infamously indiscreet man. "You know how my father has always hopped around all over the place and he never tells us where. He is very tied up with things in London."

Brice's cheeks coloured a dull red. "I shouldn't ask, should I? Not these days. Just an old habit, takin' a polite interest. None of my business, and there's thousands of folk missing their family."

"Oh, I was forgetting. Have you heard from your son?"

"No." His features drooped and Bunch was tempted to reach out and pat his arm. Brice was an old busybody but he truly meant no harm by it. "Still listed as MIA," he added quietly. "Mother is beside herself but I keep telling her, the people from the Red Cross are sayin' there's a lot of prisoners not been logged by them as yet. We've not lost hope. And Mother swears she'd know if Glyn was gone."

Bunch was amused by his referring to his wife as Mother but kept a straight face because she knew it was done with a touching amount of affection. She wished that her own family could be half so open. "I'm sure that's right," she murmured. *I hope they won't be disappointed.* "Daddy has spent far more Christmases away than at home. All terribly normal in our house, I'm afraid. The house does seem rather empty these days with…" she worked her tongue around her teeth as she swallowed down the prickle in her throat, "…with just Granny and me most of the time." She made an attempt at a chuckle. "I'm surprised we haven't had Granny's WVS chums foisting boarders on us."

There was pity now in his eyes and Bunch felt grateful and irritated in equal quantities. She had thought she was getting over her mother's death but now and again, at odd moments such as this, it caught at her as a physical pain in the gut. Yet the act of being pitied was alien to her. A change of subject was required. "Dodo insists we all gather at Banyards for Christmas dinner," she said. "And my sister can be quite insistent when she chooses. These kerchiefs are for our cousin because I understand he'll be there. I have no idea what else to get him and I am running out of time."

"I have some badger hair shaving brushes," Brice said.

"Oh yes. And a razor perhaps?"

"Ishh…" Brice breathed in noisily through his teeth. "Blades are unlucky gifts."

"Cook always says that too. It's not something I've ever believed in but I take your point. Especially since those fly boys can be a superstitious crowd. What about that brush set in the leather pouch?"

"Excellent choice." Brice came from behind the counter and picked the set from the window display. "Last one."

He held it up, eyebrows raised hopefully, and Bunch nodded. "I'll take the kerchiefs and the badger brush as well. In case we have unexpected guests." She shrugged and grinned sheepishly. "I am so behind with my shopping. Major Tinsley will be getting a half-box of shotgun cartridges from the gamekeeper's store. Since we don't have a keeper now nobody will miss them."

"And the major will appreciate them no less. Shells are also hard to come by these days."

"Are they any better as a gift than a blade do you think?"

The pharmacist paused, halfway past the raised counter flap, and considered the point. "Never heard anything of the like." He lowered the flap behind him and rummaged for butcher's paper. "Nasty business over at the gardens," he said as he creased and folded a sheet of freshly ironed but plainly used paper around the purchases and whipped a strand of thin twine around the package. "I saw you going up to Miss Cawston's flat. Quite a shock for her, I should think."

"She was surprised," Bunch conceded. "Who wouldn't be? Corpses among the cabbages are not an everyday occurrence. I suppose her not being around much is why it hadn't come to light sooner."

"There was no end of talk when she got that plot," Brice said. "Locals with families to feed could make something of it." He dropped his voice to an undertone. "There was talk at the last committee about taking it off her in the spring."

"Just talk?"

"Mr Tallboys said we should give her another season. I had a chat with him after and he says it's with her writin' for the newspapers. Didn't want us to look bad. Mother thinks there was something going there. Now, Mother and me don't argue much but I don't think our Miss Cawston would see him that way." He gave her a knowing nod. "Him though, he's always been a bit of a one for the girls."

"I'd be surprised if Tallboys carried on this close to home. Pamela would be furious."

"She would. Not that it ever stopped him, mind."

"He's fooled around before now?"

"If it wasn't for remembering his sainted mother, I'd call him a spiv. *Duw uchod.* He's had some very odd sorts down from London a few months ago."

"Really?" Bunch's antenna twitched. Small talk, Beatrice often insisted, was all about these smoky wisps of gossip that pointed to the fire. "Odd, how?"

"Not for me to say, really." He bristled visibly. "They only came the once, mind."

She waited for more but the spark seemed to have fizzled out. "I'd have thought, with Tallboys' mother's family, and Pamela's, you'd get a better sort of..." she prompted.

"Least said." Brice tapped the side of his nose. "But like I told Mother at the time, I might not renew my subs for the golf club next year. Gone downhill, it has. Westmere was his wife's family home, and her father only took Tallboys on as a partner in the golf club when those two youngsters got married. John would be spinning in his grave."

"It was part of the deal?" Bunch nodded. Such things were far from unusual. "I didn't realise you were a golfer."

"I was. Don't get up there much now. What with running the shop and bein' in the choir, Mother would skin me alive if I took off every Sunday afternoon."

"Same here," she said. "Not for the same reasons. Daddy's away too often to get carried away. Does Miss Cawston play golf, do you know?"

Brice's brows furrowed. "Not here, as you well know."

"Sorry. Of course she wouldn't." Bunch gave him a wide grin. "Silly me. I wasn't thinking. What does she do in her spare time?"

"Well now…" he frowned "…do you know, I haven't the

slightest idea. She's always very polite, chatters on to Mother when she meets us. Pays her rent regular as you like, which is what you want from a tenant. I don't know what she does in her spare time. She's not here much, see. It's with her being a journalist I s'pect." He glanced up at the ceiling. "She's quiet. Apart from the typing. We often hear her tapping away up there. At it all day, sometimes. Makes me glad our little house is away from here. Mother could never stand that row when she's listening to The Symphony Concert on the wireless."

"Not one for ITMA then?"

He made a token attempt to hide a smile. "She never had what you might call a sense of humour. Not more than she liked living over the shop. People hammering on the door at midnight for a box of plasters." He pulled a face. "You think I'm joking? People think shop hours never matter if you're here anyway."

"Terribly inconsiderate … but I must be off. Put these on our bill please. Happy Christmas, Mr Brice. And do wish Mrs Brice all good cheer for the season."

"She'll be at the carol service on Wednesday. But if not, then…" He stood back from the counter and gave a gallant little bow. "*Nadolig hapus iawn i chi*, Miss Courtney."

Bunch laughed as she gathered up her purchase. "I don't speak Welsh so I hope I'm right in saying Happy Christmas to you too."

She stepped out into the street and glanced up at the sky. After the stuffy, chemical environment of the pharmacy the air felt fresh but cold, with a hint of drizzle filtering down from heavy clouds. She sensed rather than heard the door of the police Wolseley opening.

"Chief Inspector said I was to drive you home, Miss. He said the Commissioner has ordered him straight back to Brighton once he's finished briefing PC Botting. Something big going down by the sound of it."

Bunch looked along the high street towards the Police House. If Wright's new case was top priority, she wondered what on earth could possibly eclipse murder. She realised there may be little realistic chance of resolution when the body was six months dead. *Identification will be a miracle. Finding his killer with a war on will take longer.* It was not for her to second guess Wright's priorities, however. She had more than enough to deal with, especially now she was being badgered into taking up some of her old WLA duties in overseeing land girl placements, and though she didn't object to doing her bit she only had so many waking hours. "Yes please. I have a lot to do in the office myself."

"Right you are." Glossop opened the passenger door with a flourish. "Hop in, Miss."

~~~

Bunch squinted at the horn lanterns above her head. She wondered for how many centuries the misshapen collection had lurked at the back of the storeroom before Kate and Pat had dragged them out. The lamps' windows, made from sheets of soaked, scraped and flattened cow horn, lent a sepia yellowness to the cowshed's interior; a flickering line of candle-glow along the length of the byre that threw shadow puppets of women and beasts against limewashed walls.

These archaic props had proved useful for several reasons. Firstly, because the storm lantern glasses were easily broken and replacement parts impossible to obtain; secondly, they required candles and not rationed paraffin oil; and perhaps most importantly, their gentle medieval light rendered the old hessian sacks flipped across the windows sufficient for blackout needs.

The small dairy herd, just a dozen cows in all, generated sufficient warmth for the shed to feel balmy compared to the yard outside, yet Bunch's fingers, fumbling for cigarettes and lighter, were blue and aching with cold. She leaned back against the wall, breathing in smoke over the sweetish odours of straw and bovine bodies and watched Kate saunter along the channel in front of the beasts, releasing each yoke in turn with a practised flick of one hand. It was a scene that had barely changed for centuries. *Except the lord of the manor's daughter is a latest milkmaid paddling around in the shit.*

As the last animal ambled past, Bunch closed the doors and dropped the locking bar in place. Kate was already busy swilling slurry towards the drains with buckets of water and a yard brush. "Got another one of those?" Bunch called.

"Take mine, Boss." Kate tossed the broom across to her. "I'll chuck the water and you sweep."

"Right ho."

They had almost finished the swilling down, finishing off with a very weak solution of Jeyes Fluid, when the door opened briefly and Wright slipped in, shutting the door quickly to prevent even the subdued light to escape into the deepening dusk.

"William. I wasn't expecting to see you again today." Bunch leaned her broom against the wall and reached into her dungaree pocket once again for cigarettes and lighter.

"I called at the house and Mrs Knapp said I'd find you here."

"Up to my neck in muck, as the saying goes, but fortunately without the bullets." She proffered her cigarette case. "What can I do for you, old chap?"

He declined the smoke but moved closer to prop up the wall beside her. "I can't stay. Just thought I should apologise for sending you off earlier without a word of warning. It's all got a bit … fraught." He glanced at Kate.

"I'll finish in the dairy," the land girl said. "Then I'm off to start supper. The girls will be back on the six o'clock bus and starving like wolves. Goodnight Boss, Chief Inspector."

"Goodnight Kate."

"She's a grafter," Wright observed.

"My right hand. I'd never manage here without her. I'm thinking of making her up to assistant steward because I am drowning in paperwork and she is awfully good at it."

"I know the feeling."

Bunch leaned one welly-booted foot against the stonework behind her. "You seem troubled, old thing. What's Uncle Walter flapping about?"

Wright glanced at the dairy door, clearly on edge, which made Bunch take note more than words ever could. "Very much under wraps." He spoke rapidly, in an undertone that Bunch could barely make out. "A twelve-year-old girl has been kidnapped at gunpoint."

"Oh dear lord, the poor child. For ransom, one assumes?"

"No demands have been received so far. Her grandfather is a judge and we suspect this may well be about something other than just money."

"Isn't it usually money? What makes you suspect this is different?"

"The sheer level of violence. The cook-housekeeper was killed at the scene and the words 'No police' were daubed in her blood next to the body."

"Hell's bells! Was anyone else hurt?"

"The maid is in hospital with gunshot wounds to the chest. No one else in the house at the time."

"That's bad enough."

"Just so. None of this is common knowledge, though I suspect it won't be long before it gets out. As you can imagine, it's rather a priority Scotland Yard case. I've been placed in charge of searches in our area."

"I thought the Yard and local constabularies didn't play well together."

"The man in overall charge was my senior in my time at the Yard. He wanted someone he can trust who has local knowledge."

"You're the go-between. Does that mean you're off this other case?"

"In theory I'm investigating both. In practice, investigations into the Italian's death will fall way down the list and will probably stay there."

"He was Italian? That's been confirmed?"

"He's been identified as escaped POW by the name of Nario Costa. Which explains why there were no reports of locals going missing."

"I can see how it might not be a priority for some, but the poor chap deserves some kind of … justice." Bunch paused as some detail tickled at the back of her memory. "I seem to recall there was some hoo-hah back last summer. It was just after we lost Mummy and I'd taken Dodo off up to Scotland for a rest."

"There's a report from Botting about that. It will be sent

up to you."

"Thank you. And I will do my best to find some answers. This chap was one of the enemy, yes, but…"

"I agree. And if it was a recent death he might have it. Unfortunately this Costa chap's been dead for several months. The trail will be stone cold." Wright took off his hat to rub at his hair. "The first weeks are always crucial to any investigation. After all this time any physical evidence beyond his remains will be long gone and the memories of potential witnesses will be rather hazy. We have the 'where and when', but sadly the why is not likely to be a thing we'll ever know."

"What you mean is that a POW comes way down the list?" Bunch growled. Wright's seeming dismissal of a murder, regardless of who or what they were, was out of character. "I am surprised the case wasn't handed over to the Red Caps."

"Military are leaving it to us, would you believe. And I think you know me better than that, Rose. Murder is murder, no matter who or what the victim is, was, or had been."

"I know. Sorry, I didn't mean to imply anything else. Nevertheless…"

"Nevertheless." Wright shrugged. "We don't have men to spare right now on a 'dead-end case'." He held his hands up. "Your uncle's words, not mine. As this was right on your doorstep, and you are the county's consulting detective, the Commissioner did agree that you can handle the enquiry, for now at least."

She frowned, wondering where the catch was and why her uncle had not asked her for himself. "Uncle Walter wants me to take charge? Me?"

"Not in so many words but in essence, yes. I shall be on the other end of the telephone if you need me. Use PC Botting for the leg work."

A year ago she would have given her eye teeth for this opportunity but there was something in the way Wright was avoiding her eyes that made Bunch wonder what she was being offered. The immediate family didn't approve of her involvement in police matters and made it clear that now she was rapidly approaching thirty-two years of age, the

Perringham estate should be her sole priority. She preferred to think that being Lady of the Manor was something way off in the future, but with her father so heavily embroiled in War Office business, her mother passed away, and Granny Beatrice frailer than ever, it rested increasingly on her shoulders. The Land Army girls were already under her charge and those expected to arrive in the area very soon were going to be another drain on her time.

Then there were her horses that she felt she was already giving less time than they deserved. Even the idiotic excuse for a gundog that Henry Marsham had foisted on her required hours of training she simply hadn't got to spare. These were all responsibilities that she had to engage with on a daily basis. On the other hand, she was being handed a case all of her own. How could she possibly refuse?

The soft rustling and sweetish bovine smells of the herd settling to her right, the clanking of metal churns as Kate rolled them out onto the stand ready for the early morning collection, summed up her situation in a single moment and she loved them all. At the same time she couldn't deny a deep-rooted need for something more. Something that defined her as Rose Courtney.

"It would take up a lot of my time, I should imagine," she said.

"It may," Wright agreed.

She turned away, moving to lower the lamps on their hoists and extinguishing them one by one until the final flame, which was closest to the doors, glowed between them.

The ATS had refused to pass her fit after a run in with a mortar shell in France, and she had seen the title of Consulting Detective as a compensation. What Wright was now offering went beyond that. She regretted the cause of this shift in circumstance but she couldn't deny that it was a challenge she was eager to meet.

She supressed a smile. To be so gauche as to display excitement at the mere prospect of her own investigation, and accepting it out of hand, was unthinkable. The only objection she could raise on the spur of the moment was the sordid topic of money. "Fees?" she said.

"The Commissioner has authorised the brief in full."

"In which case, I accept. I shall need all of your files, including Letham's report, and I shall expect Botting to carry out some of the work. Send me everything you have on this Nario Costa chappie – where he escaped from, etcetera."

"I did say preliminary enquiries," Wright growled.

"And I shall start at the beginning," she agreed.

"All right. I shall send over everything we have in the morning."

"Good." She motioned him towards the door and began to lower the last of the lanterns. "I do appreciate the chance."

Wright hesitated and for a moment she thought he was going to come close to her. *God forbid he tries to hug me,* she thought. *That would be too bizarre.*

"I know. Good night then, Rose. I shall be in touch." Wright tipped his hat to her and slipped out as quickly as he had arrived.

"Good night," she murmured to an empty space. She opened the lamp's hinged front and blew sharply to extinguish the candle's feeble glimmer.

Sunday 21st

Beatrice rested one hand on the panel door to the Courtney box pew and cast a critical glance around the church until she spotted the Reverend Day lurking at the vestry entrance. "This place is like an icehouse." She opened the low gate and stepped into the box, directing her words to her companion but plainly for Day's benefit. "Short sermon today or we shall all catch our deaths. Alice, didn't we spare them a cord of wood just this month?"

Her complaints carried across the transept with pin-sharp clarity to Sid West, the verger, doing his best to melt into the stonework behind him.

Bunch waited for Alice to help Beatrice into her seat and arrange a rug around the older woman's knees, before stepping in behind them and pulling the panel closed behind her. Beatrice expected to have the final word and Bunch had some sympathy for the poor beleaguered churchmen. Coal was in short supply and firewood was at a premium, but the furnaces had been lit – she had smelled the smoke from them as she came in. *West plainly didn't stoke it early enough, again.*

She looked along the pew. It was sad to see how small the family had become. *But*, she thought, *probably no smaller than it's been for years.* In the row behind them Dodo sat with her father-in-law, Barty Tinsley, and his daughter, Emma. Little Georgi, it seems, had been left at home with Nanny.

"A sniffly cold." Dodo leaned forward to mutter between Beatrice and Bunch. "And as Granny just said, the church is never heated these days. Hardly the place for an infant."

"Absolutely." Bunch didn't comment on the fact that Maurice Badeaux was there in the child's place. Bunch had nothing against him personally. She simply found him rather dull company, but it wasn't her opinion that was important but how her sister felt about him. He was one of their Stateside cousins, and distant enough by blood not to be a problem. He was a solid chap who made Dodo laugh, and who plainly adored Georgi, showering the child with rationed treats that only the NAAFI had access to. *He's becoming something of a fixture at Banyards these past few months.*

Bunch had a notion it was the spectre of George Tinsley that prevented her sister from committing herself for a second time. Dodo simply wasn't ready to leave her husband's memory behind; or she imagined people expected her to think that way. *Which is silly. George has been gone for over two years. In times like these you grab what happiness you can.* Bunch knew how Dodo had adored George, and grief did not have a time scale.

Maurice was dapper in his RAF blues, pilot wings glistening on his left breast above a lengthening line of medal-ribbons. George had crashed and died before he'd accumulated quite that many. *But they're cut from the same cloth, quietly understated hero types.* For a fleeting moment she felt a stab of jealousy that her younger sister had the gift of entering into relationships in a way that Bunch could not, yet she would never begrudge Dodo happiness.

She glanced at the line of plaques commemorating past Courtneys, stretching back through the centuries; the most recent and closest mourned the passing of her brothers in the pandemic of 1920, and had been re-cut to include her mother Theadora. Next came a marble scroll recording Edward's elder sibling Lucien, lying now in a Flanders field. Above that a tablet commemorating Charles, who passed on five years earlier, and one for his son who also succumbed to the flu. *Five male Courtneys snuffed out in two decades*, Bunch mused. *Oscar Wilde's Lady Bracknell might call that exceptionally careless.*

She turned away from the past to watch Beatrice being settled into the pew by the indispensable Alice. Her grandmother was no longer young and far from well, yet apparently indomitable. Bunch wondered if the presence of all of the plaques affected her grandmother more than the family realised. Somehow she doubted it. Beatrice had adored her youngest son, Edward Courtney, who had only inherited

Perringham Estate because Lucien had passed without issue. *Not that eldest are always the favoured offspring, but the expectations are higher.* Bunch's mother had not anticipated being lady of the manor and much preferred globetrotting for the FO with Edward. Theadora's death had saddened Beatrice, despite the two women being less than close, but in her role as Grande Dame she set such personal things aside for the sake of Perringham's legacy.

I discern a pattern, Bunch thought. *The line is about to fracture once again with female heirs and not a single partnership among us. Brood mares, that's what we are. Probably why I like the gee-gees so much. Natural affinity. What a legacy for poor little Georgi. She's going to be a substantial heiress and every eligible chap in Debrett's will try herding her to the altar. At least she has me to guide her. God knows I've had enough of that for myself to know what it's like. I had Granny to watch my back, and Father – when he's been here.*

Bunch wondered where her father was. They had all hazarded a guess that he'd crossed the Atlantic with Churchill to persuade Franklin D Roosevelt into the war more quickly. *Which is a worry given the attacks on Atlantic convoys. Unless they flew, which in December would not be a great deal of fun. Thank God he's not in the Pacific region now, what with the Japs marching across the whole region. Even the Yanks are feeling it after that Pearl Harbour raid. But we shan't know until Churchill surfaces for the press.*

"Are you quite well, dear?"

The question broke into her thoughts. "Yes, I'm fine."

"Then do sit down. You look as if you're about to make a dash for it and it's making people uneasy."

"Sorry Granny." Bunch sat abruptly and turned to study the congregation. The village matrons had flooded the space with greenery, dotted here and there with red holly berries and vast arrangements of greenhouse chrysanthemums. No mistletoe, of course. Reverend Day, she knew, was adamant on that score, believing it to be a pagan symbol. *As if the entire ritual of "bringing in the greens" isn't rife with superstition.* She had never been religious and recognised that her weekly attendance in church was out of habit, but she still found a sense of peace in the building's solidity. With the added bonus, Bunch expected, of gathering information from a captive audience.

The organist, Miss Hatcher, struck up "Hills of the North Rejoice" and the congregation stood while Scouts and Guides paraded flags, followed by the ARP, Home Guard, WI and WVS. Three flags to either side of the apses, with the Union Flag behind the advent crown, on centre stage.

Bunch was aware of a faint mist caught in a shaft of light as collective breaths belted out the final verse into the chill, and the congregation settled back into place. She spent the rest of the service homing in on those with links to the Victory Gardens. Daffyd Brice, eyes closed as he sang. His wife, Nancy, chatting with Marion Cawston behind her hymnbook, which was a surprise because Bunch had assumed the two would be unlikely friends. A few rows ahead of them sat the Tallboys. Pamela Tallboys and the children attended sporadically, but Reg almost never appeared, and Bunch watched him for a long moment noting his discomfort, and wondering what had prompted him to attend a freezing church service when he would be preparing for some golf club function where he could cosy up to the cream of local society. As if sensing her gaze, he glanced at her and looked away quickly. Bunch looked behind her, wondering if Barty was Tallboys' focus, and reminded herself to ask about the Home Guard's dealings with POWs. Major Tinsley was oblivious to either attention as he leaned behind Dodo to pass some comment to Maurice.

Today was the first morning service since the POW's body had been discovered and would be the best chance to hear whatever people had to say. Even so she would need to sprint for the exit to catch the congregation outside after the service ended because people would disperse rapidly on a cold grey day.

Bunch was certain the organist had galloped through the carols and the sermon was oddly short given the vicar's usual habit of meandering. *Granny's coded messages all received, it would appear.* She gathered up her bag and scuttled towards the doors as rapidly as she could, arriving there almost before Day was ready to meet and greet his flock. Spotting one of the villagers that she hoped to speak with, Bunch moved rapidly to intercept. "Mrs Chapel, may I have a quick word?"

"Good morning, Miss Rose." The woman was apprehensive at being hailed by a Courtney. She gestured to her brood to move ahead. "Put the potatoes on when you get in. I shan't be long," she called after them and turned to smile shyly at Bunch. "Is it about the body? PC Botting said you were helping that police inspector." Chapel nodded as if agreeing with her own comments. "I'm not sure I can help a great deal. I mean to say, it's a shock to us all. Fair gave me the shivers. Poor chap. Do we know who he was?"

"I haven't seen the coroner's reports," Bunch replied. "I thought with yours being the plot next door, so to speak, you might have noticed something going on."

"Not a thing, Miss." She had a north country burr still evident despite almost ten years of trying to fit into Wyncombe life. "I'm not there that much since Bob was called up. I don't know why he took it on in the first place. It's not like he's ever had any spare time."

"He must have known he'd be called up."

"You would think so. Sign sheet was on the bar at the Stars, I shouldn't wonder. Four of them got their papers as it happened. I put in a few hours at the gardens when I can, but the bairns took it on for themselves, especially our lad Robbie. Him and his pals in the scouts seem to have commandeered a couple of plots. They've got some sort of competition going and they weigh every ounce of produce they get out. It's been all I can do to stop the lad camping out there – because they've really taken this pilfering to heart."

"Did the scouts just take on any of the other plots of men who were drafted, perhaps?"

"No. There's a waiting list so under-used allotments should be given up to the next names. Your grandmother would know."

"I suppose she would. I shall have to ask her. One good thing is the body wasn't on yours. Would have been ghastly for those boys if they had dug it up."

Mrs Chapel gazed at her for a moment and then chuckled

quietly. "You've not had much to do wi' lads his age, have you. Blood-thirsty little tikes, they'd have revelled in it. Old enough to know what it is when they've seen dead pigs an' the like, but not old enough to realise what it means – 'specially when this bloke turned out to be an *Eyetie*." Her smile vanished. "This war's doin' nobody no good. They shouldn't know anything about people being enemies. People are people and there's not a body deserves being buried under the cabbages." She looked back at Reverend Day still glad-handing the last of the congregation leaving the church. "Will he get a decent burial? That Eyetie, I mean. They can't send him home, I know. I'd hate to think my Bob wouldn't get treated wi' respect. I were thinking... They will bury him proper?"

The question took Bunch by surprise and she felt a little guilty that she hadn't considered it herself. "I assume so. I know that any German pilots shot down are given a military funeral."

Mrs Chapel gazed at her feet, her face solemn. "That's good," she said finally. "Puts my mind to rest."

Bunch had a lot of time for Val Chapel, who had uprooted herself from the Northumbrian coal fields and come south with her husband as part of the Land Settlement scheme. They had settled in one of a series of LS smallholdings on the edge of the village. And now Bob Chapel, just a year shy of forty years old, had been called up the previous autumn, leaving his wife with the seventeen-year-old Joyce, Peggy at fifteen, and twelve-year-old Robbie. With Rookery Farm to contend with, Bunch wondered why the Chapels had taken up a Victory Garden plot – but there they were, right next to Cawston's garden with its macabre produce. "Did any of you notice anything *at all* last summer?" she said.

Mrs Chapel thought for a moment, a deep frown line bisecting her forehead. "Let me think... The plots were rotavated when we took them on. To mark the boundaries, the groundsman said, so people didn't start yammering on about who had three inches extra. I can't remember hers looking any different from mine, 'cept she never came near it more than twice from that day to this."

"I hear there was a raffle to decide who had possession of the plot." Bunch knew perfectly well that was the case but there was an edge in the woman's voice at mention of Cawston that sounded alarms and it was worth prodding for a source.

"That were Reggie Tallboys' bright idea," Mrs Chapel growled.

"He's not popular?"

"He does a lot for the village, but he's not one for doing owt for nothing." Mrs Chapel smiled, making her seem younger for a moment. "Must break his heart that your old dad don't play golf – Sir Edward that is, meaning no disrespect, Miss." Her illusion of youth vanished in a flash, replaced by weather-worn worry-lines.

"None taken, I assure you." She gave Mrs Chapel a wry grin of her own and dropped her voice to a stage whisper. "Naturally Daddy wasn't involved in too many village activities; he and Mummy trotted around the world a lot. When he's home he likes to be at Perringham, or he did before the damned Ministry took it over."

"Must be hard, losing your home."

Bunch sighed. "It's still standing so far, and I suppose we shall get it back some day. To be honest, I've had enough to do with running the farm to worry about that barn of a place. Min of Ag seems to think we have nothing better to do than fill in forms."

"Aye. They do that, Miss," Mrs Chapel agreed. "Doesn't leave us time to whistle."

"It has its compensations, though. I manage to evade a lot of village committees by pleading war work, which is not entirely untrue. Besides, Granny has ruled the parish council and the village hall board for decades. Nobody will get a look in while she has a breath in her lungs. Father does take an interest when his overseas trips permit. Mostly in the annual Perringham-v-Wyncombe matches. And he likes to hunt. We all have our pet sports. I prefer the horses."

"And me. Bob's father was an ostler. Down the pit. He taught me a thing or two about 'em."

"You still keep horses at Rookery Farm? Must make

ploughing and such damned hard work."

"It does, but we've not the brass to spare for a tractor," the woman snapped and looked away, embarrassed at her outburst.

"They are dreadfully expensive," Bunch agreed.

"Yon Major Tinsley's 'ad his lads up on the Downs on horseback these past weeks. He saw them blokes in the Lewes Home Guards on the Pathé News. The Lewes Cossacks or whatever they calls 'emselves, and he's not one to be outdone."

"I can see the sense," Bunch ventured. "They can cover a lot more ground along the coombe tracks, especially in this weather. Never get a car along them this time of year."

"Maybe. But our lad's bin using our gelding for it and it's not fit to be harnessed half the time. Not when he's been out all night. He's a willing beast but he still needs his rest."

"Has Barty – Major Tinsley – spoken with Iris Westing at the stables, do you think? With the hunt on hold I bet she knows a few people with animals in need of a decent hack across the hills."

"Dunno, Miss. I do know my eldest's still half asleep by dinner time. Worn out every night."

"You don't have any land girls to help out?" She knew perfectly well there were none at Rookery Farm and felt a stab of guilt at the oversight.

"No Miss. Bob said we never needed help. We was offered some land girl as conscripts just before he signed up. But he were dead set against it."

"Was he? Well, he's not here now to do the work. Men and their bloody pride… Excuse my language. When your eldest girl is called up next year, when she turns eighteen, it will get even harder. Please don't think I am interfering, though I suppose I am," Bunch grinned and shrugged. "I'm sure I could get you a couple of extra hands. Or better still I have some dealings with the WFGA. They are trained for market garden rather than general agriculture like most of the WLA girls. Granny is thinking of registering the Dower House gardens for food production. She had all of the lower lawns by the walled garden turned over at the beginning of the year and then most of our younger staff were called up, so it's going to waste."

"It would be good to have help that doesn't need watching every hour of the day – if I had the space to house them. I've heard some folks 'ave bin making girls sleep in barns, but I'd feel bad doin' that."

"Quite right too. And don't worry about it. I have recently rearranged accommodation and can squeeze in another two girls at our bothy on Perringham Farm. If we can lay hands on a pair of bicycles it's barely a two-mile ride from there to Rookery Farm. I shall see what I can do."

"I can't say it wouldn't help, Miss."

"Top hole. Might not be until the New Year but we can get something done. Meanwhile…" Bunch reached out to touch the woman's shoulder "…anything you can remember about the Victory Gardens, or your children can recall, anything untoward no matter how small it might seem, give me a shout."

"I shall. And thank you."

"We all do what we can. Oh … one last thing. The remains were dug up by foxes but only because the ground was disturbed by someone stealing veg. I don't suppose you have any ideas on that?"

"Sorry, no. I mean there are rumours. You know what Wyncombe's like. Mostly guesses and gossip, or summat would've been done by now. Folks take their produce very seriously."

"They do indeed. If you do hear anything that sounds as if it might be more than gossip, please let me know. It might provide us with some insight. Now you should get home out of this cold wind. Happy Christmas, Mrs Chapel," Bunch called as she moved quickly to intercept the Tallboys. "We don't see you here often. And Pamela, hello old bean." She nodded to them both but decided it was best to ignore the toddler of indeterminate gender beneath its swaddling of scarves and knitted hats, who peered agog from the pleats in the sides of Pamela's winter coat.

"Good morning." Tallboys tipped his hat and smiled the professional smile of a businessman. "I try to get here when I can. Sunday is as busy as any other day at the club."

"Rather like farming." *Dammit, the man always puts my back up.* She conjured a small laugh. "No peace for us wicked folk, hey?"

"I'm sure you're not wicked, Rose." His smile was wider.

And a little sleazy, not to mention fresh. The nerve of the man, with his wife standing right there. And I don't know him half-well enough to be on first name terms. She glanced at Pamela who seemed not to have noticed, busying herself with wiping some minute speck from her infant's face with a gleaming white hankie. *Used to going conveniently deaf and blind, I imagine.* "Not wicked perhaps, Mr Tallboys, but a few of the girls call me the dragon. They think I don't know but voices carry in the open air."

"They do indeed. I could not help overhearing your parting words with Mrs Chapel. Are you investigating our Victory Garden murder? Taking down statements?" He favoured her with another cheeky grin. "Thumb screws, I'll be bound."

"That would probably make things far simpler, but I am making general enquiries for the time being. The police will be taking statements in due course."

"Naturally. I heard it was only an escaped POW. Police probably have better things to spend their time on."

Bunch gave him a *Beatrice glare*. "Mr Tallboys, a man was murdered right here in Wyncombe and I am acting for the police. It will be my time well spent." *Uh oh, that's raised his hackles,* she thought. *Perhaps not the best way to wheedle answers from his kind.*

"I think what Rose means is that who he was makes little difference in law," Pamela added. "She's got to ask questions, Reggie. It's her job."

Tallboys was evidently unused to being contradicted and Bunch wondered if he would retaliate. "Of course," he muttered. "But we are at war with those chaps. Seems just like a waste of time to me, and I'm not sure how I can help."

"We are, as you rightly say, at war," Bunch agreed. "And I can imagine there are a lot of people who would kill him just for being Italian. All the same, it doesn't change anything for Sussex Constabulary, or the MOD, come to that. I've been asked to see what people know, if anything." She laughed, a small rumble of chagrin to calm the man down. "Reports to be made and all that. You know how it is."

"Yes … naturally, I quite see that."

Does he? Not so sure about that. "Given how long he's been dead…"

Pamela drew breath and took a step away. "Shall I wait with Tina in the car, Reggie?"

"Yes, do that." Tallboys waved his wife away. "And do try to get those boys in order. It doesn't do to have them running ragged in the churchyard."

"Sorry, Reggie. I'll wait in the car. Happy Christmas, Rose."

"Happy Christmas." Bunch watched the woman hurry away. She had known her well when she had been Pamela Reynolds. As a businessman's wife she had somehow become cut off from the usual crowd. *And we never noticed,* she thought. *Which is a little sad.*

"What did you want to know?" Tallboys said. "It's always a pleasure to talk to you but it's a little cold to stand around."

"Yes, I'm sorry." Bunch pulled her attention back to the job at hand. "Chief Inspector Wright wants to know exactly how the allotments were allocated?"

"I marked out the original plots and had the groundsman rotavate the turfs."

"I don't recall you doing that for the first gardens."

"No. More's the pity." Tallboys looked down at his shoes. "It was done to make sure people knew where their boundaries were – to save arguments." Tallboys made a show of looking up at the trees and tapped a gloved finger against his chin, as if thinking back though Bunch was certain he remembered perfectly well. "We sold tickets at a shilling a time, with proceeds going into the Allotment Society kitty. I think it may even have been your grandmother's idea."

Not according to her, and I know which of you two I believe. "So it was completely random? Anyone could have drawn that particular plot?"

"Completely."

"Have any plots been reassigned since then?"

"No. We have a waiting list, should anyone drop out or

neglect their plots. The committee made it very clear that every holder was to make his section productive or hand it back." Two lads shot past them, roaring with arms outstretched in a noisy airplane dogfight. "Reg! Fergus! Behave yourselves!" Tallboys spread his hands. "The boys are getting far too excited. I really should get them home."

"Yes. I may get back to you at a later date."

"Call in at the club and we can have a private chat over a glass of bubbly. We have a very comfortable Ladies Lounge at the club. Nobody will disturb us."

"That would be absolutely spiffing. I haven't had a chat with dear old Pamela for a donkey's age."

He flushed. The message was plainly received, although whether he was embarrassed by it or angry with her Bunch was not certain. "Yes, of course," he muttered. "Happy Christmas, Rose."

"And to you, Mr Tallboys."

He tipped his hat once more and strode away, leaving her seething. Some of the locals found him a charming rogue but Bunch was left feeling a little ill at ease after five minutes in his company. *That's why I lost contact with Pamela. Something about his teensy eyes reminds me of wild boar in Tuscany. And learned nothing new from the dratted man, to boot.*

She glanced around her at the rapidly thinning congregation for a sign of Barty, but no one wanted to hang around in the chilled air sweeping across from the Continent. *Damn it. Oh well, I shall have to catch up with him at Banyards.*

"Morning, Miss Courtney."

"Oh, Constable Botting. I was going to call on you tomorrow. Is there anything more I should know about this Italian chappie? Or the vegetable thieves?"

"Not beyond what we already know."

"I've been going back over the logs and it seems it wasn't always police business. I read that it was the local Home Guard who apprehended two prisoners on the Downs back last summer."

"Not directly, Miss. Major Tinsley's platoon was involved but it was the Storrington platoon that made the arrest. I'm betting Major Tinsley'd know more about it than me."

"I shall be sure to ask him."

"Yes Miss. One more thing, I had a visit from Maisie Armitage yesterday."

"Landlady at the Seven Stars?"

"That's her. The top floor of the Stars is occupied by Maisie and Phil and happens to be one of the few places overlooking that side of the recreation ground. She claims she'd gone up to fetch something from the flat, and that the dogs were at the window barking something fierce. She couldn't see much. With no streetlamps it's black as black out there, but she did see a couple of lads coming out of the rec with a wheelbarrow. Never gave it another thought until a couple of regulars were bellyaching – her words, Miss, not mine – about stuff being snaffled from their plots. She thought she'd better mention it."

"She has no idea who they were?"

"No Miss. She said they scooted off down the twitten, side of the church, and she had an idea they had to be local to know that way. I'd say it's locals 'ave been perpetrating the crime. Getting a barrow down there in the pitch black when it's wet like it was that night, they'd need to know it pretty well."

"Or they were parked along Church Crescent."

"Then why not park alongside the rec? No, they're locals all right, I'm certain. And Maisie said she never saw or heard anything on the night after that."

"Perhaps you are right, and it would make sense. If it was anyone thieving for a market stall somewhere they'd probably take a lot more at the time, not in dribs and drabs every other night. Do you have any suspects?"

"Maybe. There's a few up along The Terrace who'd swipe their granny's teeth if they thought there was a few bob in it."

"That's excellent. It would be rather useful to speak with our cabbage rustlers. Let me know if you get to the bottom of it."

"I shall, Miss. And I sent them files the Chief Inspector wanted you to see over to the Dower. Didn't think you'd want me handing them over in the churchyard. Too many eyes about, and tongues to wag afterwards."

"Very true. I dare say when I've read the files I shall be running down to see you, but in case I don't, a happy Christmas to you and your good lady."

"Thank you, Miss, and the same to you and your family." Botting tipped his fingers against his helmet peak and strode away.

"Miss Rose?"

"I was just coming, Alice. Run and tell Granny I shall be right there." She watched Alice hurry out to the road where the car was waiting.

There was no point in hanging around in the cold when most of the people she wanted to talk to had already gone. The investigation was proving to be frustratingly vague and she wondered what line she should take now. She could see why such cases were dubbed cold. The trail really was quite moribund. Since no one had seen or heard anything, no one was likely to remember anything useful. She knew all too well how recalling those little details after such a long time was next to impossible. *Unless it's something you'd rather forget*, she thought bitterly, given the nightmares she still had over her accident in France. Telephoning Wright for advice on her next step was not going to be an option since she had tried twice before she came to church and had been told he was unavailable.

There seemed nothing more to do but go home and read over her notes and the files, and see what she might have missed. She looked around the churchyard a final time and hurried after her grandmother and her companion.

"What did the Tallboys have to say?" Beatrice asked as Bunch settled in the car.

"Not a great deal. Pamela is a nice woman, but him? A little like our Colonel Ralph but without Ralph's breeding." She made an effort not to shudder, recalling the threats Ralph had once made her on a deserted downland track. "Tallboys thinks rather too much of himself. Those beady little eyes. *Ugh*."

"Goes with that type of man." Beatrice waved away Bunch's surprise. "Men like Tallboys and Ralph – even your friend Wright – all are popular with the people under their command. Something they all share is that they have far better roots than you might imagine."

"That is rather a sweeping statement."

"All were raised to issue orders. I do agree, however, that of the three, Reggie Tallboys has something of the weasel about him."

Bunch debated whether to take the proffered bait. Clearly Beatrice had unearthed some snippet from the Chief Inspector's past. *Is it something I need, – or indeed want – to know? Right now, I suspect it will be a distraction.* "You think I am being too harsh?"

"Possibly, possibly not. Just don't allow your own antipathy to cloud your thinking."

"About what?"

"I'm not blind, Rose. It's bitter cold and trying to rain. You would never stop to talk with Reg Tallboys if you didn't have a very good reason. Such as snooping for William Wright."

"I do not snoop, Granny!"

"What else would you call it?" Beatrice shot her a sly glance. "Not that I blame you in the slightest. It's a distraction from trying to run the estate with one hand tied behind your back."

"Meaning?"

"I understand your frustrations, slaving for the estate when by rights it should be your father's responsibility. But Edward has always been the globetrotter."

"That's a bit strong. Daddy is doing his bit for the war, you know."

"He is indeed."

"What has that to do with Reg Tallboys?"

"Nothing whatsoever, but I worry about you. Please, my dear, don't wear yourself out with this Consulting Detective nonsense. You are running the estate and now you've taken on the Land Army duties again."

"Only for Wyncombe."

"And before you know it there will be 'just Inchett' and 'just Chiltwick' and 'just Storrington', and you will be back with half the county in your charge – and run ragged. May I remind you that it's not that long ago you were an ATS driver in the thick of a war and being shipped home from France with a shattered leg. The other chap in that Staff Car died … you spent months getting back on your feet."

"It was two years ago, Granny and I barely notice it now. I am not some Victorian flower destined for a life of bathchairs and taking the waters."

"The ATS won't have you back. Unfit for service my dear, that's how much better that leg of yours is." Beatrice was not usually one to shy away from difficult conversations.

Bunch glanced at Alice seated next to the chauffeur, knowing both were listening – they couldn't help but hear. "I know you are trying to make a point Granny. Wouldn't it be easier to just tell me?"

"Don't stretch yourself too thin," Beatrice replied. "You have some ridiculous notion that you are not doing your bit, that you are missing out somehow."

"I don't."

"No? Then why did you twist your uncle's arm into letting you play detective?" Beatrice touched Bunch's arm. "You have almost the entire family's workload, and since old Parsons passed away you don't even have a steward to fall back on. I can't imagine why Edward doesn't hire a replacement for him."

"I think he intended to take it on himself, or that Mummy would be here." Bunch grunted and half-smiled. Both of them knew perfectly well that Theadora would never have taken up the baton. "I know you're right, Granny. I do need some help and I think I have the solution. Since I am allocating Land Army resources I shall take a few liberties and co-opt Kate, and perhaps Pat as well, to help with paperwork and general overseeing. They've been here since '39 so there aren't many jobs on the estate work they haven't tackled. They can move into the garage flat. We'll have new recruits aplenty to replace their other duties now that conscription is in place up for all girls over eighteen." She waited for Beatrice to object but the counter argument never came.

"You've given this a lot of thought?"

"I have. What say you Granny? A good wheeze?"

"Have you discussed this with Edward?"

"Not had the chance. Daddy has rather left it in our hands of late."

"I agree. All right, if you can get the girls to agree then by all means, though perhaps to begin after Christmas festivities have ended. Half of the girls will want time off to see their families, I imagine."

"Only two have asked. I think the party at the WLA bothy, and dances at the air base, have far greater appeal than spending two days leave trying to get home and back on the wretched trains. Provided they could even get travel permits."

"Is the flat habitable?" Beatrice asked. "I thought Edward had abandoned that project."

"More or less. The kitchen isn't up to much but the girls could eat with Cook and Knapp until it's sorted."

"Then do it. Just make sure you have enough girls to cover all the work."

"I wondered if we might snag some POWs."

"Now you would need to ask Edward about that. I have no problems with Italians, myself, but your father's current post may makes things sticky." Beatrice sat forward as the car pulled into the yard close to the stables and garages. "I am pleased you are getting some assistance."

"Thank you, Burse," Bunch said to the chauffeur-groom as she opened the door.

"Will you need the car again today, Miss?"

"No thank you. But could you get Perry saddled for me for one o'clock?"

"Yes, Miss.

~~~

Maggie, in the stall closest to the doors, snickered loudly at Bella who had scampered past on her way to investigate the empty feed bins at the far end, where mice were often to be found. Bunch grabbed a handful of hay from a pile waiting in the corridor to pacify the pony, and tapped the animal's whiskery nose lightly but the horse went in for one of her trademark nips.

"No you don't, you bad tempered old nag." Bunch scrubbed at Maggie's piebald face affectionately. "You had a jaunt out with the cart yesterday." With petrol on strict ration an old pony cart had been dragged out of retirement for local travel, but Perry, the Fell pony, was too small for the shafts, and Robbo, Edward's hunter, too large. Magpie – now Maggie – had been purchased at Storrington stock market to fill the gap.

Maggie appeased, Bunch moved to Robbo and offered him a wisp of hay, which he took delicately, rumbling quietly in satisfaction as he munched. It was the comforting sound of a childhood Bunch spent on or around horses every waking moment she could snatch. Stable time had always been her safety valve and she had been horrified when her father had told her of his intention to allow Colonel Ralph the opportunity to ride his hunter, when he, Sir Edward, was away. She had not wanted outsiders invading her private domain and in the end Edward had given way. Burse would ride Robbo out where possible, but the onus was on her now to see the horse was properly exercised. It was yet another pull on her time, albeit a small one.

"Perhaps we should hitch him up to a plough," she had grumbled to Dodo. "Fat old thing can't be much lighter than some of the dray horses I've seen."

She should have ridden Robbo out today but Bunch had a yearning for time with Perry, her aging black Fell pony. She left Robbo content with her peace offering, and smoothing her hand down his glossy chestnut neck before moving on. She promised she would get Kate to take him out later.

Bunch unbolted Perry's stall and stepped inside. "Hello, old fellow. Move over," she murmured, feeding the pony the last few strands of hay. She smiled at the familiar tickle of velvety lips on her palm. "Just a taste because we're going out." She led him into the corridor and tacked up, taking her time, adjusting his quarter sheet against the cold and checking straps were secured, talking quietly to the animal, as she always did, though he needed little calming. Satisfied at last she led him out into the yard, mounted up, whistled for Bella to follow, and headed out not to the village but uphill towards Hascombe Woods.

The quiet of the Downs was a good place to think. Her waking hours had so many duties heaped on them that solitude was hard to come by. She was thankful to have thus far avoided chairing the village committees, which her position as a Courtney tended to involve. Beatrice, despite her age, retained her vice-like grip on most of them and Bunch was not sorry. The Land Army and estate management duties she could hardly avoid. Horses were … a lifetime's passion she could not discard.

The one duty she could relinquish was her self-styled position as Consulting Detective.

Bunch pulled Perry up just short of the treeline and watched Bella snuffing her way along the fence, plunging her nose so far into the dead grass that she seemed headless. There was a wind whipping across the last sections of hillside that had remained free of the Ministry of Foods drive to cultivate every available inch of farmland. This slope was too steep for the plough.

Seeing the untouched sward all around her was welcome, in that it was as it had always been, untouched by the demands of war. But here, on this hillside she could not avoid being reminded of a similar day almost two years earlier, to the day with her old Labrador, Roger, tracking rabbits and pheasants with slightly less speed than her hyperactive springer would, but with no less interest. It was the day she and her sister had ridden this track into the wood to escape the snow – and come across the body of Bunch's first lover, Jonathan Frampton. The day she had dived headfirst into solving the crime with the inimitable Chief Inspector William Wright.

She had no regrets on that score. Solving Johnny's murder had been a labour of… *Love? I suppose it was. I loved Johnny as much as I've loved any of the men in my life. But I'm not sure I have ever been in love. Not with him, and certainly not with Henry Marsham, much as I like him, and despite what the family say.*

The sun was weak and without heat, sloping in and out behind sluggish grey clouds. Bunch took a deep breath and closed her eyes, turning her face into the wind. *This is my fifth crime to solve in two years – and this case is all mine.*

She could smell the sharp, almost acrid scents of winter trees and leaf mould. With the smell of dead and damp grasses came a faint whiff of sheep that still grazed here whilst the weather remained relatively mild. No hint of the snows of the previous two Decembers.

Bunch opened her eyes and looked over the Coombe. Across the valley she could see glimpses of Perringham House, out of bounds for the duration. The solid outlines of Perringham Farm were clearer, with few trees around it, and closer still, the Perringham Dower House. Her father had suggested it be renamed Perringham Farmhouse or even Perringham Manor to differentiate it from the military enclave, and Bunch could see the point, but somehow it felt like a betrayal.

"The Dower is hardly new. Maybe we *should* make it Perringham Farmhouse? What do you think?" Perry shifted uneasily, snickering his protest at standing around in the cold. A few drops of rain on the wind stung at Bunch's face in the same moment. "Yes, I know. Bigger fish to fry. We'll get moving now." She slapped his neck and turned him back the way they had come, whistling for Bella to follow. *Time for going into action.*

Bunch pushed Perry into a brisk walk and made it back to the stable yard just as the rain began in earnest. Inside the stable block it was warm and dry, and the sound of rain drumming harder on the tiled roof made it seem all the cosier. She was in her haven, this her solace. True, the building wasn't as well laid out as the stable block at Perringham House but the smell of hay and straw dust, and equine aromatics, were just as familiar to her, although she barely noticed them as she unsaddled Perry and let him amble into his stall. She contemplated cleaning the tack – it was a job she quite enjoyed – but left it for Burse. She gave what time she had to giving Perry a quick rub down, and was contemplating a light rug for him when the doors opened.

"Boss?"

"In here, Kate." Bunch gave Perry a final pat and came out into the aisle. "How lucky," she said as she bolted the stall door. "I was just going to come and find you. And Pat." She nodded at the dark-haired girl standing a little behind Kate.

"Boss," Pat added, grinning in a way that lit up her slightly flattish features.

The two young women waited expectantly. Kate the taller of the two. Loose, almost sparsely limbed, but deceptively strong. Wright often referred to her as the head girl, which Bunch thought very unfair, but knew what he meant. With her thick, light-brown curls styled in the new sensible *liberty* cut, and her grey-blue eyes that fixed on any subject with a direct questioning gaze.

Pat was dark-haired and more reserved, though by no means subservient. Shorter and a little stockier, she had warm hazel eyes that were never far from laughter. They were a duo, these two: both cousins and close friends who had somehow managed to swing a posting together through some connection or other. Bunch suspected they had volunteered early on for the Land Army rather than the more glamorous WAAF or WRNS for that very reason.

"We came to see to the milk yield forms and Burse said you wanted a word," Kate said.

"So we stooged around for a bit." A small crease formed in Pat's forehead. "What's the cackle? We are still getting that extra girl in that you promised?"

"Absolutely. This is something extra, which I hope will meet with your agreement. Follow me."

The garages on the far side of the yard had once been the carriage house, and the flat above them a bothy for the grooms that drove them, and after that a storage space before Edward had thought it might be suitable for his valet. Bunch had even considered making it her own but somehow it remained unused.

The door was not locked, mainly because there was nothing there to steal. She pushed the door open into the main room. The plastered walls were painted a startling white which made it a bright space despite the line of windows along the west side being very small, wedged in the space between skirting and the sloped eaves. The floor of oak boards had been shaved to a smooth finish but was unvarnished, echoing the timber beams that crossed the room above their heads. Two doors punctuated the wall opposite the windows. Both were open, the first leading to a tiny bathroom and other to a small kitchen. The wall at the end had a fireplace with a small wood-stove fire situated next to a third door, which was closed.

"Bedroom." Bunch waved towards it. "Only one but it's quite roomy if you don't mind sharing."

"Sharing, Boss?"

"Well, girls, I have a proposition. I need help with the estate office and as you are already familiar with a lot of the ministry eyewash, I want you to take some of it on."

Kate glanced at Pat, who shrugged. "Us?" she said. "You want us to be clerks?"

"I was thinking more managers. Not full time. Maybe four mornings a week? Rest of the time you would be carrying on with what you always do."

"This a promotion?" Kate's brows creased. "Will it take us out of the Land Army?"

"Not entirely. But I've not had any help since Miss Benoir left us. Parsons used to deal with most of it when he was steward. Then it occurred to me that I have you two right here, and you're chipping in so often anyway. You know the ropes… Yes, I suppose it is a promotion."

"We're shorthanded already," Kate muttered. "How will the rest of the girls cope?"

"Ah, as you know I am not asking for one extra hand but five."

"Five?"

"Three recruits for here and two for Rookery Farm. Another of the houses on the terrace is coming empty so we've billets enough for them. And there will only be plenty of room if you two move over here. Does it sound like something you could do?"

"Do we get a rise?" asked Pat.

"Oh. Yes … I suppose you will. It shall have to come from the estate because the Ministry won't cough up. The Land Army agricultural rate is sixteen shillings a week, plus board and overtime. I have given it some thought and given the new responsibilities … say twenty-one shillings a week? Plus board, naturally." She smiled at them. "And we'll discuss a further rise before the next quarter day, if it works out."

"That sounds fair," Kate replied. "And when would you want us to start?"

"No time like the present." Bunch waved around the room. "For furniture, you can move stuff down from the house. The attics are loaded with bits and pieces. Are you visiting your families for Christmas?"

"We drew the short straw for dairy duty," Pat said.

"We'll have the New Year instead," Kate added. "You said some of the girls could go on Wednesday and be back late on Boxing Day."

"You'll be on your own over Christmas? That hardly seems fair."

"No Boss. Dot will be here. She said getting home to Wales and back would be too hard, and Elsie hasn't a home to go to anymore, poor thing. Not since her parent's place in Lambeth was flattened. Mumsy and Daddy sent me a cake and some bubbly, and we've got plenty of gin and beer."

"And there's always the dance, at the village hall," Pat said.

"Sounds as if we have an agreement." An awkward silence followed. Bunch wasn't sure how to end the conversation. She hadn't imagined it could be done so easily. She wasn't even sure it was legal, given the shortage of personnel, but she'd solve that problem if or when it arose. "Well, this is rather jolly. Perhaps you can start in the morning with tallying the milk records for the month? We don't have a lot of other produce going out at the moment, as you know, so nothing else will need doing for a few days. I shall be a bit busy so—"

"That Italian prisoner?" Pat ventured.

"Does everyone in the county know about that?" Bunch raised both hands. "No, don't answer. This is Wyncombe – they all know. It would be rather nice if some of them had known that before the man surfaced, so to speak."

"Not going well?" asked Kate.

"Too early to say. Nobody can remember what happened

back in August, and no reason why they should, I suppose, but the lapse in time doesn't help matters."

"Anything we can do?"

"Some idea of who has been raiding the plots of vegetables would be a start. Foxes uncovered the body but only because the ground had been disturbed. Even Botting hasn't been able to find the thieves."

"It's not just a few parsnips at stake, is it? Whoever it was who dug up the crops probably thinks they'll get charged with murder."

"Perhaps. Well, if you do hear anything give me a nudge. Meanwhile, welcome to the Perringham Farmhouse."

"Perringham Farmhouse?"

"Daddy hopes it will stop any confusion with Colonel Ralph's bods at the big house. Somehow I doubt it." Bunch didn't voice her view that Edward was, in reality, planning against the day that Beatrice was no longer alive. *He thinks it will be difficult to remain a Dower house when the mistress is a spinster of this parish. Is that how he sees me? Or is it the image I give him?*

Kate looked doubtful. "Is that going to affect us as well?"

"Only if you notice strangers around the yard."

"Not so far."

"Then probably not. Are you on the dairy roster today?"

"Yes, but we've finished earlies. Got a few hours before late milking, if you needed something urgent doing."

"Only moving house, so to speak. See Knapp about any furniture you will need for the flat. There are beds and chairs in the attics over at the Dower – I mean the Farmhouse. Heavens, it's going to take a while to get used to that. Is there anything else you want to ask?"

"Not at the moment."

"Excellent." Bunch glanced at Pat. "You seem concerned, Pat. You are happy with all this?"

"The move? Absolutely. The bothy is an asylum most days. I shall enjoy the peace and quiet. It's what you were saying about the thefts down at the rec."

"Have you heard something?"

"I'm not sure. It was just a passing comment I heard down

The Stars a few nights back. Something about a lad keeping his head down because Botting always has it in for him, and thinks he'd not get a fair hearing."

"Who was it?"

"That's the problem. I never saw who it was. These old chaps do mumble. One of the skittles team, I think, but I wouldn't swear to it."

"Right, thank you. That could prove very helpful. Meanwhile, take a good look around and tell me what you think you'll need. And I shall find the keys for you. Well then, see you in the morning, girls. And thank you."

Monday 22nd

Catching up on the week's backlog of forms had taken less than an hour. Kate and Pat were already familiar with Perringham's office filing and worked together as one. They left by nine o'clock for breakfast. Bunch remained despite the cold. When she had called the Brighton police station she had been assured by the desk sergeant that Wright would return her call the moment he returned. But that had been two hours ago – and by now she was beginning to lose the feeling in her toes.

When she had first relocated to the dower house, Bunch had commandeered the attics for estate business. It had not taken more than a week or two before Beatrice objected to a stream of people trudging through the house and so the office was banished to a converted feed store in the stable yard, with the telephone line rerouted accordingly. Edward had his private War Office line under strict lock and key in his study; the house phone, situated in the hall, was not the place for private calls, and so there was nothing for it but to wait in full outdoor rig with a squat black Valor Junior paraffin stove crammed as close to the desk as possible without setting it alight.

The small kettle on top of the stove burbled gently. She lifted it to one side. Cold as she was, the prospect of the chicory based Camp coffee that was kept in the office was not inviting. Tea was rationed where coffee was not, but fresh beans were becoming harder to buy, and try as they might British farmers were never going to be able to grow either, no matter how much the Min Ag exhorted them to make the British Isles self-sustaining.

Beneath the desk Bella lay on her back, impossibly contorted with limbs splayed, snoring gently. Out in the yard

Kate and Pat were debating the best way to manoeuvre an iron bed frame around the right angle turn at the apex of the stone stairway clinging to the side of the building that was their new home.

She peered at them through the small window, murky with condensation, tapping the pencil held loosely between her fingers against the metal mug on the desktop. The white enamel with its blue rim was a jokey gift from Wright after he had seen her office. It had never been used for beverages; it was a memento of their first case. And though that would be two years come the New Year, she barely needed a reminder of Jonathan's ugly death. He had been such a part of her coming-out years.

She glanced at the boxes on the upper shelves that had been stored here since the family's ousting from Perringham House that same winter, when this had been more storeroom than office. They contained personal papers and photos of Jonathan, amongst others, and really should have been moved to the attics in the house long ago. "I suppose I should clear them out ready for Kate and Pat's residency," she muttered.

When the telephone finally rang it jerked her back into reality. She picked up the weighty Bakelite receiver and barked, "Perringham Farm estate office."

"Miss Courtney? I have a call for you, Miss. Go ahead caller."

The line clicked and chattered for a moment and then, "Hello? Rose?"

"Wright. Good morning to you old thing, except that it won't be morning for much longer. I had all but given up on you and its positively arctic waiting out here in this office."

"Sorry. I've only just come in."

"Is it bad? Have you found her?"

"That case is still ongoing."

"Oh dear." Bunch leaned back in her captain's chair. Plainly Wright and his squad were still searching for the young kidnap victim and it was clear that he was not going to discuss it over the telephone. "You sound tired. Have you had any sleep at all?"

"An hour or two here and there. What about you? Making any headway?"

"A little. Finding those thieves will probably be a big help. And I've still got to catch up with Reg Tallboys."

"Is he avoiding you?"

"Not sure. He's not making it easy but it's his busy time, so perhaps it will be simpler after the Christmas festivities are over. He certainly didn't seem that eager to talk to me when we spoke after church yesterday."

"Anything at all?"

"Not really, at least not yet. I've already spoken with one of the other plot holders, Mrs Chapel. Perhaps I should go and have another chat with her at home. I also had a word with Botting who seems to think Mrs Armitage, the landlady at the Seven Stars, has some information. It was local lads taking the crops, by the sound of it. Which would make sense. Can't see much of a profit in driving out to our small village to pilfer a few sprouts."

"My thoughts too. Will you speak to the publican today?"

"If I can. Catching her for more than two minutes before the holiday will be as tricky as it will be for Tallboys, and for the same reasons. The best time to call on her might be just before lunchtime closing and hope she will talk to me in the afternoon. People are hell bent on making as much out of Christmas as they can so the pubs and clubs will be extra busy."

"Who can blame them." He sighed heavily, his breath rustling across the mouthpiece. "Do what you can. I have a detective constable trying to root out some details on Costa's background. It's times like this that I miss Interpol. Even the neutral embassies are of little use nowadays. Nothing to be learned from the POWs themselves so far, and before you ask, no, I haven't had any joy getting there. The Military are being very cagey on that front."

"I spoke with Barty about that and he told me that there was a big search for the POWs and that there had been a sighting by one of his patrols between Wyncombe and Storrington. In the end, both chaps were arrested by a Canadian search party who spirited them away quite rapidly.

Hardly surprising when they'd lost the trio in the first place."

"I have put in a request for Red Cross records, asking them to look into any family links – and internment camp records. If anything turns up, I shall let you know."

"That's all you can do for now. I shall go down to the Seven Stars a little later and see what we have on these parsnip pinchers."

"Thank you. Look, I'm sorry but I have to go."

"At least try and get some rest, William. I hope you get a breakthrough on your case very soon. The poor child must be terrified."

"Probably."

"It's not going well?" she murmured.

"Hard to say at this point—" Wright's voice became muffled for a moment. "Yes, sergeant, I shall be just a moment. Sorry Rose, I have to go now. I shall talk to you soon."

He was gone before Bunch could reply. She settled the receiver back in its cradle and spun her chair around to hold her fingers over the stove top for a moment or two. She recalled Wright telling her once that kidnap cases that demanded a ransom were mostly resolved within five days, one way or another. She hated to contemplate what the ramifications of "another" were. A glance at her watch told her she should get a move on if she wanted to get to the pub before afternoon closing time. *I wonder what lunch might be available*, she thought. *I suppose I shall soon find out.*

Bunch leaned down to extinguish the heater's blue flame and hurried out. The girls had vanished, though she could still hear their voices emanating from the flat above as she opened the garage doors. She climbed straight into the MG, primed the engine, and thanked the heavens that Watson's garage had secreted a cut-off switch beneath the dash to get around the directive to immobilise unattended vehicles. She didn't envisage parachuted Nazis spies lurking at every corner, and though she did understand the fear the government had of vehicles aiding the enemy if the invasion came, extracting the rotor arm each time she left the old jalopy would be both tricky and impractical. The engine coughed a little but fired up on the third key turn, despite the cold. She breathed a sigh of relief because she really hated cranking the engine. She pulled out across the yard and turned left to the village.

~~~

The Seven Stars car park was empty save for a few bicycles propped against the side wall. Bunch parked the MG and hurried into the empty saloon bar. She could hear the slow Sussex drawl of the old hands inhabiting the public bar deliberating football and other less important news.

Maisie turned to greet her, surprised and curious but welcoming. "Afternoon, Miss Courtney. What can I get you?"

"A small dry sherry, please, and is there any food available?"

"Not hot food, Miss. I don't have many eating of a Monday, but I've got some bread still, so I can make you up a ploughman's. Cheese is from over Wiston and I makes my own pickles."

"That would be lovely."

"You just go and sit yourself by the fire and I'll fetch it."

Bunch barely had time to take off gloves, scarf and Irvin jacket before Maisie trotted in with a schooner of amber wine and a tray of food. The landlady set a plate with two hunks of crusty bread, two small pats of butter, and a slab of Forester cheese that was doubtless a week's ration for most people. With it came a pickled egg, two dark-skinned pickled onions, and a small heap of virulently coloured piccalilli. A second small plate held one russet apple and a William pear; last of all came a small willow-patterned tea plate bearing a small slice of fruit cake; without marzipan, which used precious almonds and eggs, but graced with a slender skim of icing across its top.

"A real Christmas cake," Bunch said. "What a treat!" Since the pub was officially a restaurant, she didn't doubt they could manage to obtain sufficient fruit and sugar. How much of the icing was sugar, though, and how much chalk, a trick she had read about in the papers, was anyone's guess. She still appreciated the effort.

Maisie beamed with pleasure. "My pleasure, Miss. Can I get

you anything else?"

"I shall have some coffee afterwards … and perhaps you could join me when time is called? I'd like to have a little chinwag."

"What about?"

"Well…" Bunch looked towards the bar and through to the far side "…this may be better if it were private."

"Ah, it will be."

A few moments later Maisie returned, flicked the tea towel she carried over one shoulder, and looked at the door as a bell clanged. "I asked the lass to ring time. They won't notice a few minutes early, and if they does it'll do 'em good. I'll bring in coffee once I've slung 'em all out."

"They don't mind?"

"The workin' boys are all gone off. 'Tis only Jackie Haynes and his pals left. They'll get lapsy but it won't stop 'em being back on the step when we open this evenin'."

A ploughman's lunch was a treat Bunch had often enjoyed with her ATS chums in service but seldom since. She stared at the plate for a few seconds to savour the anticipation and got stuck in. She found the bread deliciously fresh and the cheese pleasantly sharp, a natural antidote to Maisie's mahogany-coloured and eye-watering pickled onions, which she was certain must have been laid down before Chamberlain returned from Berlin. The piccalilli, on the other hand, was a little short on shallots and turmeric and heavy on the cauliflower and runner beans, but full of flavour, nevertheless. Bunch was wiping the last smears with the final piece of crust when the publican returned with a tray of coffee.

"Evie'll close up." Maisie set out cups and coffee pot and a small jug of milk and took a seat opposite Bunch. "Now then…" she pushed her brown curls away from her face and fixed Bunch with a calm, hazel gaze "…what were it you wanted to know, Miss?"

"I was hoping, since the Stars is one of the few properties with a clear view of the recreation ground, that you had some insight on the goings-on at the allotments. PC Botting said you might have a few ideas about our vegetable poachers."

"Did he now?" She poured coffee into the waiting cups and pushed one towards Bunch. "Help yerself to milk 'n' sugar."

"Black is fine," Bunch replied. She took a sip and smiled. "Gosh, this is rather good coffee."

"Almost the last. The beans don't keep so may as well enjoy it now before we're down to bottles of Camp."

"Cook was only saying this week that coffee may as well be rationed for all you can buy good beans. When and if the Yanks do come into the war I can guarantee they'll bring coffee with them."

"You really think they will?"

"We can only hope." Bunch took another sip and set the cup down. "Botting said you had seen someone crossing the road early that morning?"

"Several of them. It was just about dark, of course. I was only upstairs because my Phil was off with Major Tinsley on some Home Guard manoeuvres and he wanted me to help with his backpack. No idea what he had in it. It were heavy, I know that. The old man don't say a lot about what they're up to. Just comes back up to his ears in muck." The publican looked puzzled. "Not like 'im. We don't normally have no secrets from each other. Whenever I asks, he just says that what I don't know can't hurt me."

"Dodo has told me much the same. Barty – Major Tinsley – is in his element. And Stan Botting too, seeing as he's in the Home Guard when he's off duty. Not sure that is entirely allowed but I doubt anyone really cares that much. They're all seeing themselves as the first and last line of defence."

"And so they are. All the same, I do wish they spent a biddy bit of their time keeping thieving little herberts like the Hayneses under control. People work hard on those plots and it bain't right, them tearaways go and help themselves."

"It was one of the Haynes lads?"

"I'm pretty sure it were young Victor. He's as wild as Harry were at that age, and we know how that one turned out. It was him all right. Him and that little beggar, Micky Hurst. You never sees one without the other. Were two more lads with 'em. I didn't get a good look but if it were Vic and Micky it stands to reason those Simon brothers wouldn't be far behind 'em."

"And they were doing…?"

"They were crossing Church Lane and cutting up to The Terrace."

"They all live up there?" Maisie nodded and Bunch pursed her lips thoughtfully. "It was dark. Are you absolutely sure it was them?"

"I wouldn't have noticed 'em at all but for the major's little convoy. Him first, then Geoff Watson's van and one other behind them. Blackout headlights are about as much use as a candle in a sock, but three in a row gave me a good idea of who were going along the road."

"What did the boys do when the vehicles appeared?"

"Daft beggars were pushing wheelbarrows." Maisie paused, a crease furrowing between her eyes. "Might have been prams. Something with wheels. They got one stuck on the verge and spent a few seconds trying to pull it free before the major arrived – an' then they legged it. They all dived into the hedge pretty sharp."

"Wouldn't Barty have seen them?"

"He may have, though he didn't stop."

"Did you see them after the Home Guard convoy had passed?"

She shook her head. "I'd better things to do than stand watching them boys playing the fool. When I looked a while later the barrows were gone." She topped up her coffee and paused to gaze at Bunch with an apologetic grimace. "Things is, it really was only a liddle biddy look. I bain't sure I'd want to stand up in court and say it were them."

"Which is why you didn't give names to Botting."

Maisie shrugged. "I never thought much of it at the time. Three kids muckin' about by the road isn't something that sticks in your mind normally. It were only when Stan Botting came in asking questions that it came back to me. It was dark after all," she said, less emphatically than before. "I'm not sure and for all they might be yoysterin' little weasels, I didn't want to get them in trouble for summat they didn't do. Bain't wise to stir the pot."

It was understandable. In a small village such as Wyncombe it was never sensible to alienate the locals by spreading unsubstantiated rumours. More especially with the residents of the Terrace, it was very unwise to be seen passing on such tales to the police. There were other pubs within walking distance: The Kings Head on Worthing Road, The Stag Inn, the CIU working men's' club at Inchett, all ready and willing to take a drinker's money.

"Wise," Bunch agreed. "Still, you're fairly certain that whoever it was had been raiding the allotments?"

"Can't see any other reason four lads would be trundlin' barrows around the place at that hour. And it'd be a bit of a coincidence, them being there the same night."

"It would indeed. I shall have to pay a visit to those young gentlemen."

"Didn't Frank Haynes work for you?"

"He did. As did his parents. They've retired now. Poor Mr Haynes didn't want to, but his back let him down."

"He's fair crippled with the screwmatics. Got so bad he had to give up the darts team. Still hobbles in for his pint and dominoes, though. But Mrs H says you see them right."

"We find him some light work for us here and there."

"And got him a house in the alms terrace."

Bunch waved her hands. "He's a good man."

"And he'll be right hatchetty with those boys if they'm got into bad ways. Broke his heart when Frank Haynes took off with that no-good cousin of his." She paused and pulled an apologetic face. "But you knows more about that than most, I daresay."

Bunch thought about the time she had been investigating some missing sheep with Frank Haynes in Hascombe woods on the day that her dog, Roger was shot by poachers, how he had carried the animal back down to the farm despite his war-wound. She shook her head. "Frank was a nice chap when he signed up for service but very different from when he returned home."

"Ahh," Maisie agreed. "It happens. My old dad was never

the same after the last time."

They sat for a moment in silence before Bunch pushed her cup away. "It happens. And now I must be off. Things to do. And I still like to be home well before the blackout starts. I do hate driving without proper lights, don't you? Thank you so much for your help."

"I hate to see people's hard labour go to waste – but if you can see your way to leaving my name out of your report to your Inspector friend…"

"I am certain I can get these charmless little oiks to own up and then there will be no reason to mention you at all. I shall make other enquiries about their movements."

"I'd appreciate that, Miss."

"I agree with you about the waste of people's effort, but parsnip theft is not the main reason for my enquiries."

"The Italian?" She shrugged at Bunch's raised brow. "I don't think there is anyone in Wyncombe that don't know that much. Nor that you're on the trail. Old Roly Jenner says you'll have 'em on the run."

"He's very kind."

"He don't have a good word fer many but he thinks you walk on water. Him and his brother Fred." Maisie's hand flew to her mouth. "I'm sorry Miss…"

Bunch let rip a snort of laughter. "Jenner and I go back a long way. Ever since he rescued me from those old chalk pits up in the middle of Hascombe. I wasn't meant to be out riding on my own. My pony threw me and he caught her and got me remounted and never breathed a word."

"Mebbe he weresn't meant to be there 'imself," Maisie chuckled.

"That probably goes without saying." Bunch sighed. "I have some sympathy for headstrong children. I was one myself. What do I owe for the food and the coffee?" She reached for her bag as she stood up and opened it.

"Don't trouble yourself, Miss. My biddy maid'll have cashed up by now. I shall put it on your father's slate."

"Daddy has a slate? Oh my, I bet Granny doesn't know about that!"

"Probably not, Miss. His Lordship often pops in for a quiet drink, especially since you lost the house."

"He finds living at the farm quite difficult. But a slate? Goodness. I am impressed, and on that note I shall go. Happy Christmas, Mrs Armitage – and thank you again."

Outside in the car park Bunch wondered where she should go next. She needed to speak with Tallboys, but it was almost three thirty and it would be dusk in half an hour or so.

Putting the MG in gear she went over the crossroads and parked at the top of Church Terrace. From there she had a good view of the terraced houses that consisted of a dozen front doors. Each pair of homes shared a front path, which lead to an arch between them, but veered off to identical green doors with a window to left and right of it. The symmetry beyond that was altered by the habits of the occupants. Some were neatly kept while others were as wild as she knew the residents to be.

The Courtneys owned this terrace, as they owned a great deal of the village. Since the Perringham Estate's steward Parsons had retired, her father dealt with the running of the properties but it seemed that pressure of war work made him less vigilant than he might be. Or perhaps this was a duty of estate management she hadn't previously been aware of.

Note to myself, check with Daddy's solicitor to see if this is something I need to look into. As if I don't have enough already.

She hesitated for a moment, unsure as to where any of these boys lived, and frowned at the junk piling up in the first garden. Given the reputations of the Haynes and Hurst families, she would be surprised if one of them didn't live here. She eyed the heaps as she passed and realised they were not anywhere as random as she had first thought, but stacks arranged first by metal and then by size.

~~~

"Deidre Hurst? Michael's mother?"

"S'roight."

"May I have a brief word?"

"That Betty Haynes bin complainin' agin about our lad's collectin'? 'Tis not just from the Terrace, Miss Courtney." The woman stood in the arch between the first two doors. She was painfully thin with premature grey in her dark hair to match premature lines beneath her eyes. Her arms were folded defensively across her chest, though whether against the cold or the sight of a Courtney showing their face on the Terrace, Bunch was not sure. From a meagre roll-up between the fingers of the woman's right hand curled the merest wisp of smoke. "I told Stan Botting when he came round last week," she continued "That scrap's fer the Spitfire fund. The van'll be round to collect it next week. Don't have room out the back, see. What with the chickens an' a few rows of spuds. Dig fer victory, hey?" She raised the cigarette to her lips and muttered something unladylike as she realised it had gone out.

She began to fumble in her cross-over pinny until Bunch proffered her cigarette case.

"Ta." The woman pushed the roll-up into her pinny pocket and took one of Bunch's cigarettes. Bunch took a smoke for herself and lit both.

Mrs Hurst began to cough, hugging both arms to herself. "Sorry Miss," she wheezed. "Not used to tailor-mades."

"Do you want some water? We can talk indoors about Michael."

Mrs Hurst look wary. "What that little beggar bin up to now?"

"That is what I am hoping to find out." Bunch jerked her head minutely at the terrace buildings. "May we talk inside, where it's a little more private."

"If y'like." Mrs Hurst turned and led the way along the alley and through the back door into the kitchen, apparently the larger of the house's downstairs rooms and plainly where the family lived.

A black iron range took up most of one wall. Around it was a fire guard draped in damp washing. A rack above it dangled more shirts and underwear ranging in sizes from five-or-six-year-old to adult.

"Monday," Deidre grunted. "Washin' day. Always got a copper full with my lot. I has Mondays off."

"Off?"

"I does fer Reverend Day most mornings, and the school in the afternoons."

"Three children, is it?"

"Four."

"And Michael is the eldest?"

"No, Miss. Our Florrie is." Deidre sucked frantically on the cigarette, making the end glow cherry red. Bunch could hear the tobacco crackle under the assault. Diedre held her breath for several seconds and let go noisily, coughing a little as her lungs emptied. "Don't get much of proper fags. Not unless the mister's home on leave."

"Your husband is away?"

"Army," she grunted. "If he'd be six months older he'd've been kept back. But he wasn't and now he's gone. Still, money's welcome, and he's a good man. Don't keep much back fer his self." She scowled. "He had been 'avin' a hard time findin' work since the ladder factory shut down."

"It was repurposed for war work."

Deidre took another deep lungful of smoke and nodded. "Ahh," she agreed. "Farley only kept half the staff. Now then, what's my Mickey s'posed to have done this time?"

"I don't know yet. Is he in?"

"No. Him 'nd Vic are out collectin'. Doin' their bit."

"With a pram?"

"Yeah. They gets quite a bit. They'll be collectin' paper later this week."

"Very commendable. The thing is, I'm looking into the goings-on at the allotments."

"What're you sayin', Miss? You can't think our bwoy had anything to do with it? My lad's not goin' round killin' people. Not even Italians."

"No, no, Mrs Hurst. Please. I don't think anything of the sort. But I do believe he and Victor, and the two other boys with them, may have seen something that could help us. They were over in the recreation ground the night before the body was found."

"Who says so?"

"The Home Guard. When three of their vehicles passed by

the recreation ground the boys abandoned the old pram of theirs and took cover. Even in the dark with blackout lamps it's not likely all of the Guard missed seeing them. They are trained soldiers."

"Trained? Them? Fred Karno's circus, more like."

"A little unfair. Half of those men probably served in the trenches."

"They did. But now they struts about in khaki fer a few hours a night and then they goes home." She gazed at Bunch through the trickle of smoke from thinned lips. "You was in France."

"I was." She rubbed at her leg, all but healed now – but the memory remained. "Not for long, though."

"Must've been hard, still."

"It was, but in an odd sort of way I miss it, if that doesn't sound too peculiar. I mean, nobody wants to fight a war but if you have to then at least I felt as if I was doing something. Not kicking around in Wyncombe." Bunch took a sidelong glance at the woman, wondering why she had admitted something that she barely acknowledged to herself.

Mrs Hurst let a glimmer of a smile haunt her eyes. "I understands, Miss. 'Tis what a woman's allus done, sit around and wait. I'd have signed up now if I were still a maid. Not that I wouldn't give up havin' my kids, love 'em, but 'tis hard. My mam waited fer my dad – Bertie Hill. He fought in France. He's still there, at Richebourg, along with a lot of other Lambs." Diedre clamped her lips tight and nodded several slow nods.

It was something Bunch heard often from relatives and occasional survivors of the ill-fated Lowther's Lambs, the 12th Sussex Regiment, the closest thing to an old pals unit the men of rural Sussex ever had. She understood the woman's fear when there were at least four by the name of Hill chiselled onto the village memorial. "I've seen Mr Hill's name on the monument," Bunch murmured. "I am sorry."

"'Tis what it is." Deidre seemed to relax once more but Bunch was aware of how, for all her brashness, the woman was a bundle of nerves; and how her work-aged hands shook as she reached into her apron for her baccy tin.

Bunch beat her to it, flipping her cigarette case open. "Take a couple," she said. "For later. Look here, Mrs Hurst, please don't think I'm here because I am worried about a few missing vegetables. I may be on police business but I'm not Stan Botting. Between you and me, the owner of that plot only took it on because she thought she should do something for the war effort, and I'm certain she wouldn't want to press charges. It would be a huge help to me if you could tell me where young Michael is? I'm not trying to get him into trouble but I really need to talk to him."

"Him and Vic are on messenger duty for the spotters up by Lynch Hill, so he'll be in for his tea shortly. And the girls won't be far behind. Flo took Mary and Angie down to the swings while I got some bits wrapped for Christmas, not that anyone's got a lot this year. She a good liddle maid; helps out no end when they're all home, what with school off now, and me on me own."

The woman's nervousness was growing again and Bunch wondered why. *Does she think her son's up to something more serious than stealing a few parsnips?* "My father's away on war business so we won't see him either," Bunch said. "Feels off, doesn't it. Like Christmas and yet not."

"Ahh." Deirdre's smile was uncertain. Bunch laid four more cigarettes on the table. "Save them for Christmas. The gentlemen have their cigars and we need our little treats as well…" She was interrupted by the noise of boots in the passageway and boys chattering excitedly. "Will he talk to me, do you think? Your Mickey?"

"Yes, Miss Courtney, he will if he knows what's good for 'im."

The door burst wide letting in Michael Hurst and Victor Haynes along with a blast of cold air. The two skidded to a halt and stood gawping as they realised who was sitting at the kitchen table.

"Close the door, boys. It's terribly cold out there."

Victor took a step back but Deirdre had slipped behind them and pushed the door shut before either could escape.

"Miss Courtney wants a word." She snatched their caps from their heads and gave Mickey a little shove. "Set yerselves down. The pair of you."

The boys pulled chairs from the table as far from Bunch as they were able and sat mutely, side by side.

"Well now, gentlemen…" Bunch began "…I think you may be able to answer a few questions about parsnips. Am I right?"

Mickey fidgeted and cast a furtive glance at his partner in crime, wide eyed and a little bewildered. When he turned his attention to his mother there was a tinge of fear that made Bunch wonder what awaited him when she left the house, and finally he dropped his gaze to focus on the faded oilcloth covering the table.

Victor was a different prospect. He folded his arms and met Bunch's stare with one of his own. She guessed he was just as afraid as his friend, though again whether that was of her or the consequences he'd face from his parents was open to question. The difference was that he had enough bravado to attempt toughing things out.

Bunch directed her question to him. "You were at the allotments late on Wednesday night."

"I wasn't Miss. I were at home."

"I beg to differ. What were you up to?"

"Nuthin'."

"Really?" She slapped her hands on the tabletop and both boys flinched. "Do stop wasting my time. You were seen. Stealing is a serious offence and I cannot approve of it in any shape or form. Seeing as Mrs Hurst here doesn't know what you have been up to, I am assuming you didn't steal for the family table, so either the vegetables are hidden away or you sold them. Am I right?" She sensed Deirdre moving behind her and held her hand up. "The thing is, stealing may be bad, but murder is worse, and if you tell fibs about it when there's a murder investigation, you could go to prison." She looked from one grubby face to the other and felt bad about making hollow threats as she watched them crumble. She softened her tone a little. "You can tell me, and then PC Botting won't have any reason to take you to the Police House." The seconds ticked past and to her surprise it was Victor who spoke up.

"We never did nuthin'," he growled. "We never 'urt no one, Miss. Honest. But don't tell Bottin'. He's 'ad it in fer me ever since Harry got nicked. Mam'd get a right pucker on if I gets arrested, cos of her dodgy ticker, Miss."

"I'm sorry to hear that." She gave him a brief smile. "I don't believe you hurt anyone Victor, nor did very much that was wrong. Either of you. Nor the Simon boys." She raised an eyebrow as the lads exchanged looks. "Yes, I know about those two as well, but I shan't need to see them if you tell me what happened. The sooner you tell me what happened the better."

Victor nodded. "We never saw much, Miss. I mean it were dark." He looked at Mickey who nodded vigorously.

"And you were there to take Miss Cawston's vegetables?"

"No Miss. We never touched 'em! I bain't no scally!"

"I'm sure you're not." Bunch replied. "But why were you there?"

The boys looked at each other.

"What were you up to?" Deidre leaned on the table to glower at her son. "Don't you go beating the devil round the goosegog tree, my lad. You tell Miss Courtney now."

"We was after the sheep wire." He said at last. "An' them metal poles from behind the old cricket nets. They were just chucked in the ditch right along by Miss Cawston's. It were rusty old stuff no one wants, but the bloke doin' the spitfire salvage says it still counts."

"But why take it at night?"

"Old Tallboys wouldn't let us 'ave it," Victor snarled. "We said it was fer the salvage but I never see'd 'im so mad. 'E said the wire were there to keep the sheep out and we 'ad no business takin' it."

"We'd already 'ad the stuff from behind the pavilion and 'e didn't care," Mickey added.

"But he was angry about that wire in particular?"

"Yeah. Dunno why."

"I can show you what it were. It's out on the front," Mickey added. "We bain't done nothing wrong. Mr Jenner says there bain't never been no sheep either side've that hedge. Not for years."

"And Mr Jenner would know." She pretended to be stern. "You were taking things you were told not to touch. Junk or not, you still need permission from the Hall Committee."

"Yes Miss. We did though."

"And this was when?"

"Wednesday mornin'. Mrs Chapel said it were all right."

"Mrs Chapel?"

"Aah. She 'eard old man Balltoys…" Victor stopped, his face blanching white and then red "…Mr Tallboys sayin' we were bein' tricky. She reckoned Tallboys were bein' a jobsword."

Bunch coughed and rubbed at her mouth to hide a grin. It was not hard to have a sneaky admiration of the spoonerism. "You mean jobsworth."

"Yeah. Like we said." He shrugged. "Then she said it might be a good idea if we collected it when he weren't about, so's he couldn't start moanin'."

"I see. That explains why you went to pick up the scrap after dark. Was the plot disturbed when you were liberating this scrap? You may have heard that people have been losing crops from the gardens. Did you decide to dig up some veg while you were there?"

The boys looked at each other and the fear was replaced by questions.

"That wasn't us, Miss. Honest," Victor squeaked. "We wouldn't've taken 'em if they hadn't been dug up."

"We never had no spades with us so we couldn't've done it. The garden was already mucked about with," Mickey added.

"Really?" The boys shuffled but said nothing. "You're saying there a hole there already?" she persisted.

"Gurt big'n," Micky said.

"You didn't see anyone digging?" They shook their heads in unison. "The parsnips were laying on the top of earth? They weren't there the following morning."

Victor hesitated. "We picked 'em all up. The ones we could see anyhow. Would've bin a waste of food, else. An' teacher says that's a sin when there's starvin' kids in Africa."

"I've heard that said," Bunch agreed. "Who knew you were going that night to collect the scrap metal?"

"No one, miss."

"And you saw nobody there?"

"Like we said," Victor snapped. "Weren't nobody there. Not by the plots."

"But perhaps nearby? Where abouts?"

"There were a car out at front of the hall."

"There was? Did you recognise it?"

"Mebbe," Victor said. "It were parked right up under the oak trees and we went out through the hedge on t'other side."

"Could you make out the colour? Or the make?"

"It looked posh," Mickey said.

"How would you know that?"

"Cos the roof were lower than the gate. It were big though. Not like your little'n, Miss."

"It weren't the vicar's old Sunbeam, anyway," Mickey added. "But truly we never got a good look."

"Was there anyone sitting in it?"

"Dunno Miss. We didn't stop."

"I see. Well thank you boys, that is really helpful."

"You bain't goin' to say nuthin' to old Bottin'?"

"I doubt I shall need to." Bunch pushed her chair back. "You were collecting scrap metal and the evidence is out on your path." She winked at them both. "All for the Spitfire fund, which is highly commendable. Keep up the good work, boys. If you think you can push your pram up to the farm I shall tell the girls to look out some bits and pieces for your stack."

"Cor. Thanks, Miss Courtney."

"You are welcome. Happy Christmas boys, Mrs Hurst."

~ ~ ~

The sun had already set by four o'clock, the allotted hour for tea, and Bunch was not late; nevertheless, Beatrice and Alice were waiting in the drawing room, seated close to the fire, sorting through a stack of cards for Beatrice to sign.

"Just the staff cards left to do, Rose dear. Kate came across them on the office desk and thought you might need them,"

Beatrice announced. "I thought they had already done them but they seem have been overlooked."

"Daddy usually gets Sutton to do them but he vanished in rather a hurry.

"Rather a habit of late. In his absence I think it's important we both sign them."

Bunch picked one up and flicked at the edge. "I've sent out oodles of cards already and there are dozens more here. How did we end up with so many? They have been like hen's teeth this year."

"Edward ordered them from the States back in August. You will make sure you have time for distributing the Christmas goodies?"

"The birds are all plucked and ready. I know Daddy always did the rounds in the evening when the families were gathered together. I shall get Burse to have Maggie ready and do it Wednesday morning."

"I could help you."

"Absolutely not. You have a chill and you do not need to spend hours climbing in and out of that cart in the freezing cold. I might borrow you, Alice. If that is all right?"

"Yes Miss Rose."

"Thank you."

"An excellent idea," Beatrice said. "You will get around in half the time with two pairs of hands. Such a shame everyone can't have a goose this year."

"Granny! We're breaking all manner of rules as it is. Given what people can obtain with their ration books, I'm perfectly sure that capons will be acceptable." Bunch settled beside Beatrice and poked at the pile of cards with a finger. Any word from Daddy? Is he where we thought?"

"I had a cryptic message from his office to the effect that he will be arriving at his expected destination tomorrow. They thought we should hear it from them, rather than on the wireless. They neglected to tell me where, claiming it was too delicate to mention over the public telegraph."

"How generous." Bunch pulled a face. "They are not telling us anything and expect us to smile and say pretty thank you.

It's all codes with them. No – that's ungenerous of me. They no doubt assumed he would have told us. Not that it took a lot of working out. If Winnie was going to scuttle off anywhere after that dreadful attack in Honolulu it was going to be Washington. I hope they succeed. I'm rather afraid we're sunk if the Yanks don't come in soon."

"We shall find out quite quickly, I'm sure. Now start writing these cards, young lady. Spit spot."

As Bunch pulled a stack of cards across the table Beatrice poured her a cup of tea and put a sliver of cake onto a plate. "How did you get on with your visits today? Find anything interesting?"

"I'm not sure. I thought I had found the vegetable thieves but it turns out they were boys from the Terrace who were collecting metal salvage. They say the plot was disturbed when they got there."

"Did they help themselves to the turnips – and didn't notice a body?"

"I don't know. Little boys can be quite observant, in my experience, and I am certain they didn't see anything directly related to this Italian, but they claim to have seen a car parked in front of the hall. It's possible they disturbed our local Burke and Hare mid-excavation."

"My goodness. They might have been killed!"

"Possible, yes, though I imagine hiding in the shadows until the lads had gone rather than slaughtering them out of hand was the more logical course. Three missing children would be hard to gloss over. Which reminds me, I must ask Knapp if we have any small items of metal scrap. By way of a reward. The boys are collecting and it seems a shame not to encourage them in their legitimate endeavours."

Beatrice nodded. "I shall see to it. Now, onto happier things. Daphne wants us to go to Banyards for Christmas luncheon. She seems to think we want to spend some time with Georgi."

"Don't we?"

"I can't imagine we shall see much more of her than when Nanny brings her down for a half-hour. But she is a sweet little thing and it would be fun to watch her open her presents."

"But they are still coming here for dinner?"

"I am informed that Barty may have Home Guard duties."

"On Christmas Day?"

"He says he can't expect his platoon to turn out without him, but they will carrying out reduced patrols. Say what you like, he does take his duty very seriously. But the final duty roster has yet to be posted."

"In that case, I take it Daphne and Emma will stay over so we can have a jolly evening, with just we women together."

"Not so. I believe we shall have the pleasure of Cousin Maurice's company. He will drive them over and back home afterwards."

"Oh, I see." Bunch didn't mention the obvious, that with Edward away, and Theadora gone, Dodo would want to gather what remained of the clan. Bunch looked forward to some time with her sister; and Emma, Dodo's sister-in-law, was a long-time friend. But Maurice was a bit of a shocker. "He's there at Banyards a great deal," she said carefully.

"He is. I don't view it as a problem. Daphne is a young woman and she can't mourn George forever."

Bunch tweaked her lips in a half-smile and bent to sign more cards. Maurice was harmless enough in many ways but it was only after she had turned him down that he had made a play for Dodo. Perhaps he genuinely liked her sister, and she was willing to give him the benefit of the doubt, but she had two reservations. Firstly, Dodo had been devastated at the death of George Tinsley and Bunch could not bear to see her hurt again. Secondly, on a purely selfish note, what would happen after this war ended? What if Maurice were to sweep his wife off across the Atlantic? She couldn't imagine life without Dodo. "Well good luck to her. She deserves it."

"I wish you were settled."

"One day, Granny."

"Shall I ask Henry Marsham down for Christmas?"

"Henry? Why?"

"You like him."

"Granny, I cannot understand why you of all people, one

of Pankhurst's fighting femmes, should be so obsessed with tying me down to a life of domesticity."

"You don't?" Beatrice sighed. "I love your independence and I love that you have opportunities that I never had. But you are the heir."

"Dodo has Georgi."

"And what if she marries Maurice and rushes off to the Americas with Perringham's only heir?"

"Well … the boats sail both ways."

"Don't be flippant, Rose."

Bunch got to her feet and paused at the back of Beatrice's chair. "I wasn't. Truly." She felt guilty at being so selfish when her grandmother considered that the family line relied on her. *Just that I'm not ready to settle. Not yet.* She let her hand rest momentarily on her grandmother's shoulder. "I have a lot of work to get through in the office. I shall be back in for dinner."

Tuesday 23rd

Bunch headed for the golf club just as the sky was growing lighter, in the hope of catching Tallboys at home. On near-empty roads it was just a short drive and the sun was creating faint shadows of trees and hedges across the road. The downside of a cloudless sky in December was frost and so she drove carefully along the twisting lane leading up to the club.

Westmere's sandstone manor house still retained walls from the monastery dismantled in Henry Tudor's Dissolution. It had housed the Reynolds family for four centuries until Pamela Reynolds married Reginald Tallboys. The shaded side of the lawns, where it dipped sharply into the remains of an ancient moat, sparkled white with hoar frost. Across a dip stood the golf club's all-important nineteenth hole. She had wondered how Pamela felt about sharing the site with golfers, even though her home and the business were separated by a hundred yards of neatly manicured turf.

Bunch wondered how Westmere had escaped the Ministry of Works relentless requisitioning, or the predations on the gardens by the Ministries of Food and Agriculture, at very least. There was no hint of a Victory Garden, which even the Tower of London moat had sprouted.

But Reggie Tallboys is the kind that would have friends of friends, the kind with pullable strings, she thought.

Bunch pulled up on the gravel drive in front of the house and looked around. Beyond both buildings twin lines of trees hid the practice nets to one side and channelled the view towards the first tee and beyond. In the distance she glimpsed light reflected from the carp lake. Tallboys had stocked it with trout just before the war began, with a view to selling rods by the day; but there was a shortage of fishermen willing to pay a fee for fish that had only gone to service the club's restaurant.

As she unfolded herself from the MG and went to yank on the bell pull, she spotted a curtain being drawn aside in one of the ground floor windows and caught a glimpse of someone watching before the drapes fell back in place. She was ushered into a small sitting room where she found Pamela Tallboys, neat in a plaid skirt and cabled sweater.

"Rose. What a surprise." Pamela got to her feet, smoothing her skirt in rapid nervous movements.

"Hello Pamela. Sorry to call unannounced and I hope I shan't disturb you for long. I'm here about the awful goings-on at the Victory Garden. You may have heard I do a little work for the police from time to time."

"I'd heard, yes. Good for you. You always were the unconventional one."

"Was I?"

"Always. You and Emma Tinsley between you. She was the swot and you were quite the daredevil. I so envied you."

"I didn't do half the things I'd have liked to have done."

"You did far more than I ever managed…" Pamela looked wistfully through the window at the MG in the driveway. "Shall we have some coffee?"

"That would be lovely."

"I just had some made fresh." Pamela led the way into a small breakfast room where the table had been cleared of food but a coffee percolator still graced the side table. "Cream and sugar?"

"Cream? I thought we weren't allowed to make that now."

"It's top of the milk really. We keep two Jerseys and a few chickens to supply the club house, so it's almost as good. Sugar?"

"No, thank you." She accepted the cup and sat at the table.

"Nice of you to visit," Pamela said, "but it's early for a social call so how may I help you?"

"I was rather hoping to catch up with Reg. I have a few questions about that awful business at the village hall. But he's a very busy chap."

"Well yes, he is busy these days. I think he's over at the club house."

"Oh, all right. Perhaps we can join him there."

"Join…? Heavens no. Ladies are not permitted in the club rooms. Just into the restaurant – as guests."

"You still have no lady members?" Bunch knew the answer very well; it was one of the major reasons behind Beatrice's antipathy to Tallboys.

"There are a few wives but the club house is just for the chaps. You know how it is."

"Yes, Daddy has his club in Town." Bunch watched Pamela's hands resting on the tabletop. Resting being a figure of speech: the woman was engrossed in twisting her rings round and around. "As I'm on official business that shouldn't cause too many problems. Or would it be simpler for you to call him over, perhaps?"

"Call him?" Pamela looked up in horror with a hint of blind panic. "Oh, I don't know. He… Reggie will be in shortly, I'm sure." The barely suppressed panic in Pamela's voice was obvious.

"Then let's drink our coffee, shall we?" Bunch sipped at her cup and managed not to grimace at the flavour. *Presumably the good beans are kept back for the club*, she thought. *If not, then the members are paying a lot more in fees than they should.* "While we're waiting, perhaps you can answer some of the questions, just to save a little time."

"I'm not sure what I could possibly know. I don't have anything to do with the allotments or the village hall."

"I know, but I'm only asking very elementary questions. For instance, what car do you have."

"Car?"

For heaven's sake woman, can't you answer a question without asking a question. "Car," she said aloud. "I love motors, don't you? Was that a Jaguar you arrived at church in this week? I've not seen it before."

"How clever. Yes, it's a Jaguar. Last of the '39 models. A business associate of Reggie's was able to get it for him very recently to replace the old Alvis – Reggie said it used too much fuel. I wouldn't know about those things." She laughed nervously. "I don't drive a great deal."

"I don't blame him. We had to mothball our shooting brake for the same reason. Daddy has his official car and Granny has a small allowance for her WVS work. Even with motor spirit coupons for official usage, they goes nowhere, do they? So glad I bought the little MG for my official stuff. Nippy little thing. Practically runs on air."

"I was looking at your sports car. It's rather dashing, if rather cold at this time of year."

"It can be rather uncomfortable, I grant you. Though being brought up at Perringham has made me somewhat immune to the cold. My Grandfather didn't believe in radiators and the place is a freezing pit – which is a source of great comfort now that the place has been requisitioned by the likes of Colonel Everett Ralph. I hope they all came equipped with their flannel winter drawers."

Pamela laughed and Bunch caught a glimpse of the young woman she used to know. "I imagine all those early morning horse rides had to have had some effect. You are completely inured to the cold and I'm not. Oh Rose, don't you wish we could swan off to Cannes? Or Genoa? Somewhere you can have blue skies even in the winter. I loved Sorrento."

"You've visited it?"

"Once or twice. Reggie had business there. All of that has gone since this war started."

"Yes, our cousin Maurice said much the same thing. His family in America imported Italian leather goods."

"How lovely. What else did you want to ask my husband? Anything I can help with?"

"Something quite mundane, I'm afraid. I gather he had words with some boys from the village about collecting scrap metal from the recreation ground."

"Someone asked me about that when I was in the bakery. Apparently the boys were out collecting scrap for the Spitfire Fund. When I told Reggie about it, he explained there'd been damage done around the village hall and he'd warned youngsters about taking things without permission. Is it terribly important?" The moment of hilarity had vanished and the serious Pamela returned. "Has somebody complained that my Reggie shouted at their boys? He has such a lot to do these days, and he does expect children to show some respect. Our James and Fergus would never behave like that."

"I thought your eldest was Reginald, like his father?"

"James is his middle name, after my father. I call him that most of the time because ... it saves confusion. Having two Reggie's in one house can be a trial."

Most of the time. Bunch thought back to Reg calling the boys to order in the churchyard. *No sign of James then, so that would mostly mean when Reggie senior is out?* "I can understand that. In our family it used to be all Charleses. Eldest child of eldest child and so forth. Does gets terribly confusing, doesn't it. My grandfather broke that mould by naming his sons Lucian and Edward."

"It can. Rose, I know you didn't come to talk about names and the like. What little mystery did you imagine I could help you solve?"

Bunch smiled. "I'm also looking into complaints about stolen vegetables. I am sure Reg must have mentioned it?"

"Vegetables?" Pamela looked confused. "No, he hasn't mentioned it. I thought..." She started like a rabbit as the door opened.

She's jumpy, Bunch thought. *Is our pillar of the community a bit of a bully?*

"Rose, hello." Tallboys breezed into the room and put out his hand.

Bunch took it and shook it briefly, shuddering at its clammy warmth. *Surprisingly warm for someone who crossed those lawns in this weather.*

"To what do we owe the pleasure?" He pulled out a chair and frowned at Pamela. "Coffee?" he said.

"Yes, my dear, of course."

He watched his wife scuttle towards the coffee pot. "Fresh," he added.

Pamela hesitated and glanced at Bunch before she rang for the maid.

"Now then, Rose, did I hear you mention vegetables?" He clasped his hands on the tabletop. "They seem to be the bane of my life of late. Is this to do with the dead Italian everyone's talking about?"

"Partly, by pure co-incidence. Grandmother is on the WI and WVS committees and her ladies are concerned about the thefts at the allotments. It seems that when that unfortunate man was unearthed last week, produce from that garden has gone missing. They are naturally worried for the safety of women if they are alone there. The ladies, that is, not their garden produce. The men go after work, or at the weekends, but housewives are often putting in an hour here and there while children are at school and were already feeling nervous because of the thefts. Having a body turn up has raised their fears to the skies."

"Rightly so. Sadly, I can't tell you anything more than I have told the police. Pilfering is something that is so hard to deal with. Until we have the return of street lighting the local riffraff will come and go as they please. We had the chain-link on our drive entrance stolen a month ago. In broad daylight."

"The municipal scrap collectors took down the church railings a few weeks ago." Bunch offered him a bland smile. "Perhaps they spotted the chain-link and thought it should be added their scrap-metal pot."

"They had no right to take it without notice," he snapped. "Cost good money not three years ago."

"I should write to them if I were you."

"Perhaps, but I've told Botting to patrol a little more often."

"His special constable has opted for the army life so I doubt Botting will have much opportunity. The police are stretched terribly thin, which is why I have been tasked with finding out who is behind the pilfering. Not the greatest crime in the world, but you know how much upset it's causing. If we discover who are the perpetrators it will make your life so much easier."

"The village hall and allotment committees will be very grateful, I'm sure. Now I shall do whatever I can, but how do you imagine I can help?"

"Since you mentioned your fence being taken, I heard you

had a run in with some village boys over salvage at the rec."

"Yes. Cheeky young whelps. Are they behind all of this, do you think?"

"I've seen no evidence that they have been liberating carrots," Bunch replied. "I am just trying to piece together the facts. What time were you there?"

Tallboys leaned back in his chair and gazed up at the light fitting for a moment. "I suppose it was ten o'clock that morning. I'd only popped down to inspect the standpipe that had been leaking. We needed to get it repaired or in this the weather we shall have the pipe burst like it did last year."

"Of course."

"I left straight after the groundsman came to see to it. I had urgent work here at the club."

"Naturally. And did you go back? Later on, I mean."

"No."

"Oh. It's just that someone thought they saw a dark saloon car, like yours, parked there just after blackout."

"Not mine," he repeated. "I had a party at the club house to oversee and then I had to hurry to join my unit for late patrol. Barty…" he smiled a small triumph at using the first name of his commanding officer and her relation "…was out on manoeuvres. You did know I'm in the Home Guard as well having the club to manage?"

"I had heard."

"I failed my army medical," he went on. "But as I told Barty, even with a dodgy ticker I can still man the HQ for the night shift, at least. We all have to do our bit."

"Indeed we do. Now I must get back to Perringham. I have a farm to run and I have been wasting far too much time running around after missing parsnips."

~~~

Bunch arrived back at the estate office to find Kate sitting in the captain's chair that dominated the space, sorting ministry forms into neat piles. "Mornin' Boss." She started to rise but Bunch waved her back.

"Good morning, Kate. No please, sit down. I am sorry not to be here earlier. I had a few errands to run. Is everything running well? All tickety-boo?"

"I am finding my way. I thought I'd get the milk and egg forms sorted so we can add on the last few days, and post them straight off on the thirtieth. We've had a letter from the War Ag about a visit next week. They want to discuss putting Hascombe Down under the plough for flax."

"I thought we'd settled the Farm Survey? The Down is simply too steep for horse or tractor."

"They've appointed a new inspector, I gather. I can deal with them if you like. Shall I invite them to drive the Davey Brown across it without tipping over?" She grinned. "The argument for leaving it to sheep grazing is still a good one?"

"It is. You're terribly efficient, Kate. We'll have a word with my father when he gets back if they're still being antsy over it."

"Wilco, Boss." Kate held her hands over the paraffin heater and rubbed her palms together. "This beats shovelling out the byre."

"Agreed. Shall we go over the rest of the duties this morning? Or would you rather Pat was here as well?"

"I know a lot of it already, and I can bring Pat up to snuff later."

"Excellent. How are you getting along with moving in across the yard, by the way?"

"Very well. Mrs Knapp sorted us out with the furniture we need, plus some blankets and things."

"All set for Christmas?"

"We thought we'd spend that with the gang and move in after Boxing Day. It seemed rather bad form to leave before then. The girls have been planning things for weeks. Christmas dinner and a party. Lucky dip presents. That was Pat's idea. We all buy one present, or make it, wrap it in newspaper so they all look the same and throw it into the sack. Then we all pick one out."

"That sounds very fair. And while I mention fair ... any grumbles over your promotion? Or the new digs?"

"Not that I've heard. Well ... Elsie has dropped a few sly digs, but she does love to have a jolly good moan so I haven't taken it to heart. She will be fine when the newbies arrive and she's got something, or more likely someone, new to carry on about. I had a call from the WLA depot confirming six new girls arriving on the twenty-eighth of December. Three Land Army girls and three from the horticulture college. Is that right?"

"It is. I asked for three horticulturists. We're expanding the Perringham Farmhouse kitchen gardens so that we can feed you girls as well as the house and staff and then sell the surplus. It means more lawns on the far side, across to the ha-ha, will have to be sacrificed. I am still negotiating the croquet lawn. And as you know, Mrs Chapel over at Rookery Farm needs some help but hasn't the barrack space. She will be paying board and keep for two workers for four days a week – so the books will balance."

"I didn't realise you were turning so much of the grounds over. Are you keeping the tennis courts? They are right in the middle of all that."

"Yes, I can't see digging up the asphalt surface would be useful, and the girls need some fun. We can excuse it to the Min Ag as recreational space. I gather more farms are to be offered POW labour but we may have issues on security so close to the main house. I am hoping to snag at least one other land girl before then."

"Concern over who the prisoners are because his Lordship is a big wig in the Cabinet War—?"

"That is something that we don't discuss." Bunch was a little sharper than she intended because Kate had hit the proverbial nail on its head. She had been taken aback to learn recently that both her father and Sutton, his valet, driver, secretary and apparently now bodyguard, were frequently armed, but she knew better than to make it generally known. "I'm more concerned about the effect all that Italian charm will have on our girls." She leaned on the edge of the desk and twisted her head to look at the envelopes Kate was sorting. "Anything there that I need to know about?"

"PC Botting dropped in with an envelope. Said it was urgent. From Chief Inspector Wright."

"Indeed? I've already received the reports he promised."

She picked off the seal, unwound the cotton tie holding the envelope shut and picked out a single sheet of paper from the Brighton police station, addressed in Wright's familiar scrawl. She shook the letter out and read it eagerly.

Dear Rose,

Please excuse my sending this by messenger but I shall be out of reach today and thought I should keep you up to date. I would have called but as I write it is one in the morning and I didn't think your grandmother would appreciate telephone calls in the dead of night.

How well he knows Granny, she thought.

We have not been able to trace any of the POWs' activities before the war through our usual channels, but that is hardly surprising. I have someone working on Red Cross records and we should have something from them in a few days.

I do know that our man escaped from a small camp at Castle Goring, which is being overseen by a Canadian division, and the two who were recaptured were returned there. Sorry but I don't have a CO's name but am enclosing a number for the base. The Military Police are not being at all cooperative (nothing new!). I doubt we shall get far with them before the New Year, but if you do what you can with the thefts from the allotments I think we may at least get a sequence of events down on paper.

I will be in touch later this evening or if not then, tomorrow.

Remember me to your grandmother and your sister,

Happy Christmas and best wishes
William Wright

She set the paper down. *Goring's not far*, she thought. *Less than twelve miles each way even if I stick to the main roads. All right … it will take days, weeks perhaps, to get a visitor's pass but I can't let that stop me. I'll go on the off chance. All roads have been leading to Rome, after all. Or to the sons of Italy, at the very least. Can I afford not to? Dammit, if I want to get this case sorted on my own before Wright and Carter come swooping back it has to be done now.*

"Good or bad news?" asked Kate.

"Pardon? Sorry Kate, I was wool-gathering. I know it's really dreadful of me, but I need to dash down to Goring-on-Sea on police business."

"Today?"

"Yes. If I leave it until after Christmas, I suspect it will be too late. I should be able to make it there and back while it's still light."

"That's fine, Boss. I have everything organised here," Kate replied. "We only have the basics to keep going over the holidays."

"Thank you. It's not always like this but Wright has rather left me to it. Not his fault. I shall tell you all about it at some point." She opened the door and looked at the house. "Do me a favour and let Cook know I shan't be in for lunch."

Kate grinned. "Not going to tell her or the dowager yourself?"

"Heavens no. Tell them I should be back before dark, all being well. It's a dozen miles or so each way, although there are always so many checkpoints when you get nearer the coast, and they can take up so much time." She glanced at the telephone. "I suppose I should give them a call to say I shall be arriving."

"Want me to do that?"

"Really? That would be a huge help." Bunch scribbled down the name of the CO and his office number. "I shall owe you such a huge favour."

~~~

Bunch always had a fondness for Castle Goring, despite of or perhaps because of its title. Built by the American Sir Bysshe Shelley for his poetic but ill-fated grandson Percy, the stone battlements of Castle Goring were a gothic façade for the imposing regency residence; it went beyond eccentric into the realms of mildly insane, yet somehow it worked. Given that the far more ancient clock tower at Angmering Park, just a mile or two along the road, had been destroyed in the name of artillery target practice, she hoped it would survive the army.

"Infantry…" she muttered as she pulled up close to the barrier "…with their natural penchant for blowing things up." She reached for the sheet of paper safely stowed in her inside coat pocket, stating that Goring was home to a smaller contingent of the same Canadian North Nova Scotias that occupied Angmering, and that its current CO was one Major Harvey Campbell.

"May I help you, Ma'am?"

The sentry was so young that Bunch wondered he was allowed to wield the Lee-Enfield clutched casually in both hands. His khaki tam o'shanter, with its distinctive red toorie, was pushed back on his head in a very unmilitary fashion. She saw how he was paying as much attention to the car as to its driver, and she realised he was trying hard to appear unimpressed by his duties. She felt a pang of pity for the boy, no doubt far from home, trying to be an adult when he had barely left school. On the other hand, he needed to have the word duty impressed on him a little more firmly.

"The Honourable Miss Rose Courtney." Bunch produced her card and waved it at him. "Here to see your CO."

The lad hesitated and looked behind him as an older soldier – *Though not by much*, Bunch thought – strode out from behind the barrier with clipboard in hand.

He took glanced at the paper and nodded. "Is Major Campbell expecting you, Miss?"

"Oh, Jock and I go way back," she lied. "He'll spare me a few minutes, I'm sure."

"I shall have to call the main house."

"Must you? I'm perfectly harmless. Completely unarmed. Guides' honour." She raised three fingers to shoulder height, thumb holding pinkie finger across her palm in the prescribed salute.

"Can't let you in without a pass, Ma'am."

"I only need a few minutes of his time." She looked at the open window. "Call him, please. It's terribly important."

"Ma'am?"

"Tell him it's about Costa's parsnips."

The two soldiers exchanged glances and she could not help winking at them for good measure as she reached out to press her card at them.

"Costa is the prisoner that went missing last year. His remains have turned up on my patch and I'd rather like to have a chat."

"Patch?"

"Parsnip patch as it happens. My Granny is in charge of the gardens and she's a tad upset as you can imagine. All a bit rum I agree but it would be top hole if we could get to the bottom of it so Granny can get a night's sleep. Do call him. There's a dear"

"Parsnips," said the older man. "They belonged to your grandmother?"

"In a manner of speaking." She pulled a face at their undisguised suspicion and she could only hope they didn't see through her. *It's not all fibs. I'm only embroidering it a tad.* "I know... You would not believe the half of it," Bunch dropped the grin and met the man's eye. "Please? It is terribly important."

"Okay Ma'am." He stepped aside and wound furiously at the field telephone fixed to the gate house. He spoke for a few moments, turning to watch Bunch for a moment before nodding and replacing the receiver.

"Go on up to the house. They're expecting you."

"Thank you most awfully."

She let off the handbrake and drove up to the front entrance where a young corporal was standing next to a Humber Heavy. "Miss Courtney?"

"Yes."

He looked the MG up and down and shook his head. "You need the Nissen compound. Is this thing able?"

"I've driven rougher tracks than this one," she replied.

He hesitated and eyed the MG critically. "The tracks here

are kind of rough going and you can't go without an escort."

"Is it far?"

"No Ma'am."

"Then it's fine. Hop in."

He stepped into the passenger seat and settled his rifle across his body with the barrel pointing skyward, but in the close confines of the car it was uncomfortably close to Bunch's head. "Major Campbell'll be right down there."

"Thank you." She acknowledged him with a wide smile and gracious nod and eased the car into gear to coast down the road. The track was an unmetalled woodland lane that hugged the wall around the immediate gardens of the house, but it had been recently packed tight with hardcore and gravel and was in fact a better surface than many farm tracks she had come across.

Within a few minutes the track opened out into a cleared space, to right of which was a compound hemmed in by two concentric chainmesh fences, each with a security post guarding the single entrance. Her escort hopped out and directed her through the no-man's-land, the second gate, and to a one-storey wooden building on the right of a small drill ground. To her left, five Nissen huts fanned out in a semi-circle. Smoke curled from the pipe chimneys on each of them, and she thought she caught a glimpse of movement at one of the windows. The quiet surprised her, other than the ubiquitous gulls screaming at each other as they soared in from the sea, the wind-rattled leafless branches in the woodlands, and faint distant voices from somewhere over the wall in the castle grounds. She had expected noise from however many prisoners were held here, and that silence was unnerving.

"Ma'am? Major Campbell's waiting."

"Yes, sorry. Never been in one of these places. Grim isn't it?"

Her escort didn't reply. He mounted the steps and knocked on the door into the main building.

"Enter!"

"Ma'am," the soldier said as he stood aside to let her precede him.

Inside was warmed by a pot-belly stove and a welcome relief after the cold wind that came straight off the Channel. A tall and muscular man in his forties, rose to greet her. "Miss Courtney?"

"Major Campbell?" She handed him a card. "Very good of you to speak to me at such short notice." *And without all the usual military hoo hah,* she added to herself.

"Yes, I'm Cambell. Come and warm yourself." He waved her to a chair near to the stove. Coffee?"

"That would be lovely."

"That will be all, Corporal,"

"Sir." Her escort snapped and vanished into another room.

"Sorry not to see you up at the house." Campbell got up to pour coffee from a pot waiting on the edge of the stove and handed a cup to Bunch. "We've had a few problems here, you see. The gate sentry said something about vegetable gardens. I think you may have had a wasted trip because we've got our guys working out on farms."

"I think we are at cross purposes. I mentioned parsnips, but only half-jokingly. It's where we found your missing man, Nario Costa. Middle of a Victory Garden."

"I read the report," he replied. "There was no need to come down here and tell me that."

"It was the two men that escaped with him that I wanted to talk about. Are they still here?"

"Yes and no." Campbell poured his own coffee and sat down, avoiding Bunch's eye.

"That sounds ominous."

"Yeah, it is. Look, Miss Courtney, this is highly irregular. We may not be as hard arsed as your lot but there are still channels to follow."

"Then why let me in?"

"Curiosity. A young aristocrat playing at detective arrives at my door babbling about parsnips and calling me Jock. I wanted to see for myself."

"And?"

He glanced at the card. "I shall keep this. My colonel will want to see it. Consulting detective, hey? What did you want to consult about?"

"I really wanted a quick word with the two prisoners, if I may."

"You're talking about the two guys that some police sergeant has been pestering the red caps over? I don't want the prisoners stirred up. Not easy keeping captured men happy. We don't do forced labour so we need them volunteering for duties."

"Farming duties," she said. "That will improve with the weather."

"You know about that?"

"I hear many things. I am also a WLA co-ordinator." He was prevaricating, which she had expected. The military were invariably difficult when dealing with civilians and dealing with a woman always seemed to magnify the problem. "The reluctance to help is understandable. I doubt our own chaps in their POW camps are eager to aid the enemy."

"I guess. After we had a call from Inspector Wright's office I had a chat with the Italian Officer in Command. We have questioned those men. I was concerned about these chaps and wanted to know what the hell was going on. I only took over here a month back and I hadn't been informed there'd been a previous escape." He paused, staring at the orange glow peeking through the stove's grille. A vein pulsed on his temple and Bunch could see his knuckles clenched white. "It was a foul up somewhere along the line. We might be short on workers but it was crazy for those two to be included."

"They've escaped again?"

"I wish it were that simple. Lorenz Favero is dead."

"Oh." Bunch struggled for a reply. Whatever she had expected this was not it. "What happened?"

"Officially? He fell from a hay barn. A tragic accident."

Bunch raised an eyebrow. It was one of those statements that just cried out to be questioned. "Really?" she murmured. "He just fell?"

Campbell shrugged. "We would strongly suspect he was helped on his way. Without witnesses we can't prove otherwise. The only thing we can say for certain is that nobody admitted to hearing any sort of altercation, and if these chaps had been arguing you'd have heard them, without any doubt. Some called him *Il Cavallo,* but mostly behind his back."

"The horse? He was a big chap then?"

"Not tall, no, but solid. If he had known that an attack on him was coming, pushing him from the hay barn would have been no picnic."

"What about the other one … Vito Pavessi?" she asked.

"We're keeping an eye on him. He's been pretty nervous since then. It's another reason why I want to talk to you: I need to know what information you have that makes these fellas so interesting. If I have a murderer in the camp, I want all the facts I can gather."

"The other prisoners?"

"We kept them back for the MPs to question, but now they've gone back out to work."

"Were the local police involved?"

Campbell straightened up. "No. POWs are a military matter."

"Yet your MPs aren't dealing with the death of Nario Costa, are they."

"I've been asking myself that question." He shook his head and grunted. "You guys have his body and are already investigating his death, so I guess HQ will probably leave it to you. Costa was not an allied soldier, and beyond him being dead there isn't a lot we can do, other than taking him off the Red Cross list."

"The fact that I'm here rather points in that direction. Since I'm here may I have your permission to speak with Pavessi? Or is he out with a work party."

"No, he reported sick this morning so he was kept back in camp. Somehow, I think this illness is too convenient."

"May I talk with him?"

"Not alone. Red caps would have a seizure. But I'd like to know what he's so scared of, same as you, so sure. A few minutes. Corporal?" he shouted. "Fetch *Fante* Pavessi."

"Sir."

"Do you think it possible that Pavessi killed Favero?"

Bunch asked once the corporal was gone.

"I don't see how. He was shovelling pig shit way over the other side of the farm, with half-a-dozen witnesses."

"Thus pretty much in the clear."

"Looks that way," Campbell agreed. "He seemed rattled when he heard about it though. I don't think he was expecting it – yet at the same time he didn't seem that surprised. Just nervous."

"Is that out of character?"

"Sure. He's a bit of a tough guy. Quiet, but like he knows how to look after himself. He wouldn't say squat to the MPs so don't expect him to offer too much information."

"Do we need a translator?"

"No. He speaks pretty good English."

"Did Favero?"

"Surprisingly. They seemed like buddies. We thought they might even have been related. Came from some little village called Dogaletto on mainland Venice. I doubt they'd stepped a boot outside of it before the military grabbed them. Pavessi was the brains."

"Interesting." She looked up as the door opened and the corporal escorted a short slender man into the room.

"Thank you, Corporal." Campbell jerked his head towards the window. "How are those red caps doing out there?"

"They've finished searching the barracks."

"Find anything?"

"Nothing substantial."

"Okay. Thank you." He turned to Bunch. "Over to you, Miss."

"Thank you. Mr Pavessi, come a little closer. I'd rather not have to shout at you." She beckoned with her fingertips and the prisoner limped a few paces closer, cradling his bandaged hand against his chest like a shield.

"Who did that to you?" She turned to glare at Campbell. "How did he come to be injured?"

Pavessi raised his head to look at her. His face might have been handsome without the swollen and blackened eye and sullen expression. Every muscle was tensed and his attention flickered constantly from Bunch to Campbell.

Bunch looked to the Canadian officer once more. "He didn't get that injury feeding the pigs. Can you explain it please?"

"He says he was set on by a boar and tried to jump over the wall, and then got tore up on barbed wire." Campbell replied. "The MO says he'll be fine in a couple of days."

"Hmm, I can't think of many pig keepers who use barbed wire around pig stalls. Was he trying to escape, do you think?"

"He was back inside the pen when the guard dog cornered him."

Bunch shook her head. "Dogs and pigs do not get along. Farmers wouldn't let a dog anywhere near their sows or weaning piglets. If you want my opinion this whole story is a bit of a pig's ear – if you will excuse the pun." Bunch grinned at Campbell and seeing her joke had not hit the mark turned to watch the prisoner for a few moments, wondering what to ask. This wasn't at all what she expected and she knew she wouldn't be able to ask the all the pertinent questions in the allotted time. "Mr Pavessi … Vito … I came to ask about Nario Costa. You knew him, I believe?"

The man said nothing, his focus now on the worn toes of his boots.

"You escaped with him and your friend Mr Favero when you first arrived in England, yes?"

A small nod.

"Did you know them both before the war?"

A shrug and a shake of the head.

"I was told you were taken prisoner at the same time."

He shrugged. "Si. Like a thousand more."

"Then you weren't close friends."

Pavessi shot her a curious glance and shook his head before going back to his silent boot watching.

"Why did you try to leave the pig pens when Favero was killed?"

"I did not leave."

"You didn't try to escape?"

Another glance, this one fill with pity and a little derision.

"Is what a prisoner does. We escape," he whispered.

"But you clambered out of the pen and then returned. And were recaptured." The Italian's features tightened in a shrewd appraisal and they stared at each other for a full three seconds. "Well?" she said. "You left the pig pens and then you went back again. Didn't you?"

"No!" he spat. "Is not true. *Il maiale*, it attacked and I could not get out. And then the dog it bit me."

"Really?"

"Si. I have witnesses."

The only sound for another count of three was the tink of metal from the heater.

"All right." Bunch said at last. "A different question. Were you upset by the death of your friend?"

Pavessi seemed confused. "Yes. He was a friend."

"Was Costa also a friend?"

The Italian looked up at her and this time there was no mistaking a fleeting steel in his eyes. "No," he snapped.

"Then why did you escape with him?"

"Is what a prisoner of war does. He escapes." Pavessi hugged his injured hand closer to his chest and buried his eyes briefly against the white bandages. "We saw the chance at the same time – and we run. But I don't know him. He was not from the north."

"Where do you come from Mr Pavessi? You and Mr Favero. Who are you really?"

"We come from Dogaletto. Is in Venezia."

"Venice. Ah, I visited many times. Such a beautiful city."

"Si."

"And Signor Costa? There was no other connection between you?"

"No. Not one thing, so why you keep asking me this?"

"Because the three of you escaped together and now two men are dead. We should very much like to know why. Surely when all this is over, their families at least will want to know what happened.

Pavessi shrugged. "This happens. It is war."

"Costa was murdered," Bunch replied. "Did you know

that? Brutally murdered and buried in a cabbage patch, of all places. Then he was dug up again and the foxes and crows ate his face." Bunch heard Campbell's sharp intake of breath and avoided looking at him, intent instead on the Italian soldier standing a few feet away. "It was only pure chance that his remains were not found by children. He'd been dead since the summer so it was not a pretty sight." She got up and walked around the prisoner, ignoring the nervous tic from the guard who plainly disapproved. "But you knew that very well, didn't you. Did he have children, do you think?" she said, her lips a bare inch from his ear. "How would it be if one of your children found a dead body?"

Pavessi pulled away, tucking his chin into his chest.

"Ma'am," Campbell murmured. "Steady on."

Is he warning me that Pavessi was dangerous? Or am I overstepping the mark? Bunch ignored the officer but moved a few paces to face Pavessi. "And Favero, did he really fall from that barn? Hmm?" Pavessi shook his head again and wrapped his good arm further around himself. He was plainly jittery, as Campbell had said, but Bunch didn't have the impression he was as submissive as he appeared to be. The tension in his jaw and shoulders spoke more to her of suppression rather than fear. "Can you cast any light on the death of either of those men?"

Another shake of his head.

"Won't you help them…" she said "…their families?"

The quiet stretched for almost half a minute this time. Bunch looked at Campbell, who shrugged. "Red caps have been asking him the same kinds of things."

"I can imagine. Very well, Mr Pavessi, I shall leave you to think about it. You might remember something useful, given some time. I shall be back to talk with you again."

He said nothing, only half-turned away from Bunch.

"Turn around, Pavessi, face the door," the corporal barked.

"You may take him away, Corporal." Bunch turned away from the prisoner to take a sip from her neglected coffee, indicating the interview was ended. "I will come back when I have a few more questions."

The corporal ignored her and looked to his CO.

"Back to the cooler," Campbell barked.

"Sir."

Campbell watched the corporal march his charge back into the cold afternoon and sighed. "He seems like one scared little bunny," he said. "And you were not helping."

"I rather think it's an act."

"You do? Why do you say that? I'm not suggesting you're wrong because you obviously have a reason for thinking the way you do, but I gotta say you were coming on strong there. Like it or not, the Geneva Convention gives these guys rights." Campbell scrubbed at his face and exhaled. "Look, there are witnesses swearing Favero was alone on the hay barn. Pavessi was in that pig pen. Some of my own men back their stories. Any court, military or civilian, is gonna see this as open and shut. Convince me I am wrong."

"I can't," she replied. "There was something in those eyes. He wants people to think he's some peasant boy that knows nothing, but he's not. I know a liar when I see one. However…" she picked up her bag and gloves and moved to the door "…one thing he was telling the truth about. Costa was no friend of his or of Favero, which leaves us wondering why Costa would escape with those two. Was it really as he said, that they all saw an opportunity at the same time and took it?"

"Maybe, maybe not. For the record, they were billeted in different huts. From what my guys have said, the three of them rarely spoke amongst themselves."

"Actively avoiding each other?"

"This is all speculation, Miss Courtney. Fortunately, I am not responsible for anything that happens outside of this camp, and as far as we're concerned, in this compound nobody saw anything happen. Favero was discovered on the ground with a broken neck and as far as we can ascertain he was up there alone. Pavessi was nowhere near him at the time. Until we get proof that says otherwise, it will be logged as an accidental death."

"I understand," said Bunch, "although Pavessi's plainly lying about something through his back teeth, but we have no way to prove it."

"That's a very cynical view, if you don't mind me saying."

"It's one thing I have learned as a consulting detective, Major Campbell. When it comes to an unexplained death there is rarely such thing as coincidences. Now I must go, I'm afraid. I have a million things to do and not nearly enough time to do them all. Oh, one other thing: did he learn that level of English since he arrived here?"

"He claims he worked as a hotel porter before the war."

"That's possible, I suppose, but he still feels out of place."

"Do you want to speak with the MPs?"

"Is there anything they'd tell me that you haven't?"

Campbell eyed her warily. "I doubt it, Ma'am."

"Then I shall say thank you for the coffee, Major Campbell, and start for home. Perhaps you would be good enough to see me back past your guards?"

Wednesday 24ᵗʰ

Christmas boxes were one of the few tasks that Theadora had enjoyed at Perringham, especially after the Spanish flu had taken her sons. Bunch had a vague memory of watching her parents instructing their heirs in the old ways, leading by example. This year Bunch was carrying on that tradition alone and she felt it keenly. As tradition dictated, she was offered sherry at every door and felt guilty at declining most in favour of tea. But by the time she reached her final stop at the line of cottages that housed the land girls, she was at least relatively sober. As she stepped down from the cart Kate appeared, with Pat, Vera and Dorothy at her heels. "Want a hand, Boss?"

"Oh yes please. Take those boxes, will you." The girls grinned at each other as they took either side of a covered wooden crate that chinked gently, glass against glass, bottle against bottle. Bunch grabbed the large linen laundry bag remaining on the cart and followed them into the middle of the three terrace houses that made up the bothy for her land girls. Inside was warm and inviting and, because it was past midday and Christmas Eve, crowded with chattering women. The tree in the corner, festooned with homemade decorations, had presents piled beneath it. The two girls with family within striking distance were packing overnight bags. But most of the land girls were remaining and in a party mood. Duties for the holiday were light and would include milking and general care of stock until Boxing Day was past,

"We're all going to open our lucky dip presents after breakfast tomorrow," Vera said. "It'll be just like home."

"That sounds jolly." Bunch looked around at the decorations and cards. Precious hoards of fruits and nuts had already been laid out on the sideboard. She turned a blind eye to the catering tin of mandarin slices that someone had acquired in lieu of the unobtainable Christmas oranges. "Add these to the pile." She held out the laundry bag and beamed at them. "Name tags on each so not a lucky dip. Happy Christmas!"

"Thank you, Boss." Kate came forward and took the sack from her. "May we offer you a drink?"

Bunch patted her stomach and grinned a little ruefully. "Would you think me awful if I declined? Tea at every stop puts a strain on one."

"Understood." Kate glanced at the kitchen door. "A word?"

"Of course." Bunch followed her into the scullery. "Problems?"

"There was a call from DCI Wright's sergeant at the estate office about an hour ago."

"Oh? Did he say what he wanted?"

"He didn't seem keen to say much. I said you would be home shortly and I gather the Chief Inspector will call later."

"Wonder why he's being so secretive?" She frowned. "I should get back in that case. I have to change for tea with Granny – and there's Maggie to see to first. Burse is off this afternoon—"

"I'll come with you and put Maggie away."

"Would you? That would be a huge help."

"I have to go to the flat with some boxes, and seeing as the cart is empty now … two birds and all that. I'll get the boxes." A couple of boxes turned out to be an entire cartful and Kate made a rueful apology when the five-minute job turned into half an hour. "Pat and I didn't realise we'd accumulated so much between us in eighteen months." She climbed up to sit beside Bunch.

"I see a box of blankets. Are you moving in tonight?"

Kate shrugged guiltily. "We weren't going to but it's all fixed now. Elsie and Annie want to claim our room before the new girls arrive." She shot Bunch another guilty glance. "Ours was the front bedroom and the biggest so I can understand their wanting to parachute in."

"You're not having trouble with anyone over the new job?"

Kate shrugged. "Not really."

The gesture was unconvincing and Bunch had another twinge of doubt about her plans. The young women had always appeared to be a tight-knit group. They had been drawn closer together by the tragic murder almost two years before of Mary Tucker, one of the original intake of Land Army girls. She hated to think that her plans would fracture that unity. "I'm sorry," she said. "You can turn it down if it's causing problems, though I suspect it will be tricky putting the genie back in the bottle."

"No, really. Give them a week to get used to the idea and we'll all be tickety-boo again."

"Let's hope so. And I am sure you will be … but if it becomes uncomfortable having your dinner with the other girls let Cook know. I'm sure she can make room for two more in the kitchens."

"I think we should stick with dinner at the Bothy. But – may I make a suggestion?"

"Certainly."

"Maybe move Elsie up the ladder?"

"Ah." Bunch didn't say more as she turned Maggie into the stable yard and pulled her to a halt by the steps to the flat. Elsie had been Mary Tucker's friend, both from the same part of the East End of London, and Bunch could quite see how she would feel aggrieved that others had been promoted above her. "Does she feel slighted?"

"She's been here as long as we have so yes, a little."

"She thinks I've left her out. Why? Because she's a Coster's child?"

Another shrug.

"Ruth and Annie have been here every bit as long – you all came in the first intake." Bunch saw a flash of guilt in Kate's expression. "But I take it that it's Elsie who has had her nose put out?"

"I wouldn't say it like that, exactly."

"I imagine she's spitting blood, all the same." Bunch climbed down from the driving seat and went to give Maggie a pat as a distraction while she considered Kate's request. She had chosen Kate and Pat to step up to the challenge of responsibility because, of the six land girls who had first arrived at Perringham, they were the natural choice. Ruth was a good worker but lacked initiative; Annie had the respect of her team but with writing skills that were close to non-existent; and while Elsie had intelligence she also a volatile nature that never failed to put someone's back up on a weekly basis.

"Here you are Maggie old thing." She reached into her pocket for a carrot and offered it to the horse. "You deserve a treat— No, Maggie…" she pulled her hand away and grabbed the head collar "…not my fingers. I swear this animal is part bear. Grumpy old creature." Bunch slapped the animal's neck affectionately as she turned to face Kate. "The thing is, I don't believe Elsie's ready for promotion. Just yesterday she reduced young Vera to tears when the poor child couldn't start the Davy Brown, and we all know what a pig that thing can be when it's cold. Added to which, I don't believe we need promote anyone else, or we'll be all gold braid and no Tommies."

"Yes, Boss," said Kate. "I wouldn't want to sound too cocky but I do agree. I think our moving here will help make the changes easier. Nothing worse than sharing a bathroom with someone on the next rung up, no matter how long you've known them. Too easy for people to assume they can take liberties."

Kate's tone was heartfelt and Bunch had to wonder why. "Did Elsie ask you to put her name forward?"

"Well … I said I'd ask. It seemed only fair."

"My instinct is to decline. She has a gift for making waves. Perhaps we can put her in sole charge of something specific? Poultry perhaps?"

"Dairy?"

"No. Her form-filling skills are not up to snuff. Better than Ruth's, but she's more than capable of counting eggs. I shall leave that with you as your first order to be issued. Start as we mean to go on."

"Chickens it is then. I shall tell her later. Thanks again."

"It's never easy having to give orders to people you know

but I'm sure you'll cope. Now, do you need a hand up the stairs with this luggage?"

"No. By the time I've got Maggie settled Pat will be here."

"Excellent."

"Thanks Boss. For everything."

"My pleasure. And do speak to Cook if you feel the need." She rubbed her arms and looked up at the sky. "It's getting cold. Make sure to get enough logs stacked to keep a fire in for a few days."

"Yes Boss."

~~~

Bunch hurried to her room to wash her face and change for lunch. She had serious concerns whether her new regime was going to succeed. Kate's comment didn't totally surprise her. Elsie was lively and noisy and as generous as they come, but there was no getting away from the fact that she liked to get her own way. There had never been any hint of physical force but Bunch had seen enough at boarding school to know how these things played out. Queen bees brooked no arguments and every hive had one. *They will sort themselves out. Whatever I say will only add fuel.*

Bella, who had shadowed her, as she nearly always did, let out a single muted *gruff.*

"Quite right. One can take being the beekeeper analogies a little too far." She ruffled the dog's silky topknot and went to the mirror for a final check on her appearance. She was almost ready to go down to see Beatrice when there was a tapping, and Lizzie peered around the door.

"Beggin' your pardon Miss Rose but Cook only just told me you came in through the kitchen."

"I came straight up from the stables. Is something amiss?"

"There was a call from Chief Inspector Wright's sergeant a few minutes ago with a message. I was to tell you that he has a new case and that you were to meet him at the golf club, and to bring your hat and coat because you may be standing around outside for a while."

"Nothing more?"

"The sergeant wasn't very forthcoming, Miss."

"He never is. I suppose I had better go then."

"Without lunch, Miss? Her Ladyship will have something to say about that."

"I shall sneak out the way I came in. Just don't tell Granny."

"Miss…"

"It seems I must dash. Take Bella with you. And have someone to take her out for a run later."

This sounds ominously like another murder, Bunch thought. *At the club?* Her immediate thought was for Pamela Tallboys. Had her visit had prompted some act of violence from Reg? *He might be a bully but I can't see him killing anyone.* Thinking it didn't prevent a chill of apprehension that the woman she knew of old, and had only spoken to the previous day, might be dead.

Bunch quickly swapped her dress for slacks and sweater and took her flying jacket from the cupboard. After a moment's hesitation she took a dark brown fur hat from the shelf above the rack. She stroked the fur smooth. She had a vivid memory of the last time she had seen her mother wearing it at an embassy event. It was one of those rare times that it had snowed in the centre of London and Theadora had been laughing as they descended the steps to a cab. She recalled how snow had settled on the fur; and how her mother had been so merry, in every sense of the word. Neither Theadora's excesses nor that hat were Bunch's style, *but it* is *a Charter original,* she thought. *Far too good to give away.*

"Perhaps I should offer it to Dodo? She does have the full-length coat that went with it."

She put the hat on and smiled at the effect of a flying jacket topped with couture head gear. She might have been setting a trend on the piste at Innsbruck. "Except there's not a flake of snow forecast," she said to her reflection, "and the chances of seeing the Alps anytime soon are excessively remote."

~~~

Bunch slid the MG next to the police cars and ambulance, waved to Wright's driver, and strode towards the knot of men gathered near the Westmere clubhouse. Wright peeled away from the group and came to meet her.

"William," she called. "We must stop meeting like this."

"Or people will talk?"

"People will always talk," she replied. "Good thing too, or your job would be a great deal harder."

"True."

"Let's put that to one side, hey? What's happening here?"

"A body in a lake."

"Oh my goodness? Who?"

"It's yet to be confirmed but it looks like the owner, Reginald Tallboys."

"Heavens." She stared down at the lake and blew out her cheeks. "I was only talking to him yesterday."

"Is there anything I should know?"

"Not sure. I glimpsed a side of Tallboys that the great and good of Wyncombe wouldn't like very much. He has always been full of himself but generally ingratiating. Oleaginous, as Granny would say. Yesterday, that mask was categorically slipping."

"In what way?"

"He was very rude to me. Quite aggressive, I'd say. He was a man on the edge of blowing his top, if ever I saw one. His wife Pamela seemed positively frightened of him."

"Do you think he was violent towards her?"

"I don't know. Before yesterday I'd never seen any evidence to suggest that, though to be honest I haven't seen much of Pamela since the wedding. Us spinsters rather fall off the married woman's guest list. Unless it's out of pity or they have a bachelor to be entertained. We're an ever-present threat to husbands, so I am reliably informed by Granny."

"She avoided you? Hard to imagine."

Is he making fun of me? Bunch thought. *Damned cheek.* Except that she knew he was perfectly correct. "I was away a lot and we just stopped seeing each other," she said. "Reggie was very keen to curry favour but Daddy didn't much like him so he was never terribly welcome at Perringham. One has to admire the man's persistence: he was on every committee going."

"Do you think it's possible this tension between the Tallboys was recent?"

"That's possible. I hadn't heard suggestions of any tension

before, and in a place like Wyncombe tongues would wag however quiet they tried to keep it."

"That I can well believe. It's something we can ask Mrs Tallboys later. For now, let's go to the scene. It's…"

"I know where the lake is," she snapped. "Where is Pamela? And the children? They all know, I take it?"

"The greensman came to find Mrs Tallboys when the body was discovered. We have a WPC with her now, and the doctor's given her something for the shock. I'm not sure if the children have been apprised. As you know Mrs Tallboys, it would be useful if you could help with an interview."

That explained why she had been called in such a hurry. She nodded. "Later, though. Shall we get down to the lake first?"

"By all means."

"Has your other case been closed?" she asked. Wright looked grimly ahead of him and she feared the worst. "It ended badly?"

"The child was recovered," he said. "More or less unharmed, no thanks to her fool father."

"What happened?"

"He went behind our backs and paid the ransom."

"Presumably that was part of the kidnappers' deal. One can hardly blame a parent wanting to avoid giving villains the excuse to harm their child."

"We suspected he'd do just that or we wouldn't have put a watch on him. It all ended out on the marshes at the backend of Stanmer village. He had handed over the cash but the kidnappers clearly had no intention of leaving witnesses. Left him and the child trussed up like Christmas geese and sinking rapidly in the mud."

"You found them both alive. That has to be good news."

Wright sighed. "Yes, we got to them in time. But he's had the brass neck to make an official complaint. Claims we'd made such a hash of things that he'd been left with no choice but to take matters into his own hands. Your uncle is looking for heads to sever."

"Oh dear. Uncle Walter is a sweetheart but he can act up. Fortunately for you, it's Christmas Eve and he has a Christmas lunch ahead of him, with all the appropriate wines and after-dinner brandy to guzzle, and then a few days at home to calm his nerves."

"I can only hope he's too short on inspectors to actually bust me down to constable, as he's been threatening."

"He actually said that?" Bunch pulled a face. "He's venting spleen. Don't take him too much to heart."

"Finding a rapid answer for this new case is rather important. Which will not be easy over the holidays. People will find all the excuses possible to postpone making statements."

"Then we shall have to make sure we succeed by other methods."

As they neared the dip in the land that led to the lakeside a gaggle of people came into view. They had gathered some yards from the water's edge in two distinct groups. PC Botting and a second younger constable with a couple of estate workers, and closest to the body were two ambulance crew waiting to remove the corpse, and the pathologist Dr Letham with his assistant.

"Miss Courtney, hello." Letham doffed his hat and beamed at her. "I wondered if I'd see you, with this being your neck of the woods. How are you my dear?"

"Very well, thank you, Letham. A little cold."

"It is, but I see you've come dressed for the conditions." He grinned at her. "I gather it is supposed to snow tonight so the quicker we get this poor chap tucked up in my mortuary the better. Hello, Wright. I heard about your other case. Bad do when people go off half-cocked. That's the best thing about my subjects. They tend to stay put. Charming hat by the way, Miss Courtney, wouldn't you agree Wright?"

"What?"

Bunch smiled grimly, as much at Letham's gallows humour as at Wright's perplexed expression.

"Miss Courtney's hat?" Letham arched a brow at Bunch, who hid a smile.

"Oh yes, very fetching." Blissfully ignoring the exchange, Wright gestured at the body lying under a pale canvas. "Cause of death was drowning, would you say?"

Letham rolled his eyes at Bunch with another impish grin. "Straight to business, hey? Jolly good. I won't know if this poor chap breathed in any water with his last gasp until I've conducted the postmortem. Did he die by drowning? That's highly unlikely – my money's on the bullets through his thorax. They made a bit of a mess."

"Could it be suicide?" Wright asked. "Rose seems to think he was acting out of character yesterday."

"Not unless he was a contortionist," Letham replied. "Damned hard to fire two rounds into your own heart from behind. A third projectile severed the spinal cord, which is unusual. Most assassins prefer the head. The weapon was held close to the neck and destroying vertebrae four, five and possibly six. Not the heavy calibre weapon used for the lethal shots or his head might have been blown clean from his shoulders. No call for precision, however. When a gun is fired at such close range my cat couldn't miss. Doubtless intended as a warning for his associates. I've seen it before."

"How ghastly. What sort of message could they possibly want to give?" said Bunch.

"That he lacked spine my dear."

"There's no sign of that weapon?" Wright said.

"None."

"And that's another murder on our hands."

"More of an execution I'd say. A professional job. I would say two perpetrators from the marks remaining on the lakeside, after your people have clumped around the scene like a herd of bullocks." He glared across at Botting and his sidekick. "The victim was most likely walked to the site and made to kneel by the water's edge where his killers stood behind him and…" Letham held his arm out straight and mimed a gun "… pow, pow, and that was that. By the time he was in the water he was almost certainly dead."

"Has anyone taken photos of the scene?"

"Already on their way to be developed. Some of us have been here for a few hours. I've done my job and told you as much as I am able. The who and why is your department."

"I got here as soon as I could, Letham." Wright walked carefully across to the bank, examining the ground as he went and pulled back the sheet.

Bunch could see Tallboys lying on his back and not face down as Letham had described. His head and upper body were streaked with mud and frosted duck weed, which gave Bunch the bizarre image of a macabre kind of toffee apple, one half-covered in sticky goo and the other pristine white. His face was turned away from her so that she could only see a partial profile, but it was unmistakably Reginald Tallboys, a man, the locals said, who could persuade an Eskimo to buy an ice chest. She felt sorry that a person had died but no sorrow for a man like Reginald Tallboys. She considered whether her fifth murder investigation was making her callous. *It's still a horrible way to die, even if he wasn't a terribly likeable person.*

"Do we know the time of death?" she said.

"Five and twenty past nine," Botting had wandered over and piped up. "Those two blokes heard the shot." He gestured at the two workmen. "They came running because there's still the odd pheasant left over from when the estates had shoots and there's poachers in every thicket this time of year."

"Instead of which they found their guvnor already dead." Wright let the sheet drop and stood up, scanning the ground around them. "I don't suppose they saw the gunmen?"

"They say there were a few people on the links but none of 'em was acting suspicious."

"If these were professional hit men then all they'd need would be a golf bag and decent windcheaters to fit right in."

"Yes Sir."

"All right. Statements from the groundkeepers and anyone booked to play this morning. Miss Courtney and I will go and talk to the wife. Anything more you need from me, Letham?"

"These charming ambulance ladies need to stretcher our Mr Tallboys back to the van so they may require a little help. It's going to be a four-handed job to get across that fairway. Or more accurately eight-handed." He chortled at his own joke.

"PM tomorrow?"

"On Christmas Day? My dear chap, you may have no life but my good lady wife would not forgive me if I spent my time carving golfers in lieu of a goose. But never fear, I should get it done on Monday. I shall let you know my findings as quickly as possible."

"Monday? Letham! I have a murder to investigate I need answers—"

"Chief Inspector." Letham glared, more annoyed than Bunch had ever seen him. "Half my staff are off for the holidays and I already have two poor sods waiting in my mortuary from last night. They died of natural causes, so no drama involved, but their families also need answers. When people get themselves murdered on Christmas Eve, in the middle of a war, things tend to get delayed."

"Sorry Letham." Wright lifted his hat to pass his hand over his head. "It's not an excuse but I am rather tired. Had about six hours sleep since Sunday. It would be useful to have an idea of the weapon they used."

"Quite understandable. I doubt the postmortem will tell you much more than I have already stated. Two rounds went straight through his chest. We may be lucky and find one still lodged in his skull that we can identify, but do not hold your breath. At an educated guess, I would say .38 calibre handgun. Impossible to give the make."

"Thank you, Letham. When you can. Happy Christmas and enjoy your goose."

"Happy Christmas, Wright. Miss Courtney." Letham raised his hat briefly, grabbed his bag and started off towards his car.

Wright pulled the tarp firmly back in place and stood to stare across the water. "Come on Rose. We have to go and speak with the widow."

~~~

They found Pamela in the drawing room, an untouched cup of coffee on the table next to her already forming a skin. Bunch wondered how many cups had been made and thrown away. The WPC got to her feet as she recognised Wright.

"Anything to report, Constable?"

"No sir. The doctor came and gave Mrs Tallboys

something for her shock."

"Thank you. Mrs Tallboys, I am Chief Inspector Wright. I'm in charge of the investigation. I believe you know Miss Courtney?"

Pamela looked up at him and then at Bunch, her expression impassive, uninterested.

"May I sit down?" Wright asked, his voice soft.

"Yes, do." Her voice was even softer, barely audible even at a few feet distance.

"Hello again, Pamela. Don't see each other for who knows how long and then twice in as many days." Bunch indicated the cup. "Would you like some fresh coffee? Or tea perhaps? Constable, would you go and ask the cook to make some fresh?"

"And then help PC Botting close the club," Wright added.

"You have a club house manager to deal with that?" Bunch asked.

"Yes. The steward," Pamela murmured.

"And what about you? Is there anyone who can come and stay? You probably shouldn't be alone."

"I have Cook. Then there's Nanny and the live-in maid," Pamela replied. "We don't have guests often enough to need a housekeeper. Reggie holds all of his business dinners over at the club – *held* dinners. So hard to think of him gone." She smiled weakly. "He always said the clubhouse was set up for service and it was a waste of money not to use it. I suppose he had a point."

"Bit rum," said Bunch, "having formal dinners without a hostess."

"He says – I mean said – it was all about men talking business and I'd be the only woman there."

"Did he indeed. Pammie, we should contact your family. You really shouldn't be on your own."

"None are close by," she muttered. "Not now."

Bunch knew her family was small but had to wonder if Pamela was speaking geographically or emotionally. "What about Reg's family?" she persisted.

"His sister Anne is up in Cumberland. Her husband's a vet.

His brother is away. You must remember Leonard?"

"Doesn't Leonard run the nursery?"

"Not anymore. Reg hired a manager last year when Leonard joined up," she said. "I don't think Lennie would have stayed for much longer even without the war. He cared for their parents until Mother passed away in '39. The old man had left the place to Reggie because he was the eldest, which always seemed terribly unfair. Leonard had no reason to stay."

Wright raised his eyebrow at the hint of a suspect. "Where is Leonard now? We should probably speak to him. Just to … to complete our enquiries."

"I'm not certain. He was out in the Far East last time I heard from him."

"Unlikely to be a suspect, in that case," Bunch whispered to Wright. "What about his sister?" she said to Pamela. "Anne, isn't it?"

"Anne?" Pamela turned slowly to face Bunch. "She and Reggie had the most terrible row over their father's will and she swore she'd never speak to him or visit here ever again." She stared at the cup by her side then shook her head, a move that reminded Bunch of a horse shaking out its mane. "I do apologise. These powders Dr Lewis gave me makes thinking a little hard."

"Mrs Tallboys," Wright said. "Can you tell us what happened today?"

"No, not really. I mean … I don't know what happened to Reggie. Cook had lunch almost ready, and I was going to call over to the clubhouse and then someone was hammering at the door saying Reggie was in the lake." Pamela paused, frowning at a knock at the door that seemed to echo her story.

"Your maid will answer the door," said Wright. "You were saying that someone came to tell you your husband was in the lake."

"I went down to see what the fuss was about – and there he was. His good suit was all wet and muddy. He won't like that when he wakes up."

Bunch and Wright exchanged glances.

"Then what happened, Pamela?" Bunch touched the

woman's hand. "Tell us what you did then."

"I sent for Cooper."

"He's the steward?" Wright asked.

"Yes. Ben Cooper."

"One of your groundsmen said they heard a single shot. Did you hear anything at all?"

"Shots? We're not by the range. People tee off from…"

"Not that kind of shot. A gun going off, several times."

"No. At least I don't think so. But the boys were racing about like crazy. I allow them to let off steam when Reggie is out of the house. Tina was fussing because she was cold, so it was a little noisy."

"Where are the children now?" Bunch asked.

"Up in the nursery." Pamela pulled a face. "Nannies are worth their weight in gold but so awfully expensive, aren't they."

"I would imagine so," Bunch agreed.

"What about other people outside," Wright asked. "Did you notice anyone unknown around?"

"Outside?"

"Did anyone call at the house? Or perhaps standing around outside?"

"Oh…" her brow creased as she struggled to think "…a couple of tradespeople called at the kitchen, I think. And the postman, too. There are people coming and going at all hours here. And as soon as it's light the members are out on the links and then drinking in the club house – until all hours." She glanced at Wright and shrugged. "Private club, you see. Licensing hours don't apply."

"There's nothing out of the ordinary that comes to mind?"

"I … I'm so very fuzzy right now. I really can't recall anything much."

"That's quite understandable when you've had such a shock."

"Beg pardon, Mrs Tallboys." The maid came halfway in the door. "But there's a Miss Cawston to see you."

"Mrs Tallboys is not seeing anyone just now," said Bunch over Pamela's hesitation. "Tell Miss Cawston to come back after the holidays."

"She says it's very important, Miss Courtney."

"I bet she does. Mrs Tallboys is not seeing anyone today, however, nor tomorrow."

"I should—"

"No, do not speak to the press, Pamela. It never ends well."

"I suppose you're right."

"I know I am. And we should leave you in peace."

Wright got to his feet. "Yes indeed. Thank you for your assistance. We shall tell Miss Cawston you have no comment to make on our way out."

"Thank you."

"There are a few extra constables to assist Botting in taking statements from your staff, but that will be done over at the club house."

"You should try and get some rest." Bunch touched Pamela's shoulder as she passed. "I shall drop in again very soon."

~~~

Wright escorted Cawston to the Wolsey and settled her in the back seat. "Perhaps you can tell me exactly what you are doing here?"

"I'm a journalist, Inspector. I follow news stories, and you have to admit that murder comes high on the list."

"How did you know there's a story here?"

Cawston grinned. "I live above the biggest gossip in Wyncombe, who also happens to be a member of this golf club."

"And you thought a murder was a good fit for your Family Life column?" Bunch asked.

Cawston spread her hands. "A story is a story."

"You don't think it might also be a problem for you?"

"Not really— Oh, you mean because of Tallboys and the Victory Garden affair? Between you and me, I kind of avoided him. Bit of a creep, if you get my meaning. Got a lot closer to me than a girl wants from his kind."

"Yes, I heard he could be rather familiar," Bunch agreed.

"You might call it that. He was a phoney. I've been poking

around here over the past week. Reginald Tallboys' fingers were not just the wandering kind – they were roving around in all sorts of pies, and I have heard not all of them are entirely acceptable. What he does, or rather did, is legitimate interest."

"Mr Tallboys was murdered in cold blood," Wright snapped. "His widow would appreciate a little time to come to terms with that."

"He was murdered?" Cawston tilted her head and met Wright's anger with a satisfied smile. "Nice to have the police provide me with a straight statement, Inspector."

"We can confirm a murder has taken place but no more than that at this time – and it's *Chief* Inspector."

"I'm sorry." She leaned a little closer. "I would still like to speak with Mrs Tallboys, if I may, *Chief* Inspector? I like to have my facts straight before I send in copy."

Wright moved to cut off Cawston's step forward, meeting the journalist eye to eye. "Mrs Tallboys is not seeing anyone," he growled. "There's nothing anyone can tell you at this stage in our enquiries."

"Never met a copper yet that doesn't want things kept quiet until they have the case all wrapped up in pretty ribbons. May I quote you on his death having possible links to organised crime?"

"No you may not. And may I remind you we are still investigating the death of an Italian POW found on your Victory Garden."

"I know that Inspector, but that death had occurred before I took on the garden. Which does put me in the clear and gives me a vested interest at the same time." Cawston pulled her lips into a thoughtful moue and then gave Wright a single nod. "Okay, I'll go quietly and give the widow some space, for today at least. I still have an article to write for my commission, 'Christmas Eve Church Services in Times of War'. I guess those cosy stories won't be needed if Mr Churchill gets to talk to Congress but meanwhile, there's a church service at three o'clock in lieu of midnight carols – and I have a deadline. I guess I shall see you there, Miss Courtney? You being the Lady of the Manor and all that jazz."

"Not titled, and I never will be, thank heavens."

"No? Now that would be worth a few column inches, if you're willing. Why a lord's daughter can never be a lady?"

"By all means." Bunch looked around her. "How did you get here? I don't see another car."

"Bicycle. It's only two miles."

"May I give you a lift back?"

"No. I need to make some other stops on the way. I'll call on you about that article at some point soon."

"If you feel able to come along later, in the blackout, we have a small cocktail party at the Dower."

"Don't let me hold you two up," Wright said, his eyes sparkling with something not quite mischief.

"I shan't. Goodbye Inspec— I'm sorry, Chief Inspector. I'll maybe see you this evening, Miss Courtney." Cawston waved as she climbed out of the car and walked away without looking back.

"Damned woman," Wright muttered. "There's a killer out there somewhere and I can't worry about civilians dabbling in things that don't concern them."

"I remember you saying much the same about me."

"And there are times when I wish you had stepped back. It's a dangerous business for a—"

"For a woman?" Bunch said.

He looked away and coughed. "For anyone," he muttered. "See here, Rose. This has all the marks of a gang killing, and it could get very, very ugly. I only called you here to help me question Mrs Tallboys because you do know her, and this is your neighbourhood. I don't want to have to answer to the Commissioner if anything happened to you."

"I'm good for chatting to the ladies and tracking down missing parsnips, but not asking questions that really matter?"

"You have a habit of walking into dangerous situations and the Commissioner expects me to keep you safe. I can't do that if I am not around and I can't be here every time I hear you're up to something."

"What tosh. Uncle Walter gave me a job as a Consulting Detective. I even have papers to prove it, and I shall consult with whomever seems to be the best witnesses in order to solve a case, and I have not needed a nanny since I was twelve years old!"

"Sorry." Wright turned half-away, removed his hat and rubbed at his hair before tugging the Homburg firmly back in place. "Rose, I asked you to make preliminary enquiries and that was all. After the business with the Suitcase Killers your uncle made it patently clear – through official channels, I might add – that the kind of case you are permitted to consult on should be far less dangerous to your life and limb. I am the one who is going to get roasted if anything happens to you. So please, for pity's sake, woman, show a little compassion!"

"Really. Well, that hasn't worked out so well for you because now that I have been consulted, I shall go where the evidence leads me – right through to the end. So, if you don't mind, I have things to do."

"Rose, I didn't mean—"

"Happy Christmas" she called over her shoulder. "I shall telephone you if I have anything new to report."

Bunch waved as she passed Cawston peddling madly towards Wyncombe, but didn't stop. Marion Cawston might well be just the person to empathise with over Wright's patronising habits, if she were in the mood to speak to anyone at all, which she wasn't. *If he thinks I can't do any more than hold the widow's hand he has a shock coming,* she thought. *I don't doubt he's tired. And I know he doesn't mean it, but this is 1941. Women are welding aircraft frames and driving trucks. I've no time for his nonsense today. Or Uncle Walter's. I have a jolly good mind to call the old fossil and tell him exactly what I think!*

She wondered what Wright had against Marion Cawston that made him object to her so strongly. *Is it that she's still a suspect, whatever Letham's findings might say, or is it her being a journalist that gives him the jitters?* Uncle Walter was another matter. As Bunch began to come down from what she knew was sheer pique, she had to admit that Walter was quite within his rights as a Police Commissioner to dictate who worked for the constabulary. *I do, however, draw a line with him setting Wright on me like some sort of guard dog.*

She toyed with the idea of calling on her vegetable thieves but decided Christmas Eve was not the best time to expect children to concentrate on anything other than what Father Christmas was going to bring them overnight, whether they actually believed in him or not. Now was the time to go home and prepare for her own Christmas at Perringham Farmhouse.

~~~

The drawing room at the Dower House was far smaller than that at Perringham House and the open invitation to the neighbourhood to celebrate the season had the room pulsated with a constant ebb and flow as guests fitted their social calls around family or else Home Guard and Civil Defence war work.

Beatrice was in her element holding court from her chair while Alice ensured that no one person outstayed their welcome with the old woman. Bunch worried that it was all too much for her grandmother and had charged herself with the duty of circulating, taking measured sips from a flute of champagne, and ensuring no guest was left out. Last year both of her parents had been here. Edward, affable and urbane in full ambassadorial mode, and Theadora, elegant and poised in spite of her illness.

Bunch scanned the gathering and spotted Barty arrive after patrolling with his unit. He stood with Emma in an intense huddle with Maurice.

"Hello old thing." Bunch dropped a light kiss on her sister's cheek.

"They're all dying to know about Reg Tallboys," said Dodo.

"Everyone wants to know about Reggie. I feel sorry for Pamela. Completely shellshocked."

"I know how she will be feeling. Do you think I should call on her? It's not as if I know her well."

"She was part of the usual crowd before she married Tallboys."

"You didn't like him."

"Why would you say that?"

"Your expression."

Bunch raised her shoulders. "None of us understood why

she married him. If he had been my husband I think I might have shot him myself."

Dodo put her hand to her mouth. "You don't think she did it?"

"No, no. Far darker forces did away with Reginald Tallboys. I think Wright believes Pamela may know who did, but I don't believe she was a part of it."

"Part of what?"

"Not sure. I think it's almost certainly to do with that dead Italian, but the how and why, I have no clue,"

"Doesn't Wright agree with you?"

Bunch took a larger mouthful of Moet and paused as the bubbles threatened to engulf her from the inside out before replying with a cynical grunt.

"I take it, that is a no. I thought you'd made friends again."

"I think we have. That doesn't mean I don't find him desperately annoying. He was also very odd with Marion Cawston."

"The journalist who had the plot where the Italian was found?"

"The very one. She came to speak with Pamela Tallboys and he was terribly rude, which surprised me. Not the best course of action to take with a journalist. He's experienced enough to know she could harm his career with a few well aimed barbs."

"Would she?"

"Perhaps. She obviously feels a need to clear her name over the dead POW, which gives her quite an incentive for following the story. However, she knows she'll learn more by keeping the police sweet."

"Sounds as if he hasn't taken her off his suspect list." Dodo looked into her glass and took a deep breath. "Bunch, darling, changing the subject entirely, there's something I rather need your opinion on."

"I will do my very best. Fire away."

"It's Maurice," she whispered. "He's just asked me to marry him."

"I see. Are congratulations in order?"

"I haven't given him an answer." Dodo folded her arms around herself and stared at the rug at her feet. "I'm not sure he's right for me. Terribly sweet and all that but… He's insisting I give him an answer tonight."

"I say, that's terribly unfair. You're quite entitled to think it over. Say so."

Dodo nodded. "You're right."

"Do you love him?"

Dodo spread her hands.

"If you did you wouldn't be seeking advice from an old maid. For my money, if you aren't madly in love with him then say no. Or at best that you'll give him an answer by New Year. He can't expect any more."

"You think so?"

"No question— Oh hell, what's he doing here?"

Dodo turned to see who Bunch meant. "Henry? I imagine Granny invited him. She still sees dynastic possibilities there, you know."

"I wish she wouldn't. I have said no to Henry Marsham at least four times."

"Full marks for persistence. And he did give you his dog," Dodo reminded her. "For a hunting and shooting man like him, that's about as personal as it can be."

"A dog that is bloody useless," Bunch snorted. "It wasn't any great favour." She drained the last of her champagne as she watched Henry talking with Beatrice. She hadn't seen him since they had spent a night together in the Courtney house in Thurloe Square. In theory, nobody knew about that liaison, but it had been a memorable night taken at terrible risk of discovery. It was impossible to hide those kinds of things from the staff and she always had the sneaking suspicion that it was a secret that was no secret. But who else knew? Beatrice? Edward? Both? She deposited her empty glass on a tray and swept up a fresh glass as Henry sauntered across to join her.

"Rose." He leaned in to land a chaste peck on her cheek. "Happy Christmas. And to you, Daphne." He smiled as Maurice came to join them, casting a knowing eye on the younger man's uniform.

"I can't recall if you two have met. Maurice, this is Henry Marsham. Henry, meet our cousin Maurice Badeux."

"Good evening, Maurice."

"Sir." Maurice snapped to attention and swung his right hand up to his brow.

Henry tipped his fingers casually to his forehead. "It's Christmas – no need for all that."

"Thank you, Sir."

Henry chuckled. "At ease Badeux, we're supposed to be having fun."

"Have you boys finished?" Bunch asked. "Right hands are for holding a glass this evening. Hello Henry, what brings you here at Christmas time? Haven't your people gone up to their Yorkshire lodge, or some such?"

"They have." He rocked on his heels as he looked around the room. "I heard you're on another case. Something about dead golfers?"

"Gosh that was fast." She turned to look at the clock. "You arrived ten minutes ago and straight to business. Yes, the local golf club owner was shot."

"Reginald Tallboys."

"You knew him?"

"I've played that course a few times with Larry Parrish."

"Really?"

"Larry's only a member because it's nice and local, so he can snatch a game when he's on leave. I'm singularly unsurprised that somebody swung for Tallboys. What was it? Three iron to the back of his head?"

"Why would you say that?"

"From what Larry has said, one should do well to ask his wife."

"Pamela? If anything, she was frightened of him."

"Interesting." Henry took a swallow of his drink.

Bunch narrowed her eyes. "What are you saying?"

"Your dead Italian's name came up in our office. He had connections with some underworld families in New York."

"Does Wright know?"

Henry shrugged. "His sergeant has been making enquiries,

unfortunately not the right enquiries. One can quite see why policemen have a reputation for flat feet."

"Yes, quite." *So that's it,* she thought. *Wright and Carter are being given the run around by Daddy's birdwatchers.* She changed the topic. "Did you want to see Bella while you are here?"

"Is she out in the kennels?"

"No, she's down in the scullery. The stupid creature howls if we leave her in the dark on her own." Bunch beckoned him to follow her. "I shall never know how your loader managed to get her to do as much as she did that day at that shoot. Damn all use as a gundog, but you knew that didn't you?"

"Sorry old thing. I couldn't take her up to Oban, and Pa was going to have our keeper shoot her if I left her behind."

"So you lumbered me with her. You're such a clot head, Henry Marsham."

"I knew you'd take good care of her."

"Because I'm a push over for waifs and strays? Hello Cook, just showing Bella to Mr Marsham."

"Yes Miss Rose. I've been stopping her raking out the bins again. That animal will eat anything." Cook opened the scullery door and bent down to block the dog from shooting into the kitchen. "Sit, Bella. Sit."

The dog lowered her rear end, moaning gently, and paddled her front feet, her claws clicking on the stone floor sounding like a tapdancing chorus girl as Marsham knelt down to scritch and ruffle her neck and back.

"Thank you, Cook," Bunch muttered.

"Yes Miss." Cook didn't attempt to hide a knowing smile as she turned away.

Bunch waited until the kitchen door closed. "Now that we have no flapping ears – dog excluded – what else can you tell me about Nario Costa?"

Henry gave Bella a playful pat to her side, not looking up at Bunch as he replied. "Everyone wants to know about Nario Costa."

"What do you know?"

"He was Italian."

"How perceptive. What about the two other chaps he

escaped with?"

"Rose, there are some things I can't tell you."

"Not even a little hint?"

"You have heard of the official secrets act? I could be hanged. Not to mention the flak I would get from your father."

"Not even a teeny tiny hint?"

"A hint?" He frowned. "None of the players in that little drama are who they claim to be. How they all got over here is the mystery."

"The one that called himself Favero is dead. He mysteriously fell off a hay rick a few days ago."

"This we know. But who was he? Ask yourself that."

"I should go down to Goring for another chat with Pavessi."

"I wish you success, don't I, Bella?" He gave the dog a pat and straightened up.

"We should get back before we're missed." Bunch signalled the dog back to her basket and put her hand on the door. "It's like a Greek Tragedy. A man who may not exist was pursued by two fascist goons, one of whom was killed for reasons unknown by other persons unknown. Add in escaping POWs – one really has to wonder how secure those compounds are. Yet somehow it all ties in with Reginald Tallboys?"

Henry smiled and shrugged. "You're leaping to some unproven conclusions there."

"That is rather the definition of the leaping – and you haven't denied any of it. Is that why you came? To tell me that the military have lost our only potential witness?"

"I came because your grandmother, the Dowager Lady Chiltcombe, sent me a royal summons. I wouldn't dare refuse. I even have the offer of a room for the night."

"Oh dear God, you fell into one of Granny's traps? See here, Henry, I do like you. You're a dear sweet man but you know we would never work. We'd kill each other in the first week."

"Rose…" He moved closer, stroking her shoulder, his face close to hers. "The last time we met—"

"No." She couldn't prevent a blush as she recalled their

steamy night together. Putting both hands on his chest she gently pushed him away. "We had a perfectly lovely time, and I have no regrets, but I distinctly remember telling you there were no strings attached."

"You did warn me." Henry sighed. "The thing is, when I've always had this reputation for being a bit of a silly ass you couldn't expect me not to pursue in spite of it."

"Now who's the actor?" She returned the hug, her head on his shoulder, both hands spread across his back, and realised he had begun to shake. *He's laughing*. "What is so amusing, Henry Marsham?"

"You're a special person, and when I am in a position to marry then you will be top of my list of—"

"Shh…" Bunch laid a finger across his lips. "Let's rejoin the party before either of us say anything we shall regret."

"Indeed." He grabbed her hand and kissed the ends of her fingers. "Are we still friends?"

"Always friends."

Thursday 25th

Dodo had pulled out all the stops to make a Banyards Christmas for Georgi. In spite of the dearth of tinsel and lametta in the shops, the six-foot tree in the entrance hall was a cascade of glass baubles and bells and coloured lights. Swags of greenery swathed the banister and sills and continued into the drawing room where a second huge tree was surrounded by gifts that Dodo had wrapped in butcher paper.

"Patterned by mine and Georgi's own fair hands with potato stamps and ink." Dodo laughed at Beatrice's raised eyebrows. "Nanny showed me how and we had such fun with it. Oh, I know Georgi won't remember it," she added as her guests admired her handiwork, "but I want her to grow up with all of the traditions that I did. Not on Perringham's scale, but the trees and bringing in the greens and everything."

"It all looks splendid," said Bunch. "Where's Maurice?"

"His CO called him early this morning," Barty replied. "Some sort of flap on."

"Will he be back this evening?"

"He hinted he wouldn't be back before tomorrow."

"Do you think he knows where he's off to?" Beatrice asked.

"He would be hard pressed to complete a mission if he didn't," said Emma. "He's a good pilot. It's why they chose him."

"I know," Dodo replied. "I just wish they could have waited a day or two."

"He'll be back," she said. "Some missions, though, simply can't wait."

"And best not to ask too much." Barty avoided Dodo's gaze and busied himself with pouring a fresh glass of sherry. "Can't expect a chap to say too much," he added. "Walls have ears."

"Not in one's own home, surely," Beatrice said.

"Best not break the habit. Slip of the lip, as the saying goes. Eh, Henry?"

"Absolutely," he replied.

"I don't disagree," said Beatrice. "I simply prefer not to trot out every ministry poster imaginable as a topic for polite conversation. It's not good for the digestion."

"Er, no. I was just … um … ahh, there's the gong." He offered Beatrice his arm and led them into the dining room. The tree there was smaller and decorated more simply, as were the swags on the mantle, but the table made up for any lack of glitter. The pure white damask tablecloth could barely be seen beneath the settings. Though it was daytime, candles had been lit in silver candle holders positioned down the centre of the table, along with two large silver bowls crammed with winter greenery plus a few strategic and, Bunch suspected, unfeasibly hard to obtain, red and white roses.

It reminded Bunch of dinners at Perringham House. *Which is obviously what Dodo was intending.*

"Miss Tinsley," Henry called across the table. "I hear you went to Albert Hall last week."

"It's Emma, please. And yes I did, indeed. They were performing *Messiah*, which did surprise me a little. German composers are not terribly popular."

"Handel doesn't count," said Beatrice. "He's buried at Westminster, if memory serves. And they have had *Messiah* at Albert Hall every year since 1871."

"They have," Henry agreed. "Except last year. The Blitz rather made people nervous of big events. And yes, Handel was a British citizen at his death. I think the point Emma was making, however, is that Teutonic names tend to have a dire effect on people in general. You only have to look at the attacks on shops and cafes with German names. Or Italian, come to that."

Beatrice glared at him. "Thank you, Henry."

Oh Henry. House marks will be deducted because Granny really does not appreciate being corrected. Henry caught her eye and winked, and Bunch smothered a laugh. *So that's his plan, to make himself a less desirable prospect. Bravo, Henry, one has to admire your chutzpah.* She sat back and listened as Henry and Emma launched into a lively discussion about which orchestras were still performing and where. Bunch admired their skill in the art of what Edward dubbed Whitehall whitewash, guiding the conversation into safer waters, and she wondered how much they knew about Maurice's mission. Emma held her own corner, arguing like the ardent academic she was, or had been before so much of the Oxford college had been requisitioned. She wondered if Beatrice had also noticed. *Though the wily old bird would never let on if she had.*

It wasn't until lunch was over and they had returned to the drawing room for coffee that Nanny appeared with Georgi.

"She's a tad young to sit at table but we thought she would cheer people up," Emma muttered to Bunch. "Father will be doling out presents so come on old girl. Stir your stumps."

Bunch watched as Georgi helped pick parcels from under the tree and, with a little encouragement from Barty, who took her by the hand to guide her, delivered them to each person.

"This one is for Auntie Rose."

Barty led Georgi across to where Bunch sat. "Give the present to Aunt Rose."

"Ibbons," Georgi replied and turned away to pick at the scrap of scarlet ribbon holding the parcel's wrapping in place. "Ibbons," she repeated and tugged at the bow.

"Ribbons," Bunch agreed. "Red ribbons."

Georgi paused to gaze at her aunt, her face solemn.

"Give it to your Aunt Rose," Dodo said.

"Ribbons." The toddler reached up to touch the bow in her own hair, which had been so fair at birth but was rapidly darkening to match her aunt's.

Barty reached across to take the parcel.

"Mine." Georgi tottered a few paces away and paused, with her back turned firmly on her grandfather, to examine the bow closely.

"Chip off the old block," Barty chortled. "Knows her mind, that one."

Dodo exchanged looks with Beatrice who shook her head.

"I think we can all see another family resemblance," Beatrice demanded. "Georgianna, give your Aunt Rose her gift. If you are very good she may allow you to keep the ribbon … now please."

Georgi cast a sidelong glance at her great-grandmother, recognising the tone. She glanced at Nanny rising from her seat at the back of the room and turned to beam at Bunch. "Wose," she said and dumped the package in her aunt's lap.

"Why thank you." Bunch gave Georgi a brief hug. "Shall we see what's inside?"

"Ribbons?" Georgi asked, hopefully.

Bunch gazed at her niece for a long moment, struck for the first time how Courtney features were emerging from Churchillian baby dimples. *The heir apparent. My heir.*

"Do hurry up and open it, Rose." Dodo, in childlike anticipation, pulled Bunch back to the task in hand.

"Give me a chance, old thing." Bunch peeled the paper from a lidded box which she opened to reveal a small leather sheath with a folded top fastened down by a single press stud. She looked at Dodo thinking, *Not a weapon surely.* Bunch pressed the release catch on the case and tipping it slightly allowed the contents to slide out. "Oh!" A magnifying lens lay in her palm, its slender brass bezel embossed with a laurel wreath pattern. At the bottom was a round button which she gently eased out and smiled in delight as it extended into a telescopic handle. "Dodo, how lovely." She stared at it for another moment and looked up at her sister. "It's perfect. Thank you so much."

Dodo beamed. "Well, we can't stop you getting involved in your crime-solving capers so I thought what does every consulting detective need, and I saw the posters for *The Hound of the Baskervilles* film at the Regal. It was that or a meerschaum pipe! Next year I plan to buy you a deerstalker hat."

"You should and then Basil Rathbone will have to watch out. What do you think, Georgi?" Bunch held the glass over the ribbon. "It's a magic glass. Makes things look bigger."

"Ribbons," Georgi chimed in.

"Here you are darling." Bunch handed Georgi the ribbon

and the child ran to the hallway, her prize clutched in one chubby fist, with Barty in hot pursuit.

Nanny stepped in as they passed and turned the toddler around to face the room. "What do we say, Miss Georgi?"

"Thankoo," Georgi breathed, and shrugged free of Nanny's grasp to scuttle out of sight.

"You are most welcome."

"You should come round more often," Dodo said softly. "She does like her Auntie Rose, you know."

"I don't get much chance in the daytime, but I shall try."

"Georgi!"

"Sounds like Barty is in trouble." She turned back to her sister. "Come by next week, please?"

"I shall. And if not, we have the shoot tomorrow, and the New Year do at Bellcroft House."

"Yes." Dodo frowned. "But Georgi won't be at either. Now I suppose I must go and rescue Barty."

"Dodo…" But her sister was already heading for the door leaving Bunch to give her gift the attention it deserved. She was still examining it when Emma came to sit beside her.

Emma reached over and took the lens. "Very pretty," she said. "Daphne had it made specially for you."

"She's a peach."

"She misses Theadora," Emma replied. "I know your mother wasn't around much in person, but for Daphne she was always there in spirit. They were closer than most people realised, especially since Georgi arrived."

"I suppose they were. I *shall* try and get over more often. At least you are here this week."

"I should be but I'm off back to Town tomorrow."

"Oh Emm! Not staying for the shoot?"

"Me?" Emma barked a sharp laugh. "You do remember me at school? Squelching around freezing fields with you sporty types was always my idea of a good day wasted."

"You were brought up here. You should be used to a little mud."

"And left it behind as soon as I was able. My mother didn't bestow a great many of her attributes to me, thank God, but a liking for staying warm and dry was one."

"Do you have a flap on? That's why you are off tomorrow?"

"Not as such. More Henry's game than mine."

"Then he knew Maurice was off on a jaunt?"

"We both did."

Bunch looked across at Henry, busy trying to convince Barty of the virtues of a semi-automatic pistol against the revolver. "The old fox," she muttered. "Not just here because Granny said so."

"Henry?" Emma gazed across at him. "There's not a lot that goes on in the darker corners of Whitehall he doesn't know about."

"Quite enjoying his war, is he? Daddy suggested something of the sort."

"That's a little unfair, old girl. But yes, it has brought forth hidden depths. He's not quite the vacuous numbskull we all thought, hey? Has he dropped any hints about your current case?"

"Nothing that makes too much sense. He can be annoyingly cryptic."

"The chaps you are looking into are extremely dangerous. Mussolini's more dedicated fanatics have a disturbingly long reach. Mostly the States, so far. With any luck a lot of those communication lines will be cut in the coming months. Speaking of which, be careful what you say to our society journalist. She is a great deal more than she appears."

"Cawston is a spy?"

"Not exactly but she has 'sanctioned' affiliations in America. I can say no more."

"Be careful what you say, Emm. That man has an uncanny ability to lipread." Bunch waved at Henry, who was now watching the two of them as he listened to Beatrice. "She's reeling him into her web."

"Your Granny's never going to get him interested in 'socks for sub mariners'."

"Granny has very little interest in it herself these days. She handed that crusade over to her WVS minions months ago.

What you are seeing there…" she rolled her eyes and sighed "…is matchmaking."

Sunday 28th

The lack of people willing to brave sleet-laden winds had ended the Boxing Day shoot before it had begun and, with nobody willing to break off festivities to discuss murder, Bunch spent the day making small talk with Beatrice. When people remained stubbornly unavailable, the next morning she made a start on neglected estate paperwork. The call from DS Carter to tell her that Wright was on his way was a welcome relief.

Wright had not contacted her over the holiday and she was prepared to be suitably aloof when he arrived at the stable yard in the middle of the morning, but she emerged from the estate office trying hard not to laugh at the incongruity of the rangy detective crawling out of a battered Austin Seven.

"Not a word," Wright groaned as he stretched his back.

"What on earth do you call this?" She walked around the car, running her finger over the scatter of scratches and dents in its body work. "It's a wreck."

"In a better state than most of our fleet. The Wolseley was in the repair shop at Portslade when a couple of Jerrys decided to fly a dawn tip-and-run raid. Missed the airfield and scored a direct hit on our garages, and the whole building collapsed like a pack of cards. I ended up with this rattletrap because it had been left in the rear yard. A twenty-mile drive never felt so long."

"We all have to make sacrifices," she replied. "I hope nobody was hurt."

"Nobody there except for the nightwatchmen, and they take to the cellars when the sirens sound."

"Well, that's something. What brings you all the way here in this splendid machine?"

"I'm on my way to have another chat with Mrs Tallboys. Need to bring her up to speed."

"Couldn't Botting do that?"

"Yes, but I want to get her reactions face to face. The BBC said that we may have snow tonight so let's get going. Hop in." He folded himself back into the Seven and leaned over to open the passenger car door.

Bunch was accustomed to having car doors opened for her, but times were rapidly changing and when she thought about it, he had "opened" the door after all. There was no rule, she thought, to say he had to be outside of the car even if etiquette dictates that he should. She slid into the narrow seat and knew that she would suffer for it in due course. "Anything new over the holidays?" She pulled the door shut with a little more force than it really needed and smiled sweetly. "I have got absolutely nowhere. No one wanted to talk."

"Things tend to grind to a halt over Christmas. This year more than ever," he replied. "People want to be with those that matter to them, if they are able."

"It's also frustrating," she replied. "Anyway, William, you must have something new to ask or you wouldn't be driving all this way."

"A few things are gradually coming to light." Wright turned the car around and headed north. "It would appear that Tallboys' contact with fascist groups prior to 1939 was not confined to Italy."

"A lot of people had those contacts. Look at the supper club Larry Parrish belonged to." Bunch frowned at the reminder of the showdown at the Parrish farm earlier in the year. "Larry hasn't a fascist bone in his body but he ran with some sympathisers simply because they were on the same social round. I don't, however, recall Pamela being one of them. She was always one of those obedient debutantes that stuck with their chaperones and were tucked up in bed before midnight. It was such a surprise when she married Reggie Tallboys. I mean to say, his mother came from an old family but not his father. Terribly snobbish, of course, but most people viewed him as a poor catch."

"Did he have money to make up for it?"

"Yes. He inherited from his mother. And he certainly had enough knack for business to add to the pot."

"If Mrs Tallboys' family were on their uppers that would do it. We should also find out who his associates were in America."

"Nazis?"

"I think 'criminal fraternity' is more accurate in this instance. He exported vast amounts of scotch to Canada."

"There is nothing illegal in that."

"Most of it took the usual prohibition route across the border into America." Wright pulled a face. "Proving that he knew those goods were to cross the border isn't the problem. It's his continued dealings with those American agencies that Scotland Yard are looking at."

"The Mafia?"

"I think we may safely assume that much."

"Pamela did mention Tallboys had crossed the Atlantic a few times."

"And now claims she can't find his passport."

"Protecting him is probably second nature to her. Or perhaps she really doesn't know where he kept it."

"She produced her own, which has no travel stamps for some years."

"How singular. We all travelled before the war. Even those folks with sprogs," Bunch replied. "Buzzing off to Paris or Rome is something I miss. As for the rest, it's all rather circumstantial."

"It often is, except that Tallboys was playing a dangerous game. It's no secret that there is a grudge match between the Mafia and Il Duce. If Tallboys was running with the hare and the hounds, which looks increasingly likely, we may have found a motive for his murder."

"I gather Cawston is also sniffing around his overseas contacts." He glared and she wondered if throwing Cawston into the mix was entirely sensible. Wright was not predisposed to liking journalists any more than he did Whitehall intelligence services. "Do you think Mussolini had him killed?" She chortled, more loudly than intended. "The idea of Reggie being murdered by Il Duce's thugs right here in England is a little bizarre. Even supposing dictators want to stop criminals,

Tallboys would be rather small fry. And I can't imagine Pamela having anything to do with anything like that."

"Which is what we want to learn," Wright replied. He pulled into the golf club and came to a halt in front of the family home.

"Doesn't seem to be anyone here…" Bunch looked across to the club house "…which is odd for a Saturday."

"The first two fairways are a crime scene," Wright replied. "The rest of the course has been closed while we complete preliminary investigations and it's unlikely to be reopened before the inquest. If nothing else, the ACC has ordered the lake dragged for weapons as a matter of procedure. Though not even he imagines we shall find anything in there but lost golf balls and broken driving irons. A professional killer would never leave the tools of his trade behind. Botting assures me that the dredging should be completed in the next few days." He turned towards the house as the door opened by a fraction. "Ah constable. Right on cue."

"I didn't recognise the car, Sir. I thought it might be more reporters." The WPC opened the door fully and saluted. "You'll find Mrs Tallboys inside."

Wright handed his coat and hat to the maid waiting on the step and headed for the drawing room where there was a healthy fire in the grate. Pamela Tallboys was huddled in an armchair almost within arm's reach of the flames.

"Chief Inspector Wright. And Rose." She turned on a weak smile. "Do you have any news for me?"

"I'm sorry to say I don't. However, there are a few questions I need to ask about some of Mr Tallboys' business dealings."

"I shall help if I can Chief Inspector, though Mr Cooper is the steward so he would know more about the running of the club than I do."

"PC Botting is making enquiries in that area. At the moment I'm more interested in Mr Tallboys' personal business. Do you happen to know if your husband had any recent business in the USA?"

"Possible. Reggie had quite a portfolio in the city and he

went over to America several times." She shifted nervously. "I couldn't tell you who he dealt with. He was always adamant that business and home affairs should maintain a distinct distance from each other."

"Were your own affairs kept separate from the club's?" Bunch asked. "The house for instance."

"Oh yes. There's a board of trustees who control shares and such like. Daddy set it up before Reggie and I were married. Reggie was a little put out at the time but he said later that it's been quite useful in the end. I don't really understand why. I'm a bit of a dunce when it comes to those sorts of things." Pamela looked down at her hands clasped tightly in her lap. "I know I shall have to look at the papers soon, but not yet. I can't. I simply can't."

"I do realise it is very upsetting and we shall try to keep this visit as short as possible," said Wright. "Had your husband any dealings with his former associates in Italy?"

"No, of course not. That would be illegal. I mean, all trade from the Axis powers is out of the question. Isn't it?"

"It is. There was nothing with Switzerland, perhaps? Or Portugal?" Bunch asked.

"There are club members from allied forces. Not as many as he'd like. It's been far quieter all round."

"Were finances getting tight?" asked Wright.

Pamela looked away. "Reggie never discussed money. You should ask Mr Cooper about that."

"I need to ascertain motives for Mr Tallboys' murder and money is often at the top of the list." Wright softened his tone. "Had he borrowed money, perhaps?"

"He never said a thing to me." She turned to glare at Wright. "Reggie had his faults and yes, my family had doubts about him when he presented plans for this club, but it pulled the Westmere estate out of a hole. They didn't like it but he proved himself." She looked at Bunch, fleeting anger showing in the set of her lips. "There are a few in the family who hated him for that. Jealousy. There's a motive for you Inspector. Good old-fashioned jealousy."

Bunch nudged Wright into silence. "We didn't mean to

imply otherwise, Pammie. What the Chief Inspector meant was that we've heard Reggie's businesses were … varied. Was it possible, do you think, that there were foreigners trying to buy the club, or part of it?"

"No," said Pamela. "He would have told me. Anyway, he can't sell Westmere without the family trust's agreement. Mortgages against the house would be impossible."

"Mr Tallboys may have gone outside the accepted avenues," Wright replied.

"My Reggie is not – was not – a criminal."

"Could he have borrowed without involving the trust? Intending to pay it back, naturally."

"No! It's impossible I keep telling you that. Why won't you believe me!"

"I'm sorry, Mrs Tallboys, I must ask these questions."

"Perhaps you do, but Reggie would never sell Westmere." Her voice rose an octave as tears formed in the corners of her eyes.

"What if he had no choice?" Bunch rested her hand over Pamela's. "People do odd things out of desperation. What if Reggie thought you and the children were in danger? That's why we are asking these things. Was there anyone in the past few months who seemed out of the usual kind? Anyone who made Reggie uneasy or especially angry? Think as hard as you can because it could be important."

"There was this one chap about two weeks ago," Pamela said softly.

"Around the time the body was found on the allotment?" Bunch asked. "You never mentioned it at the time."

"I forgot. He came here late in the evening. Reggie didn't know I was on the landing. I only overheard a little because Reggie bundled him out. Something about having a nerve showing up after the last time."

"So this man had visited the house before?"

"Yes." Pamela paused. "Back in the summer. It was the night of a club tournament. The trophy dinner was over but these things do go on long into the night. You know how it is."

"What happened that night?"

"He and another chap came hammering on the kitchen door. I was already in bed and Cook sent them over to the club. Reggie was furious at being dragged away."

"Chaps, plural?"

"Yes, there were two that first night."

"Did you hear what they said? Do you think you could you describe them?"

"No and no. I'm sorry. I only caught glimpses of them from the window."

"One of these men returned when Mr Tallboys was killed?" Wright asked.

"Yes, I think it was one of the same men. I really only caught a glimpse. Dark haired is the best I can do."

"Was he taller than Reggie? Shorter?"

"Umm … let me think. Shorter? Possibly?" Pamela steepled fingers of her right hand against her forehead. "I'm sorry, I'm not being very helpful, am I?"

"You are being very helpful. If we brought you some photos, do you think you could identify this man?"

"No. And Cook never opened the door to them so she would have no idea."

"Perhaps your steward saw him. He lives on the club premises, I assume?"

"The old one had his call up last year. Reggie had been doing most of the work. The chap we have now is quite new. There should be records of any dealings in the club office."

"I'll get Carter to check that. Mrs Tallboys, thinking back to that summer visit, did you see the two men leave?"

"I heard the car go out so I assumed he ran them back to wherever they came from."

"Was he gone all night?" said Wright.

Pamela lifted her shoulders. "He was here at breakfast." She smiled shyly. "He often sleeps in the dressing room if he is up late."

"You have no idea where he went?"

"I didn't ask. When he's in such a terrible fug it's best to let him get over it. Was, I mean. Hard to think of Reggie in the past tense. He wasn't an easy man but I was always terribly grateful to him. I mean, he saved Westmere from the bank. And we got on quite well while Mummy and Daddy were still alive. Over the last few years, however, it hasn't been quite so easy," Pamela admitted. "I have no doubt the staff will tell you that much."

"You argued?"

"That takes two. Reggie had a terrible temper at times and he could be quite loud. I found it was easier to wait the storm out and avoid arguments."

"Was he ever violent?" Wright asked. "I'm sorry to ask this…"

Pamela looked from Wright to Bunch, her face impassive but her hands were clenched together so that her knuckles gleamed blotchy white. "Not very often," she whispered. "He wasn't a bad man. Poor Reggie. It was such a shock seeing him lying there, all wet and muddy." She shook her head and laughed without humour. "He'd have hated anyone to see him so – unkempt. It was one of his redeeming features." She put both hands to her forehead and leaned forwards. "Sorry. The powders Dr Guest gave me … they are making me terribly woozy.

"We'll leave you in peace in that case. If you can think of anything else, Mrs Tallboys, please pass it on to WPC Atkins, or telephone me at the Brighton station. You have my card."

"Or just call me. You know where I am." Bunch stood as the maid entered to show them out. "No, you stay here and look after Mrs Tallboys," Bunch said to the maid. "She and the children will need a little cossetting. We'll let ourselves out."

Once outside they both looked at the clubhouse. "There's a fire lit in there." Bunch pointed at the chimney. "Chat with the manager?"

"Not yet. Botting took a statement yesterday and seems to think the man knows very little. I'd like a chance to delve into Tallboys' finances first. Something for Carter to do. I think we should take a spin down to Castle Goring now to see what our remaining POW has to say."

Bunch went around to the passenger side, opened the door

for herself, and flounced into the seat. "You don't honestly think Pamela shot Reggie, do you?"

"Most murders are domestic, committed by a family member, and we usually investigate that aspect first and foremost." Wright settled behind the wheel and took a last look at the house before turning the car around. "I rattled the bars a little to see how she reacted."

"And your opinion?"

"I think there was little affection between the Tallboys. The majority of police detectives, me included, would consider there are grounds for a case of mariticide."

"But you don't believe Pamela is capable of murder, do you?"

"Given sufficient provocation most people are. In my experience people will do extraordinary things in the heat of the moment, especially in defence of themselves or of others. I don't think Pamela Tallboys is any exception to that rule. Reginald Tallboys, however, was murdered in cold blood." He held up a hand as Bunch prepared to argue, eased the car into gear and headed out onto the southbound road. "In the heat of an argument," he continued, "someone might push their spouse downstairs or hit them over the head with some suitably heavy object, or even stab them with a kitchen knife. If someone has a loaded pistol they invariably have death in mind. But all evidence points towards Reginald Tallboys being executed by a professional and I very much doubt Pamela Tallboys fits that bill. My honest opinion? She did not shoot her husband." He glanced at Bunch and grinned. "Had she planned to kill him, I do believe she would have slipped something into his supper."

"I do believe you're correct." Bunch returned his grin. "And a simple no would have sufficed."

~~~

They were not escorted to the compound this time, but shown to Major Campbell's office in the inner sanctum of the house. In better times it had overlooked a formal garden with topiary and knot gardens and walkways. Now it was a wide expanse of rough ground that housed a collection of tents and equipment.

It made Bunch feel sad for her own family home, knowing it was suffering a similar fate.

"Good morning Chief Inspector, and Miss Courtney." Campbell shook their hands and signalled them into comfortable chairs to one side of his desk. "I gather you're here for another chat with Signor Pavessi."

"We are." Wright sat back, legs crossed, his hat resting on his knee, seemingly relaxed; but Bunch recognised a terrier-like readiness. She said nothing and waited. "Is that a problem, Major?"

"I am afraid you've both had a wasted trip. Mr Pavessi is no longer with us."

"What? We weren't informed. You do know he's a person of interest in a murder enquiry. The police really should have been notified!"

"And you were. We contacted your HQ as soon as we discovered that Mr Pavessi had escaped."

"Again? That seems a little careless."

"He slit a sentry's throat, Chief Inspector," Campbell snapped. "I'd call that murder."

Wright looked away for a moment, his frustration evident in every muscle. "I am sorry you lost one of your own. Obviously, I shall look into why I wasn't informed at my end," he growled. "When did he escape?"

"Christmas Eve." Campbell glanced at Bunch. "Just a few hours after you left, Miss Courtney. Guess you spooked him a lot more than we realised."

"It wasn't worthwhile putting an extra watch on him?" said Bunch. "How did he get away?"

"After he killed the sentry he went over the wire."

"The dogs were unable to stop him?"

Campbell grunted. "This guy's a pro. Seems he already had an escape in mind, and when you showed up asking questions he decided it was time to leave. He'd smuggled a bag of pig shit from the farm..." he gave Bunch an apologetic shrug "...and used it to lay a false trail and the dogs led us straight out along the river. We put out all the usual alerts but apart from one unconfirmed sighting in Rustington he's gone to ground."

"Rustington? That's west, isn't it?" Wright asked. "Logically, I'd have thought he'd go east towards Brighton or head for London."

"We're guessing it was a bluff, unless he was looking for a handy boat to steal from along the river at Littlehampton."

"Good luck with that." Wright waved in the general direction of the coast. "There isn't a beach or mooring that isn't barbed wired or mined. Or both."

"There've been no reports of boats going missing so far," Campbell replied. "We're still searching. There is a high alert at all our units, and at the main depot in Chichester. I had a lot of chaps pretty put out at having their Christmas leave cancelled. The only good thing is, this is an island so pretty hard for him to get far without help. Most times escaped POWs are caught stealing apples or eggs by some farmhand with a pitchfork. Cold, hungry, and looking forward to bed – even when it's a Nissen Hut bunk." He poured coffee and handed cups to Bunch and Wright. "Sorry you had a wasted trip – but we did file a full report."

Wright took time to light a cigarette, giving himself a moment to digest the implications. "Major Campbell…" he said at last "…in light of what you have said, I have a very good reason to believe Pavessi was involved in a murder just north of Storrington after his escape. Properly, we should call it an execution. A man was marched from his home while his wife and three children were sleeping – and was shot in the back."

Campbell stared at them for almost half a minute. "I have two kids back home," he said at last. "Every father's nightmare when they head into war is leaving them behind." He leaned across his desk and picked a folder from a small stack. "This report came in yesterday. Favero and Pavessi did indeed have links to crime in their youth."

"Nothing since?"

"This report…" he tapped the file "…says they were recruited as muscle for the more secretive of the police services, but their more recent past history was somehow … mislaid."

"And Costa?"

"That's where things get weird. We double checked with the Red Cross and they insist he was already dead."

"That happens," Wright replied. "Lot of chaps in the last lot were listed MIA or killed and turned up in a field hospital or got separated from their unit after a push."

"Yeah…" Campbell tapped the file again "…except Costa died when he was five years old."

"Five? But how—" Bunch hesitated.

"This is interesting." Wright flicked through the scant four or five pages in the manila folder. "How did you manage to get this information?"

"*La Croce Rossa Italiana*. The Italian Red Cross. Surprising what information passes between these people that they'd never think to tell us." He spread his hands. "A man wants to reinvent himself, this is one way to do it. Births are seldom listed in the same books as deaths."

"Any idea when this Costa signed up with the Italian army?"

"Our guys were still trying to verify information. His military ID doesn't check out. We assumed that's why he made a run for it in the first place. We're assuming he wasn't with the same outfit as Favero and Pavessi but we have no idea where he did come from. We don't know how he ended up as a POW either, other than he was picked up somewhere along the North Africa campaign."

"What does this all mean?" Bunch asked.

Campbell pulled a face. "Out of my hands now. It's been handed it over to Military Intelligence so I don't suppose I'll ever find out."

"Was he was an allied spy?"

Campbell puffed his cheeks. "I doubt it. If he was, why not check in the moment he hit these shores?"

"Russian?"

"Unlikely. Other prisoners said he was Sicilian and a bit of hard man. Handy with sharp implements, if you understand my meaning. We don't have a lot of trouble with the prisoners in general, but Costa had problems with taking orders from our officers. It doesn't help you much but honestly, I was glad to see the back of him. My colonel is taking the line that as these guys apparently didn't exist within the military establishment, so were effectively civilians, and with two of them now dead, we have no escaped prisoners. But if Pavessi was involved in another killing he'll have to rethink that, and if he is recaptured I can't see him being returned here. He'll be handed straight to Intelligence."

"Quite likely. May I take this file?"

"What file would that be?" Campbell slid the folder back into a pile on his desk.

"Major Campbell, I have a murder investigation to conduct."

"Then you'll need to go through channels."

"Which could take months."

Campbell got to his feet and held out his hand, the universal signal for an interview coming to its end. "I wish you all the luck with that, Chief Inspector."

~~~

"That was illuminating," Wright muttered to Bunch as they squeezed back into the Austin. "Not helpful but … illuminating."

"Many more questions than answers." Bunch wriggled around to look at him. "Look here, William, if we have to come out again in this sardine can, let's not. My MG has more space than this thing."

"I shan't have this for long, believe me. For a senior officer to be reduced to something so…"

"Undignified?"

"I was going to say so farcical."

"There, there, my dear William." She patted his shoulder and laughed at his expression. "I'm sure your superiors won't like a senior officer being seen in this either. Unless the fuel savings are worth it."

"Do not – even – think it."

"I shall try very hard not to. So what now? Should I try a few contacts of my own to track Costa, or whatever his name is?"

Wright scowled. "You mean Marsham?"

"Possibly. Look here William, I cannot for the life of me think why you should be so set against Henry. Stop it this instant. I can have more than one friend."

"And more than one kind of friend."

"I wasn't just thinking of Henry, as it happens. There's also Marion Cawston."

"She is suspect. What is a journalist from an American family magazine doing in a backwater like Wyncombe?" He held a hand up to stem her indignation. "I know what you are going to say, why not Wyncombe? The point is, I did not swallow her relocation story. There are plenty of places to rent just a mile or two out of Worthing or Brighton."

"Are you suggesting she's not a journalist?"

"Not at all. She does write about British life during the war. She was also put on a flight out of Egypt only two days before the crash that killed her husband – which is curious."

"The question, then, has to be what is she doing in Wyncombe?"

"She has claimed it's because your mother's death was reported in the society magazines in America, but your Marsham and his pals should have been all over her. Or maybe they have and we haven't been told. That would be standard for their type. You said Marsham was with you over Christmas? What made him come to Wyncombe of all places?"

"Henry is terribly sweet if you took a little time to know him."

"He's a Whitehall *birdwatcher*. Military Intelligence. None of his breed can be trusted to give you the whole story."

Bunch couldn't argue with that assessment. She knew from experience how Marsham had developed a habit of steering people around him with slivers of information to suit his own ends, and she knew for a fact that he worked for the Whitehall security department headed by her own father; a small detail she could not discuss with Wright. *Not talking is simply how it is.* "Yes, and it's amazing how people step up when needed. Henry has proven to be quite a revelation. Before the war began I thought he was a very nice but rather ordinary sort of man. A nice chap but nothing out of the ordinary. As for why he came down for Christmas, that's simple. Granny invited him. She has been trying to pair us up ever since my Coming Out ball."

"If you say so. But be careful, his sort are dangerous men to be around."

She let out a belly laugh. She couldn't say it didn't rankle that Wright's warning hinted as petty objections, which were as much personal as professional. He didn't trust her judgement? "Henry has never lied to me," she said.

"You seem very sure."

"I am." She felt annoyed at Wright, thinking he was being childish, even if a part of her was flattered. She couldn't deny that Wright was handsome, and she found his humour and intelligence attractive. *He would be a pleasing partner but at what price? But it's easier to flirt with Henry. We see each other so seldom that there are no consequence. Wright is a colleague – and that has far deeper connotations.* "He may not tell me everything," she said aloud.

"I should hate for you to be chewed up in the Whitehall wringer and then spat out in little lumps."

Bunch sneaked another look at Wright's profile and saw genuine concern there. *Touching,* she thought. *He's wrong about Henry but Marion Cawston may be a different matter.* "Remember who my father is. I've been part of that rigmarole my entire life. I know how to be careful." She grabbed at the door strap as Wright came to a T-junction and swung right without pausing, and she was fairly convinced that the nearside wheels had left the tarmac for a second or two. "Good God, William, no wonder you usually have a driver. Next time we go out I am taking the wheel."

"Not a hope," he growled. "Anyway, I need to take you home and then get back to Brighton."

"What about Costa? What are our next steps about him?"

"Forget him. Looking into Tallboys' business dealings is our next priority. Not the golf club side, though; that all seems to be very much by the book."

"Tallboys excluded Pamela from the club business because of the men-only rule." Bunch snorted. "It's one reason why Daddy would never join it. He always says he has enough of that in the Civil Service. And Granny, too. She still has tea with her old suffrage campaign chum, Princess Sophia, when the chance arises. She wouldn't stand for it."

"Are you name dropping?"

"Shamelessly. But getting back to Pamela – she was frightened of Reggie. I think if she knew anything about any dubious deals she would not hold back now he is dead." She stared at the road ahead. "Marion Cawston seems to know more than she should. I shall see what I can wheedle out of her."

"Be careful there. I never trust the press. They may be nice people – until they sniff out a story."

"That sounds rather bitter."

"Let's say I have been singed in the past." He glanced at her. "Be … very … careful."

Tuesday 30th

"Miss Cawston. How lovely to see you." Bunch rose as the journalist was ushered into the drawing room.

"Miss Courtney." Cawston came to shake Bunch's hand. "I got your message. Sorry not to have come before now but I've been up in Town. Pursuing Tallboys' city connections."

"You have?" *And what is provoking you to tell me?*

"Our Mr Tallboys has a more colourful past than I am willing to bet the parish council are aware of."

"How fascinating. As it's almost luncheon would you care to stay for a bite? We can have a jolly good chat."

"Lunch would be lovely."

"My pleasure. May I offer you a small sherry? That at least is not on ration – provided you can get hold of it."

Bunch got up to ring the bell. "Knapp," she said when the housekeeper appeared, "please tell Cook that Miss Cawston will be staying for lunch. Will Granny be here? I know she had some meetings this morning."

"Her Ladyship assured me she would be back by midday."

"Thank you. And could you let the girls in the office know I've been delayed."

"Yes Miss."

Cawston watched Knapp leave, one eyebrow raised. "Do you have a housekeeper and a cook?" she murmured. "So many people seem to have trouble finding staff."

"There's also our maid Lizzie," Bunch replied. The question puzzled her and she wondered what she might be giving away. "When I was younger, when we had the big house, there was a small army of indoor staff. But with Daddy's globe-trotting for the Diplomatic Service, my parents were hardly there – and I was at school."

"And your sister?"

"She often went with them. Too sickly for the average

boarding school and even my parents thought she shouldn't spend her childhood with just a nanny for company."

"A latter-day Jane Eyre?"

"Rochester's ward was Adele Varens. Jane Eyre was her governess." Bunch sipped at her drink and took in the familiar patterns of the Turkish rug. "I'm sure my domestic arrangements are not that interesting."

"But they are. My editor wants an article on how the war is changing life for every family. Staff for example. How does staffing here compare with the golf club?"

"You can't compare them at all."

"Exactly. For example, you've never had a lady's maid."

"I have been dressing myself since I was sent away to school so engaging a maid as an adult always felt rather a backward step."

"How very modern."

"It's realistic. Hiring staff before the war was hard enough. I can't see it getting easier in the future. The Great War began it, then the flu, and the Wall Street crash gave it another kick. I suspect this war is going to see the end to a great deal more than lady's maids." Bunch poured two more glasses of sherry, handing one to Cawston. "The call up is making changes to how people view themselves. Ladies' maids, footmen, boot-boys – they are a luxury most houses will have to learn to live without. Much as some will fight against it, the cold hard fact is that old ways are vanishing, Miss Cawston."

"Does that worry you?"

"Worry me?" Bunch gazed into space and then shrugged. "Much as I love the place, I do realise that a house like Perringham is going to be increasingly difficult to keep afloat. Tallboys, for all his faults, was quite visionary in turning Pamela's family home into something useful without the family having to sell up. Many of the old places became schools and hotels after the depression and were lost to the families themselves because the old guard couldn't adapt."

"Is Mrs Tallboys in a better position than most?"

"If you mean she has a business to fall back on, then perhaps. It will depend on the bank balance Reggie left her. It all comes down to money, Miss Cawston."

"Marion, please."

Getting chummy with this woman went against logic, but Wright wanted to know what Cawston knew. "Then I am Rose." Bunch proffered the cigarette box and selected a tailor-made cigarette for her own ebony holder.

"Thank you." Cawston gazed around her. "What a lovely room. So elegant."

"Granny has impeccable taste, and technically this is still her home. I am a refugee. Only here under sufferance until we get Perringham back. If we get it back."

"You think we may lose the war?"

"I hope not but I am realistic. And luckier than most because I could flee to America at a pinch."

"I detect column inches there. Titled daughter's life in potential exile."

"Not titled, other than being an 'Honourable'. Daddy may pass on the estate to me but the title will go to some cousin or other." Her lips twitched. "Which you are well aware of, I am sure."

"Ah yes. The anachronistic rules of heredity." Cawston waved a hand around the room. "It's very quiet. You don't have anyone billeted here? Evacuees or refugees?"

"Daddy's job is rather sensitive and he can't afford to have strangers cluttering up the place, besides the land girls on the farm. No more – he cannot allow anybody to publish details about his home."

"Is it any different than writing about Buckingham Palace?"

"It's the same," Bunch laughed. "Nobody *writes* about Buck House. Not beyond the stuff you can read in the guidebooks. Surface details only, never what goes on beneath it."

"It will make for a short column unless you can give me something. Why did you ask me here?"

"You rather invited yourself, as I recall." Bunch smiled. "You are not here for a column on houses. I said yes because I think we could help each other in this investigation into Reggie Tallboys."

"Does your father approve? I've heard your family doesn't

agree with your consultation work. He isn't here, I take it. Your father, I mean."

She knows rather too much for comfort. "Daddy doesn't disapprove, but he does worry. And no, he isn't here right now."

"I heard he was in Washington."

Bunch tapped cigarette ash that had barely begun to accumulate into the glass ash tray while she considered her reply. "I don't have his diary to hand," she drawled. "I can't possibly predict what he does or where he goes."

"I think we understand each other." Cawston nodded her approval. "I gleaned that little snippet from gossip in Mrs Crisp's village shop."

"The village is generally very protective about the family so I do find that hard to believe. However, my father's whereabouts has nothing to do with what is happening in Wyncombe right now. Let's lay our cards out. Starting with a reasonable certainty that the same people who killed the POW also murdered Reginald Tallboys."

"I agree."

"And Reginald Tallboys is a good place to start. Tell me what you know about him."

"He's your neighbour. I imagine you know more than I ever would."

"You said you were looking into him."

"Amongst others," Cawston conceded. "Tallboys is an interesting character. He had links before the war with both Italian fascists and with organised crime in the USA."

"I know." Bunch felt some satisfaction at the surprise that flicked across Cawston's eyes. Here was a woman unused to finding the secrets she had gathered were already known by others. "The question is," she continued, "which side wanted him dead."

"Both and neither," Cawston replied.

"That's not helpful."

"Okay, then let's begin with one fact: the body in my allotment was identified as Nario Costa but his true identity is in doubt."

"Where did you hear that?"

"The Red Cross." Cawston drew on her cigarette and chuckled quietly on the exhale. "I've also been making discreet enquiries among the POWs themselves."

"How did you manage that?"

"Simple. They're marched out to various farms to work as labourers. It's easy enough strike up a conversation whilst they work."

"Surely they're under guard."

"They are, but toddle up in a green sweater and dungarees with a spade at the ready and you're next to invisible," Cawston replied. "I was in North Africa long enough to gain a working knowledge of French and Italian. It was essential to get by."

"Did you turn up anything useful?"

"I discovered that Costa was from southern Italy. Rumoured to have criminal links – that I have yet to confirm. Some seemed to think he may have put that around himself, as protection. No one had served with him before he was captured. Many of his compatriots suspect he was some kind of spy. Most were certain that Costa escaped for reasons beyond the usual homing instincts."

"And the two chaps who escaped with him?"

"There the plot thickens, as the saying goes. The official story was that Costa, Favero and Pavessi were stragglers from another brigade swept up in the melee as the allies advanced over the Libya-Egyptian borders. I thought that sounded pretty fishy – but the POWs were certain of it." Cawston leaned forward, her right forearm resting on her crossed knee. "Favero and Pavessi made their mark early on with beatings dealt out to those who crossed them. And Costa seemed to have had contacts of his own because he categorically had help in escaping. I have been doing follow ups elsewhere."

"How have you found all this out? Not all of it from prisoners surely."

"A journalist never reveals her sources."

"Egyptian sources?"

"Working for an American publication, I can still gain information on the Axis countries and on the people of two continents with relative ease. So far, anyway." She leaned a little further in. "Most of my sources say your father is quite a big cheese in the war business."

Bunch retreated behind her sherry glass as she recalled Wright's comments on this woman's presence in Wyncombe, and wondered if Cawston was trying to impress or threaten. *Is she here because of Daddy? Should I tell her we already know most of this?* "Daddy never tells the family anything," she said slowly, "and I am my father's daughter. I know all about how to maintain diplomatic silence."

"I'd expect nothing else." Cawston turned to look at the fire and back again, meeting Bunch's gaze head on. "Honestly? I was interested in stories of your police." She sat back, a little smug in her revelation. "You have to admit it was a hunch that's paid off, though there will be far bigger stories now that US forces are here."

"The Yanks are already here? I thought Congress was still debating."

"There has been a small force of US engineers quietly working in Londonderry since June. They have been setting up things in anticipation of the major influx. Nothing much gets past the press but quite naturally a firm lid was slapped on it."

"You seem certain that it will all happen."

"Pearl Harbour made sure of that. Hitler has already declared war on the US. All Mr Churchill is doing over there is hoping to persuade Roosevelt he should commit his main force to Europe rather than the Pacific."

"You *are* very well informed."

"I wouldn't be much of a journalist if I wasn't." Cawston grinned. "And I think you of all people will agree, snooping is such terrible fun."

"Which brings me back to why you came here today."

"Other than keeping tabs on you? Like I said, your exploits with the police have not gone unnoticed in the US. You like to be in the thick of it. I also heard a lot of rumours about what goes on in your old home but I suspect that's not something I should examine too closely. Digging around official secrets is a good way to get arrested." She chuckled quietly. "Which for someone in my business is generally all the more reason to look. That dashing chap in charge is rather a hound. Everett something?"

Bunch was sure Cawston knew exactly who he was and wondered what she was playing at. "Everett Ralph," she replied. "Colonel in His Majesty's Services."

"That's the one. He's had an interesting career. A girl needs to have her wits about her with his sort."

"And you think he needs watching? As you said, that could get you arrested. Perhaps as a spy."

"I was not investigating his official business, though for the record he seems to be squeaky clean so far as that goes. Career army carved right through him. It was rumours of a few secrets of his own, in his personal closet, that make interesting reading."

"Have you found something awful?"

"Yes, that he is a bit of a hound. No secret that he has very few women in his staff. Naturally, his superiors don't see anything wrong in that, but he does have a few skeletons involving young men rattling around his particular closet. And that could get him thrown out double quick."

"I shouldn't waste your time." Bunch would not lose sleep over anything that happened to Ralph but thoughts of her old friend Johnny Frampton and his own secret liaisons made her less eager to judge. "What people do in their own time is not our concern," she said. "So … Nario Costa?"

"When he was captured he had a map of Tangiers and Tunis on him. He claimed he had a cousin in the latter, which may be true because it's only a skip and a jump from Sicily. And it fits with my theory that he's working for one of the Cosa Nostra families," Cawston replied. "Costa is a common enough name. Choosing a name that plays on words does seem to be a rather audacious choice."

"It's all getting terribly complicated, assuming he was all you seem to think. It could be that he really was a soldier trying to get back home."

"Costa was working for the Sicilian Mafia. Quite what he was up to still needs investigating but I can guarantee it wasn't anything to do with serving the Italian state. Mussolini put a lot of effort into stamping out the dons before the war, and there's nothing like a common enemy to set aside old grievances between them. The various *coscas*, the clans, have been joining forces and looking for a way to unseat him ever since he came to power." Cawston took her glass and swallowed half the contents in a gulp. "Which brings me to Pavessi and Favero. You went to their POW camp. Did you discover anything about them?"

"I'm still looking into details." The reporter's level of knowledge was alarming and Bunch was unwilling to admit how much greater it was than the local constabulary's – or her own.

"What do you have on Tallboys?"

"Oh gosh, again it's all— Oh, hello Granny." *Thank heavens for my grandmother riding in like the cavalry.* "Granny, this is Marion Cawston. She's a journalist. Miss Cawston, meet my grandmother. Beatrice, Dowager Lady Chiltcombe."

"Ma'am."

"Miss Cawston. I have heard much about you from Mrs Brice. She is one of my WVS. Having a pharmacist's wife on that team is terribly useful. Did you know she also qualified as a chemist? Or she would be if the Oxford Colleges weren't stuck in the eighteenth century. Mrs Brice tells me you are writing for American magazines about life under siege. Perhaps you can write about her. Awfully clever woman in her quiet way, all but overlooked."

"Of course. And please, call me Marion."

"Marion." Beatrice sank into her chair close to the fire, a moment of pain appearing on her face.

"Granny, good WVS meeting?"

"Excellent. Daphne and I have been going over the new booklet that the Country Herb Committee has prepared on what they most need to be collected. Your sister is rather upset that you are missing the New Year ball committee's lunch. You do remember the ball is tomorrow?"

"I left her a message." Bunch rolled her eyes at Cawston. "'Ball' is its traditional title but it's been cut back so hard a dance would be more appropriate. We used to hold them at Perringham but that's out of the question now. Granny and Dodo have persuaded the Ramplings to host it. Their house is a lot smaller, but they do have a ball room of sorts. They expect ticket sales to be far lower with so many folk away. It's in aid of the Refugee Fund. If you want a ticket I'm sure Granny has some about her person. Sherry, Granny?"

"How splendid. Now then, I take it you are also discussing the golf club? Emma Tinsley was there." Beatrice took the sherry Bunch had poured for her and sipped appreciatively. "She called on Pamela Tallboys yesterday and said she was surprisingly bright for a recent widow."

"No love lost there," said Bunch.

"Love being lost is quite likely the entire the point," Beatrice said. "Though one has to wonder if it was ever there in the first place. Pamela had proposals from men far better suited then Reginald Tallboys. Connie Frain and I were trying to recall if she had two or three beaus before Tallboys came into the picture. What she truly saw in him is beyond us."

"Reggie bought his own way in. He wanted Westmere as an upmarket base for his wine business."

"I can quite believe that. Connie's son plays at the club. He told her that there was a quite the kerfuffle over there still being so many Italian wines on their lists, but the steward corrected that with burgundies and champagnes."

"Wine traditionalists don't see Italy as a wine-making country?" said Cawston. "I'm not sure if that is a parochial attitude or downright snobbery. Hundreds of new vineyards were planted after Mussolini's 'bonification' program, and my father claims they aren't half bad."

"That may well be the case," Beatrice replied. "But I gather the club committee demanded chateau vintages."

"And did they?" Cawston asked. "Get the vintages they wanted."

"I honestly could not tell you."

"I can get Botting onto that," said Bunch. "Or perhaps I need to chat with Pamela again."

"Never given any thought that he was a spy?"

"Given his activities in America, I rather think he is more attracted to pounds than politics."

Cawston tilted her head to regard Bunch critically. "You didn't much like him, did you? Why was that?"

"Frankly, I didn't know him well, which is quite a feat when you think how small Wyncombe is. Granny knew him better because of all her committees."

"I did," Beatrice agreed. "He had the breeding. I knew his grandmother and she was devastated when her daughter married him – a gardener – but the girl was happy. Reginald's father was a rougher diamond but a good man who married well. Reginald was rather more educated but far more obsessed with money."

"I suppose one can't blame Reggie for that. He made a lot of money and was still being treated like the poor relation. Almost makes one feel a little sorry for him."

"It was not all about money or breeding, my dear. Reginald simply lacked charisma."

"Knew the price of everything and the value of nothing, as Mr Wilde would have said?"

"Possibly," Beatrice replied. "Reggie made himself indispensable with the least possible involvement. He knew how to delegate without people realising they were being recruited to do his bidding. He was known for being a man who got things done."

"But?"

"Some of his methods were … ungentlemanly."

"How?"

"He made himself indispensable so that people seemed to end up feeling they owed him. I think that could qualify as lacking good manners," Beatrice snapped.

"Was there any suggestion of blackmail?" Bunch asked.

"Not in the way that William would view it, no."

"But he gets things done by calling in favours." Cawston chuckled. "Not illegal."

"That we know of," Bunch added. "Is it possible somebody objected to having that favour called?"

"Or vice versa."

"Reggie owed someone, but who? That could explain a lot though hard to see how he could owe favours to POWs."

"Unless they owed him and they objected to paying him back," said Cawston. "And the payback wasn't what he expected."

"Now we are drifting into the realms of fantasy." Bunch frowned, reaching out to fiddle with the lid of the cigarette box, opening and closing it with her forefinger. "How would these POWs end up owing him in the first place?" she said finally. "Do we even know there's a connection?"

"One of them ended up buried under my Victory Garden," Cawston replied. "And Tallboys was the one handing out plots. What if he banked on my being a poor tenant? A car very similar to his was spotted at the village hall the night Costa was dug up. Was something buried with him, do you think?"

"That's rather farfetched. One would assume those who buried Costa would have searched his body. What could Costa possibly have that warranted three men being killed?"

"There is that," Cawston conceded, "except that we know Costa was not actually Costa."

"What difference would that make?"

"Maybe he—" Cawston flopped back in her seat and massaged her forehead with stiff fingers. "I have absolutely no idea. Sorry. This how I work up a story. Not terribly logical at times. I suppose you are more used to working up a case from the evidence."

"Not at all," Bunch replied. "Eliminate the impossible and whatever remains, however improbable, must be the truth."

"Sherlock Holmes."

"Indubitably."

"Ah … Consulting Detective on your police card. You are a Holmes devotee."

"I've read the stories, but not especially. The consulting detective title began as a little gentle nose-thumbing. Wright was rather reluctant to have me investigate the murder of a dear friend, especially when his colleagues had quickly dismissed his death as suicide."

"And it's stuck with you."

"It has rather. Whatever the origin, it's a theory that withstands the test."

"Then test our theories and see if any of it sticks in place. And I have leads to follow up via my Italian contacts."

"And I shall look into Tallboys' business dealings. Perhaps too his political leanings need a little scrutiny."

"Then we have a plan."

"Lunch is served Ma'am, Miss Rose." Knapp drew a breath and lowered her voice to add, "Chief Inspector Wright's car has just arrived."

"Right on time. Best set another place, Knapp." Beatrice shook her head and chuckled as she got to her feet. "I swear," she added without turning back, "when it comes to sniffing out food that man has all the instincts of a Labrador pup."

"Won't he find it odd, me being here?" said Cawston.

"Not for him to question. Much as I like our Chief Inspector, his opinion on my choice of guests is not of any great import."

"I'm pretty sure he has me down as a suspect."

"I would be surprised if he didn't." Bunch patted Cawston's arm. "There isn't a detective alive who wouldn't – at least in the first instance."

"But you don't?"

"Honestly? I did. I am sure now that you're not part of the plot. It thus makes perfect sense to use your assistance. Wright makes no secret of the fact that he uses my position in society to winkle out the secrets of families and networks he would never be able to negotiate in the normal run of things. You are a journalist with contacts in places that Wright wouldn't be able to access without first facing miles of red tape. There isn't a great deal of difference between us."

"You sound as if you don't like Inspector Wright."

"Not at all. I'm really very fond of him. I simply don't always agree with his methods and have the luxury of not having to abide by his rules."

"Good enough. Let's go and face your Labrador."

"Let's. Come on Bella. Lunch." The springer, who had lain quietly all the while the women had talked, needed no second telling where food was concerned. Her claws scrabbled up the edge of the rug as she got to her feet and trotted off after Beatrice.

The three women were seating themselves at the table when Wright was finally shown in.

He came to greet Beatrice first. "Lady Chiltcombe."

"Always a pleasure, William. Do sit down. I think you know everyone?"

"Hello Rose…" he smiled at her as he took a seat "… and Miss Cawston. What a surprise. I was hoping to speak with you later."

"Of course." Cawston's wry gaze flicked towards Bunch.

Bunch herself was amused that Wright was avoiding her eyes as he sat down. She could almost feel the waves of disapproval and anger radiating from him. He didn't exactly suspect the journalist but he certainly didn't trust her. *An occupational hazard, I imagine. A persistent investigator such as Marion Cawston could cause havoc with a case.* "Cawston came to see me with some interesting information," she said aloud. "It would appear that we have a far bigger case than we first imagined."

"Bigger than murder?"

"Costa escaped because he had something Favero and Pavessi wanted."

"Do you know what? When these men were interned they were searched over and over. They couldn't take a pencil stub into the camp that wasn't inventoried – probably in triplicate, if I know the army."

"People can be quite inventive. One hears of all sorts going on with the secret services."

"You think he's an OVRA agent." Cawston rolled her eyes as three people stared back at her. "*Organizzazione per la Vigilanza e la Repressione dell'Antifascismo*, or in English, The Organization for Vigilance and Repression of Anti-Fascism."

"I have heard them mentioned," Bunch replied, unwilling to admit otherwise.

"Italy's secret police. Very, very secret," said Cawston. "Top grade fascists."

"I've never heard of them," said Wright.

"Not many have. One thing the Italians are exceptionally skilled at is secret societies."

"Hardly surprising," Beatrice said. "The Roman Frumentarii turned intrigue into an art form. Don't look so surprised, Rose. I do read occasionally."

"I know you do, Granny, but Ancient Romans are not going to be a great deal of help here."

"Except that this OVRA does not sound so dissimilar," said Wright.

"Perhaps. If Daddy were here I'd ask if he knew anything about them."

"What about asking Everett Ralph?" Beatrice said. "He seems to have a finger on that sort of thing."

Bunch glared. She despised the CO of the unit that occupied her old family home less than half a mile from where she currently sat. And even if she didn't loathe the man she knew perfectly well that the chances of him telling her anything that smacked of military secrets was as close to zero as made little odds. "I would rather put both feet in barrelful of starving rats," she growled.

"Rose! That is not entirely called for."

"Perhaps not rats," she conceded. "But you know I'm right. I may be able to scrounge up some info from Emma Tinsley. Is she still at Banyards?"

"She went back up to town on Friday," Beatrice replied. "She does have a ticket for the ball. Two tickets in fact – and being quite mysterious about who the second was for. I imagine you will see her tomorrow night."

"Want me to take a crack at Colonel Ralph?" said Cawston. "I have asked for an interview a few times."

"You might have better luck with him than me," said Bunch. "I think perhaps I should have another word with Pamela Tallboys this afternoon."

"Again?" Wright said. "What are you hoping she'll say?"

"In the absence of any other leads, I'm hoping she will remember something … if I get her chatting. Would you like to come with me?"

"I thought you'd never ask."

~~~

"I really can't tell you much. It's taking all of my time trying to make any sense of all this." Pamela Tallboys leaned back in the office chair to gaze at them. "I know that Reggie had a lot more business in America when I first knew him, but after we married he only went there a few times. His business switched to Italy because the wineries in California were ripped up when prohibition came in."

"We only know the bare bones."

"Sadly it's all I have. You know how he was, Rose. You saw…"

"I did. And I am sorry."

"I know and I appreciate it. I've had a chance to look through my situation and I've been left in a rather difficult situation. This place is mine – the buildings and the land. It would appear that the club itself, the business, is a rather different matter. My solicitor is…" Pamela glanced at Wright "…I don't know why I'm telling you all of this." The set of Pamela's jaw made Bunch certain there was more to come, but now was not the time.

"You are having to cope on your own and that is never easy. I know exactly how that is."

"It's not really sunk in yet. The coroner still hasn't released Reggie's body so I can't even bury him."

"We'll do what we can to hurry it along," said Wright. "Nothing is likely to happen until after the inquest, I'm sorry to say, which may be delayed until well into the New Year."

"I do understand. It's hard to do anything at this time of year when it comes to banks and wills and such."

"Did Reggie leave a will?"

"Reggie thought he was invincible, so not that I am aware of. I asked him once and he said it was best left to him and I wasn't to concern myself. I've been trying to go through the paperwork and it's all a little over my head."

"What do you think Reggie meant by 'best left'?"

"That it would all come to me I suppose, rather than his family." She looked down at the desk. Her face calm but a trembling in her hands betraying her turmoil.

"Look … if you need any help, you know where I am," Bunch said. "Granny knows half the men on the golf club committee, so if they are giving you any trouble, or anyone else is putting pressure on you, give us a call."

"I have a New Year's party at the club to service – and getting nowhere with it. Half the suppliers listed in the accounts have gone out of business."

"Isn't that the steward's business?"

"It should be but he's gone."

"Vanished?"

"In a manner of speaking. He was … being difficult about my asking questions. I had to let him go."

"Goodness." Bunch would have reached across to squeeze Pamela's hand had the desk not been quite so large. "That does not sound like the actions of a reasonable man. You are better off without him, in that case. And you best check the wine cellar. Ten to one, he's been making off with the vintage port. Or selling off lost golf balls as new. Hiring wheelbarrows for golfing trolleys. Making plus fours from old parachutes…"

Pamela began to laugh. "All of those things! He was a rum sort." She pinched at the top of her nose and the laughter died in a single cough that wasn't quite a sob. "I don't know, I won't know, until I get this mess sorted out. Staff to pay and suppliers to contact…"

"Who were his business contacts in Italy?" said Wright. "When he had them."

"Vintners in various areas," she replied. "He imported directly back then."

"Did he ever take you on trips there?"

"Yes, before the children came along. We stayed in Rome and Naples. Venice once, which was lovely."

"You must have visited the vineyards."

"He always insisted that business and family should never mix. My husband was not a man to argue with, except…"

"Except…?" Bunch asked gently.

"I did meet one of them. It was on my last trip. We were in Naples and these men came to the hotel. Not at all what I was expecting. Reggie was all smiles but absolutely furious when they'd gone."

"How were they not what you expected?"

"There were three of them. Father and two sons. What shocked me was that the sons were both armed. Quite openly."

"Really?"

"Yes. It was hot and they had on light jackets, unbuttoned, so I saw the guns quite distinctly." She patted under her left armpit. "Like George Raft or one of those from the gangster movies. Quite took me aback because they were so brazen about it. I was left to serve them coffee while the father took Reggie aside to talk business."

"Satisfactory business, was it?"

"I haven't the tiniest clue."

"Can you recall anything, such as their names? It could be important," Wright said. "Did your husband seem pleased with the business?"

"I can't remember their names. It was a while ago, as I said – and I only met them that once." She pursed her lips and then shook her head. "Reggie was preoccupied by whatever the older chap was telling him but seemed pleased by whatever deal they had struck."

"Wasn't he at all troubled that these men were armed?"

"Quite the contrary. I think he found it amusing. He certainly had a laugh at my expense when I mentioned it. He told me that it was perfectly normal and I should stop being such a ninny." Pamela flushed and glanced down at her hands for a moment. "Something of that kind. Then he said the hill country where they grew the vines was full of bandits. Which was true enough. The hotel manager had already warned us not to drive too far out of the city. He insisted the local brigands knew all the hire cars by sight."

"Would you think that in all probability they *were* the bandits," Wright asked.

"Looking back, I suppose that may have been the case. I was rather naïve, I'm afraid. Daddy and Mummy were very protective so I'd never come across the like. I'd handled guns naturally. We had shooting parties here when I was young. Never held pistols though. People didn't have pistols, did they?

Not normal people. It's different now, with everyone in uniform. But that's the difference, isn't it? Military weapons are not the same."

"They can all kill," said Bunch. "It must have been frightfully alarming for you, that meeting. Are you sure you don't remember their names?"

Pamela shook her head. "Truly. I only met them once. Our first child arrived that year so it was my last business trip."

"And that was your last holiday in Italy?"

"No. We went to Rome after that, and Venice too. There was the odd Swiss skiing week. But once we had the three children Reggie bought a house on Guernsey. A far better spot for young children to holiday than racketing around the continent. Or it was before the Germans walked in. Heaven knows what's happened to it now."

Bunch could not help feeling Pamela was paraphrasing, that Tallboys was still exerting control from the grave. *Or in his case, the mortuary slab.* "I can imagine how the Channel Isles would be lovely with a young family. Taking three children anywhere always looks like hard work to me."

"I doubt I will ever go back there now," Pamela replied. "It was Reggie's dream and an expensive one. From what I have managed to understand so far, Reggie was juggling accounts. And now, trying to get my bills paid when the bank will only deal with a man who is dead is rather an uphill task."

"We can understand that," Wright replied. "May I ask one more thing? We believe your husband was near to the Victory Gardens the night before the Italian was discovered. And you yourself have confirmed he left here that evening. Do you have any idea why he would have gone there?"

"Are you asking if he dug up a body?"

Wright gave a small shrug. "Do you think it possible?"

"If you had asked me a day or two back I would have said no," she replied. "He was in charge of the gardens. I'd have told you that it's more than likely he was called out to another report of intruders. There have been petty thefts going on there for weeks." Her features set into a quizzical scowl. "That was before he was murdered. You are asking me today and I have to say it would not surprise me."

"Was he capable?"

"Of what? Do I think he killed that poor prisoner? Was he capable? Perhaps, but he was not the sort to indulge in manual labour … though he certainly had the muscle and the nerve. We went shooting up on my cousin Iain's estate and Reggie ended up helping the ghillies with the stag he brought down. Not quite the thing, but there had been some sly mutterings and I think he felt a need to prove his worth. If he had a good enough reason I think he had the nerve for almost anything."

"What reason could there be?"

"Reggie was really only interested in money." She met Wright's stare with far more strength than Bunch imagined her capable of. "And status. It was all he really cared for and he knew one was the means to gain the other."

"I see. Thank you for being so candid Mrs Tallboys. It can't be easy for you." Wright got to his feet. "We shall leave you in peace. If you come across those names in your husband's papers do call us."

"And if you need any help with your committee do give Granny a call." Bunch went around the desk to give Pamela a peck on the cheek. "She will crack the whip for you. Perhaps you might want to consider delaying the club's New Year party? Hold it on Saturday perhaps? More convenient and would give you a few more days grace."

"I think I would be lynched if I tried to interfere with the members' shindig."

"They should be ashamed of themselves expecting you to supply them with entertainment when you are in mourning."

"Keeping busy helps a little. And as people have already paid for tickets and most of the stock has been ordered in it would be very difficult now."

Bunch patted her shoulder and hurried after Wright into the cold of the afternoon. "Our grieving widow seems to be taking to business rather well," she murmured.

"I've seen it happen," Wright replied. "She has her family home to protect, and her children to support. You should recognise duty when you see it. Now get in. Things to do."

"I suppose so. Where to now?" she asked.

"When I have dropped you home I shall be going back to Brighton," Wright replied. "Seems your journalist friend was right about Tallboys' links to crime in Italy."

"And America from the things Cawston was telling me."

"Then I have a lot of enquiries to make."

His whitening knuckle at a mention of the reporter didn't go unnoticed. Bunch wondered what he had against her. *It can't be because she was initially a suspect. So what?* "Anything you want me to do?"

"Keep an eye on that woman," he snapped. "I want to know everything she knows."

"Pamela?" Bunch asked, not entirely innocently.

"No. Marion Cawston."

Wednesday 31ˢᵗ

The ballroom at Okeside House was smaller than that at Perringham, and Beatrice had claimed it didn't matter when there were far fewer people available to fit into it. Bunch had to wonder if that were true as she sidled through an overcrowded room. She knew most of the gathering and considered many of them to be friends. *But God in heaven, they can be so tedious.* It was not an entirely fair assessment, she knew, yet it all felt so brittle, so artificial, with people avoiding any mention of those missing from their ranks through duty or death. Or when they did, it was in hushed tones. All hoped that 1942 would be different, that the Americans joining the war in Europe would make that difference.

Bunch watched the dancers and listened to the band, who, she had to admit, were very good. The crowd were on the dance floor quite early in the evening, with waltzes and foxtrots for the older members, but increasing the swing tunes, faster and louder, as the ball progressed. Bunch was willing to bet that the daughters of the house had chosen the band because she could see some pained expressions on the faces of her parents and their older friends.

Open fires at each end of the room were adding to the tobacco haze above the crowd, filtering off to the high ceiling where a net, loaded with as many balloons as the hunt committee had been able to scrounge, had been strung. It was swaying in a draught, casting shadows on the crowd, and Bunch hoped it would stay intact until midnight. The draughts came from the French windows opened to freshen the air despite the cold night, and the breeze was strong enough to move both the heavy drapes in front of them as well as the nets above her head, so the whole room almost appeared to Bunch to be breathing. "Have I had that much?" she muttered and prodded her cheek with a forefinger, feeling the pressure of her nail and smiled to herself. *No. Cheek test says I am sober.* She wandered to the refreshments table.

"Ma'am?" asked the waiter dispensing drinks.

"I need some refills." She waved away a glass and snagged an iced bottle of bubbly before drifting to the table claimed by her family.

"If they can be persuaded," Barty was saying, "we stand a chance. But the Japs are keeping them pretty damned busy."

"I fear it may be a little late," Beatrice said. "I assume you've heard the dreadful reports from Hong Kong?"

"Ghastly."

"I heard we're making good in Libya," said Barty. "Now if…"

"Daddy," said Emma, "this is a ball. People having a good time."

Barty cast a chastened glance around him. "It was all in *The Times*," he grumbled. "Not giving away any state secrets."

"Even so." Emma rolled her eyes at Dodo. "Can you believe him, Daphne?"

"He's a sly one," Dodo agreed. "Though he is right. Maurice was only saying a few days ago that they need more pilots than they can possibly train."

"We need more of just about everything. And right now we need more champers." Bunch poured herself a fresh libation from her snatched bottle and then topped up her sister's flute. "No Maurice?"

"Not as yet." Dodo forced a smile. "Peter Hope is here. He's Maurice's squadron leader. He told me that Maurice and few others had been seconded for something special and that he wasn't surprised we'd heard nothing, and that I shouldn't worry."

"Maurice is probably on standby for something that won't ever happen. He'll get stood down and be back before you know it. Happens all the time."

"That will be it. I gather some of the chaps were doing regular flights across the water for—" Dodo glanced around them and mimed a camera.

Barty patted her arm. "This Peter chap had no business worrying you like that."

"I would rather know."

Dodo tossed back her champagne and held out her glass. Bunch refilled it, raising her brow at Barty, who replied with a tiny shake of his balding head. To speak the obvious was to invoke a jinx. Maurice had only been away for a few days and that was far too soon to be classified as MIA.

"Excuse me." They watched Dodo hurry off to the front of the house. "She is desperately worried, poor creature," Emma murmured, leaning close for Bunch to hear her over the music. "Odd how often history repeats itself."

"It hasn't yet."

"Do be realistic. He's been missing for days."

"I know." Bunch offered her cigarette case to Emma and selected one to slot into her own holder. "It would be awful for her to lose Maurice the same way she lost George."

"So much death," she said. "Though I suspect you and I are sadly more accustomed it these days, given our chosen work. I hear you are looking into Reggie Tallboys' murder."

"I am," Bunch leaned closer still. "I wonder, do you know much about him – in your line?"

Emma grinned. "Rather thought you might ask."

"And?"

"I made some enquiries. Nothing top secret, obvs, but possibly things your Chief Inspector won't have access to, and Wyncombe worthies may hang on Tallboys' every word. You know about his right-wing links back in the '30s?"

"In fact I've been getting a picture of more of an opportunist. He had many associates in Italy, some political and others not, and all of them cultivated for money."

"You know he made his fortune exporting booze to Canada?"

"Destined for south of the lakes to bypass prohibition. Yes, I had heard all of this."

Emma nodded. "Well, those connections have remained active. Same families but on two continents. We suspect Costa was working for an Italian crime family and cosying up to the

Italian hierarchy at the same time. Dangerous thing to do."

"I came to the same conclusion. And the other two were working for Il Duce."

"The question is, why did they choose to clash on British soil."

"I think Costa was carrying something of value. Wright says a POW couldn't smuggle a matchstick through the camps, they get searched so often. I suppose he might have been carrying verbal messages, but why go to such lengths when a coded message could be sent via telegraph. No, it has to be something physical."

"Agreed. And these chaps are very skilled at smuggling," Emma replied. "If you saw some of the tricks our agents get up to."

"Such as?"

"Couldn't possibly say. Signed the King's pledge and all that." She put her cigarette holder to her lips and looked across the room.

Bunch noted a new poise and elegance in her friend. Emma had always been different but the Emma Tinsley of old, immersed in a world of academe, had gained something that was more than the hint of lipstick and shingled hair that London living had enticed her into wearing. "And?" she said.

"You could ask your friend Colonel Ralph," Emma replied. "Right up his street."

"And I could swallow swords as an encore," Bunch snapped. "You are not the first to suggest him. Ralph is a snake."

"That may be a little strong. But it gives you some idea of what you're up against. Devious does not begin to cover it. Rest assured, your Signor Costa was a courier and whatever he was carrying meant something important to his mafia bosses."

"Which ended up with Reggie being killed for what he might know?"

Emma shrugged. "We're both extrapolating the slender facts we have to hand. Rather what I do these days: second guessing the weasels and worms. Quite an eye opener, I can tell you."

"Well thank you. I hope you don't get into trouble for this…" Bunch hesitated "… and who told you what I was looking into?"

"I think you can guess. He is quite besotted, you know."

"Henry?"

"Never said a word." Emma looked up as a shadow was cast on them.

"Emma, would you care to dance?" The man in the uniform of the King's Own was offering his hand.

The smile Emma gave him made it obvious the invitation was not unexpected. "Iain, hello. Rose, this is Iain Kerr. Iain, this is the intrepid detective I told you about. The Honourable Rose Courtney."

"A pleasure."

"Likewise." Bunch nodded to him and eyed Emma, straight faced but eyes glittering.

"And the dance?" he said.

"Why thank you. I'd be delighted."

Watching Emma swirling onto the dance floor, Bunch felt a little envious. Prof Emma had a gentleman friend. Older by at least fifteen years, Bunch would estimate, tall and grey, with slightly hangdog features, but, from that fleeting acquaintance, good humoured and intelligent. He was plainly the mystery recipient of Emma's second ticket. "And she shall go to the ball," Bunch murmured.

"Some chap she works with I gather." Barty came to sit next to her to gain a better view of his only daughter. "I was resigned to Emma being the eternal spinster."

"Is she engaged?"

Barty slugged back half of the scotch in his glass and grimaced. "She's said nothing to me, or to Daphne. Emma has mentioned him a few times but I hadn't met him before tonight."

"Then perhaps it's a little early to have her tripping down the aisle."

Barty grunted and emptied his glass. "You know, for all her faults it's times like this I almost miss Olivia. This sort of thing needs a woman's touch." He waved down a passing waiter and replaced his empty glass with a fresh one and cradled it between his fingers.

"I hardly think Olivia would have had much influence." Bunch thought back to Barty's wife, the glamorous and, as it turned out, deeply criminal Olivia Tinsley. *Without wishing to speak ill of the dead*, she thought, *Olivia and her machinations were one of the reasons Em dived into academe in the first place*. "Emma has always known her own mind."

"She has. You are two of a kind: modern young things doing all sorts." Barty grunted again but more in amusement. "She says they're only friends but I can still hope."

"Emma will go back to her books when this is all over," Bunch replied. Her serial one-night stands with Henry Marsham were a relief against the constant feel of impending doom but she never envisaged them being anything more. Bunch could not blame Emma for doing exactly the same, however unexpected. "Emma is having a little fun while she can. I'm more worried about how Dodo will take Maurice not turning up."

"He's a good sort but understandably miffed when Daphne turned him down."

Bunch blinked rapidly. When Dodo had told her about Maurice proposing, it was clear she was fond of the man all the same. A flat out *no* was a surprise. "What was his reaction?" she demanded.

"He just went terribly quiet and left a few minutes later. To say he seemed stunned wouldn't be too far from the truth. I'm glad Daphne didn't accept just for form's sake but I did feel rather sorry for poor Maurice."

"Should we be concerned for him?"

"Not yet. Chaps often have to put down at other fields if their kite is damaged."

"Or if they are…"

"Let's not think about that just yet."

"Let's not."

"I meant to say before, I hear you collared those scallywags stealing vegetables."

"Yes, we tracked them down."

"I haven't seen the case come up on the Magistrates schedule as yet for the coming year."

"And you won't. They were very helpful in some other … areas, so Botting has them working off their debt. We thought it was better than wasting the court's time and giving them criminal records over a few parsnips." She paused for the bluster. Barty Tinsley had spent years on the magistrate's bench, and she knew he felt keenly over his removal from it after his wife Olivia's fall from grace.

He only nodded. "As long as they are."

"You saw them that night, I gather."

"I didn't, I'm sorry to say. Rather poor show on my part. Shan't happen again."

"Perhaps you noticed some other vehicles. The boys claim they saw a saloon car in front of the hall that may have belonged to Reggie Tallboys."

"Let me think." He took a contemplative sip at the scotch. "It was dark," he said at last. "Obviously. That was why I didn't notice the boys. We were on manoeuvres, don't you know."

She nodded, not wanting to speak and derail his thoughts.

"I don't recall seeing anything by the hall but looking back … yes, I do remember thinking I saw a car by the church, tucked back under the trees. It was a Daimler, I think. Yes, a Daimler. Or perhaps a Packard." He smiled an apology. "It was a dark-coloured car under trees at night. One of the lads spotted it as well."

"Was there anybody in it?"

"Possibly. I sent someone back to check when we reached the school but it had gone by then."

"Not a car you recognised as being local?"

"Lord, no. It was the sort of vehicle we all mothballed right at the start of the war. A thing like that would guzzle fuel like a dammed camel. Only government wallahs can get the juice for such a car. Or villains." He reddened. *He probably remembered that Daddy has such a vehicle*, thought Bunch.

"Some might say they were one and the same thing."

Bunch turned to the speaker and chuckled. "Henry. What are you doing here?"

"Came down with Iain Kerr. Didn't have a ticket but our host's an old friend. Good evening, Lady Chiltcombe." Henry Marsham bowed his head at the matriarch before he slid into a seat alongside Bunch and set his glass next to hers. "What are you investigating? Same case?"

"Reggie Tallboys. Yes."

"Ah, yes."

She waited for him to go on. "No little titbits for me to puzzle over?" she prompted.

"Me? No. Local villainy is not my jurisdiction."

"And that's what you think this is?"

"Tallboys was a businessman who skated very close to the wind. Case closed. Dance?"

"Later," she replied. "Not had nearly enough champers to make an exhibition of myself."

"Daphne?" He stood and held his hand out as Dodo approached the table. "Fancy a turn?"

"That would be lovely, Henry, if Bunch doesn't mind."

"Rose has already turned me down. Yet again. My heart is broken and I look to you for consolation."

"You're a silly ass, Henry Marsham," Dodo replied and let him lead her out onto the floor.

"One of these days, Rose, he will stop asking and then where will you be," Beatrice murmured.

Bunch stared at Beatrice. Her grandmother had been so quiet she'd almost forgotten she was there. "I don't set my life on what Henry Marsham says or does, Granny. Why would I? And I don't say that because he's dancing with my sister."

"Henry isn't worth just a little pique?"

They gazed at each other in silence and it was Bunch who broke first. "Granny you are too, too wicked."

"It's the only pleasure I have these days. Especially with all of this noise. Really, these orchestras get louder every year. I can't hear a word anyone is saying. Though being the observer has its advantages." She gestured across the room. "Rose dear, isn't that the Cawston woman trying to catch your eye? The club sec seems reluctant to let her in. One can't blame him, I must say. She's not exactly dressed for the occasion."

"Oh, yes it is. You will have to excuse me, Granny. I must go and speak to her." Bunch hurried across to where Cawston lurked in the doorway. "Hello. I was expecting to see you earlier."

"So was I." Cawston looked around her. "We must talk."

"That bad?" Cawston's face was affirmation enough. "Of course. A little cold to step out into the garden, but they have a splendid solarium here, although you'd need to be desperate to be in there tonight. At least we won't be competing with the band. And you won't attract quite so much attention." She looked pointedly at Cawston's tweed slacks and jacket.

"Long story, but we must talk so lead the way."

The solarium's domed ceiling and decorative glass side panels were vague breaks against a dark night sky. Vines, fixed across the arching glass, were no more than a faint pattern. What little light there was turned the larger ferns and tropical plants gathered in the centre into an undulating shadow dotted by pale curves of insulating sacking wrapped around the pots. Olives and lemons, which graced the loggia during the summer, were clustered at the far end like a small forest, casting darker shadows onto a small scattering of chairs and low tables. Bunch stood in the doorway and took in what little she could see, recalling the orangery at Perringham and wondering what had happened to the plants there, or the fragile glass structure itself.

"Nice and quiet in here," Cawston observed. "Bit chilly for evening dress. Are you all right with just that wrap?"

"I shall be perfectly fine for a few minutes. Shall we sit?"

"Rather keep my blood moving if that's okay with you." They made a cautious way inside, growing more confident as their eyes became accustomed to the dark, and almost immediately put a young couple to flight, like a brace of pheasants on heathland. "Doing them a favour, I should think. Ardour can't possibly keep them that warm. We should make certain there are no more young swains." They paced toward the far end and, once certain the space was empty, stopped by the silenced fountain.

"I think we're alone," said Bunch. Her voice weaving up

through the greenery to echo back at them from the glass above. She dropped her voice to a whisper. "Now what is it that needs so much secrecy?"

"The rumours were right about Pavessi and Favero," Cawston replied. "They were pursuing Costa. I don't know what for as yet."

"And you came here just to tell me that? Old news, I'm afraid."

"I now have it on good authority that Pavessi did kill Costa."

"We had come to that conclusion already. How Pavessi knew to involve Tallboys is the question. That, and why they needed to dig up Costa again."

"Presumably because whatever they thought Costa was carrying hadn't turned up anywhere else."

"All right, I can see that. But doesn't help us work out who killed Tallboys."

"Somebody thought Reggie had taken possession of whatever Costa was transporting." Cawston reached into her pocket and handed over a sheet of paper. "When I came back from Town today I found this shoved through my letter box."

"'Miss Cawston…'" she managed to read in the gloom "'…we ask for you to leave Costas to us. Do not interfere as Tallboys did.' The writer was clearly not English but English speaking."

"It's none too subtle and not at all helpful. I left a message with your Inspector Wright saying where we'd be and came right on over to warn you."

"Well thank you." Bunch gazed around them the solarium that was so full of shadows. "Interesting that it mentions Tallboys in particular. He had been keeping the seamier side of his life well away from Wyncombe."

"And was shot in his own back yard, so that didn't work out too well. It came to Tallboys out of the blue."

"Whatever they are after is so valuable that it warranted three corpses … something small enough that Costa could hide it while incarcerated in a POW camp. I've heard there are … *places* to hide things that I would rather not think about, but for six months? And what is it?"

"If we knew the answer to one of those things——" The far door squeaked open and a rowdy group entered the orangery. Cawston drew Bunch to the far side. "Do you mind if we step outside for a few minutes? Even glass walls seem to have ears."

Both women drew breath as the wind cut into them. "Bracing." Bunch held her hand out and examined a few specks of dampness. "I can't see it being much colder but it's going to get wet."

"Outside. I shall be quick I promise." Cawston guided Bunch under the very slight overhang of the roof. "Whatever it is that Costa had been carrying has remained here in Wyncombe, yes?"

"Tallboys must have known what it was, at the very least. We don't. Looking for needles in haystacks would be a breeze in comparison." Bunch pulled her wrap closer round her shoulders. "I'm getting cold and we're getting nowhere. Come back with us tonight. We'll sleep on it and start looking tomorrow…" the sound of cheering and the band striking up the New Year anthem filtered through to them "…make that later today."

"That is very——"

A sharp crack – and glass exploded close to their heads. Both women instinctively threw themselves at the freezing stone paving. Neither moved for two whole bars. Across the terrace "Auld Lang Syne" drifted through the open windows along with cheering and applause.

"Happy New Year," Bunch whispered.

"And many more of them," Cawston hissed back.

"I didn't hear a shot."

"Silencer,"

"Are you hurt?"

"Not from a bullet. I may die from exposure, however."

"Sorry, it's my own fault. I should never have come here. On the bright side, had they wanted to kill me they'd have emptied the clip."

"How comforting. What now?"

"We need to get into cover." Cawston peered across the

lawns. "The shooter will have moved by now. Wriggle back toward the door. When I open it we both make for the far side of that central display. Kick off those heels and run for it."

"Across broken glass?"

"Better cut feet than a punctured heart. Are you ready? Go."

Cawston reached up to the handle and flipped the door with one hand and caught Bunch under the arm with the other. A second pane of glass exploded around them, and a third. Shards skittered across the shiny floor all around them, crunching painfully under Bunch's stockinged feet. Out in the corridor they straightened up and ran straight into Marsham and Kerr.

"We heard glass breaking— Rose, your face."

"What?" Bunch put her hand to her cheek, felt the stickiness of blood, and stared at her reddened fingers in surprise. She hadn't felt anything cut her and almost doubted it was her blood at all.

"Tell me what happened." Henry grabbed her by the shoulders. "Quickly."

"Somebody took a pot-shot at us. Several shots, in point of fact."

"Good God." Henry opened the door into a small drawing room and pushed the two women inside. "In … and stay there. Iain, go and fetch Tinsley."

"I'm all right, Henry," Bunch protested. "Takes a bit more than a bit of broken glass—"

"You're shaking."

"Shivering. There's a difference. It's very cold out on the terrace."

"What in hell were you up to out there? No matter. Here's the cavalry. Look after these two, will you Tinsley? Come on Kerr, we'll check outside."

"I imagine they will be long gone now," Cawston replied. "They've made their point."

~~~

The night dragged on in a welter of police statements but eventually people were allowed to drift homewards a few hours before dawn.

Bunch delivered Beatrice into Alice's hands and retired to the kitchen with Cawston, Wright and Marsham. It was the warmest room in the wee small, frosted hours when Cook's range remained banked up all night. "That's a New Year ball we won't forget in a hurry, hey Henry?" Bunch had set out cups of chocolate, liberally laced with brandy, and slumped into one of the painted pine chairs. She was more tired than she cared to admit.

"Must be the first New Year shindig I've left sober since the school," said Marsham. "Little more lively than last year's."

"You weren't at last years' do."

"Wasn't I? Must've been in my cups somewhere else. They know how to celebrate Hogmanay north of the border." He winked and blew on his cocoa. "Are you sure you're all right? Both of you."

"Shaken," Cawston replied, "but not seriously hurt." She dabbed at her cheek with a piece of gauze and sighed at the dark smear across the threads. "Why do little cuts always bleed out of all proportion? You would think we'd been attacked by cutlass-swinging pirates."

"As opposed to the gun-wielding variety?" Wright pushed his own empty cup to the middle of the scrubbed wood table and sat back to survey the gathering. "I would love to say I am surprised by tonight, but God in heaven, Rose, you do attract trouble. Now, may I have the real story?"

"It was not me, for once," she replied. "Cawston was their target."

Wright took the note Cawston offered him and read it quickly. "You know what they are looking for?" he asked.

"Something portable and valuable."

"But not necessarily precious?" Marsham got to his feet. "I need to be in the office by nine. You know where to find me if required, Chief Inspector. I feel very bad about having to leave you to clear up after this but I need to start enquiries from my end." He hesitated by the door. "I suppose you wouldn't rethink a hotel stay?"

"Not a hope. Granny would never agree."

"And I need to return to HQ." Wright paused by the doorway. "Rose … I can still assign a police watch. I really don't like the idea of you being here alone."

"Or I could ask Everett Ralph to extend his sentry patrols," said Marsham.

"No," Bunch snapped. "I have a farm to run and we can't do that if we're tripping over sentries at every turn. Daddy has guns here. I shall look after myself. And to repeat, it was Cawston they were chasing, not me."

"Who is just leaving as well," Cawston said. "I also have things to do. Drop me off in the village, would you, Marsham?"

"I'm not happy about this but have it your way," he replied. "But like it or not, I shall have to notify Ralph there are enemy agents in the vicinity. Do take care, my dear. I know you've handled a few scrapes but you are nothing like invincible."

"I shall sleep with my Webley under my pillow," Bunch replied. "Now go, both of you, and let us get some rest."

"If you are certain. Lock this door behind us."

"I fully intend to."

"You're a dark one." Cawston whispered as she got up to put the cups in the sink. "Two chaps hanging on your every word."

"Nonsense. Henry can be a bit of a puppy dog, but not William."

"Were you serious about the gun?"

"Perfectly."

"Me too." She reached into her bag and exposed the handle of a revolver. "I can't see either of us sleeping a great deal."

~~~

Bunch had barely dropped into deep sleep when Bella woke her with a constant and quiet invective growling and yipping and staring at the curtained window. "Hush, girl. Quiet now." She stroked the dog's head and listened for a hint of what had disturbed the creature, but she could hear nothing unusual. Manic though the spaniel could be, she wasn't usually so vocal indoors; there had to be something amiss. Bunch grabbed the Webley and padded across to the window, pushing the heavy curtains from one side rather than parting the middle, which might be noticed from outside. It was still some time before the sun would rise, and the sky had clouded over so that the driveway, which was her view from the large window, had lost the silvery highlights of a large moon.

She crossed to the smaller side window that looked at the stables and peered into the gloom. She caught a brief flash of light from the direction of the stable yard. *Kate and Pat, perhaps?* She thought. *Or they've also heard something.* Bella reared up to put one paw on the sill and looked with her, shivering with excitement and uttering small gruffs as she stared intently at something only canine eyes could make out.

Bunch looked harder but still couldn't see anything except the gardens that the new horticultural land girls were already transforming, ready for spring planting. *Perhaps it's nothing. Probably is nothing,* she thought. *Silly pooch has heard that vixen and wants to give chase.*

She eased the casement open and leaned out, breathing in cold air, listening intently. There were the familiar sounds: a male Tawny's "twit" answered by a female's distant "woo". As the vixen screamed from the copse close to the farmyard Bunch looked at Bella, who glanced back unperturbed. These were familiar noises heard night after night and the dog would not be agitated by them.

Bella's ear's pricked briefly and she leaned out a little further. Noises carried pin clear on the cold night breeze but Bunch could discern nothing unusual. She waited for a few moments more. *Perhaps it was something inside the house?* Bella gruffed quietly, as if reading her mind. Bunch was about to close the window when the shaded ruddy glimmer of the vehicle's rear lights coasted along the lane, gathering speed down the hill before the sound of its engine coughed into life, quietly as the driver no doubt intended. A few seconds later it was gone.

Bunch waited, head cocked to catch any tell-tale sound but all she could hear were foxes and owls. She closed the window and looked down at Bella. The dog was far from relaxed. "Dammit," she muttered. Turning down not one but two offers of guards was feeling like a huge mistake. She hurried to pull a coat on over her pyjamas, slipped the Webley into the pocket, and crept out onto the landing. Common sense dictated it would be piling madness on madness to venture outside but she knew she would not rest until she had checked the doors at very least.

She made her way downstairs in minimal light, feeling behind the curtain that obscured the glass panels to tug at the bolts and handles of the front door. It seemed secure so she moved to the windows and then worked her way around the doors and windows on the ground floor with Bella close at her heels as they came to the kitchens.

The baize-lined door to the kitchen was slightly ajar which made her pause. The door was never left unlatched. Bunch laid a warning hand on Bella's head, the other fist wrapped a little sweatily around the Webley's Bakelite grips.

The passage that led past Cook and Knapp's rooms was silent but a chill breeze indicated that the outside door had been opened. Wright's parting words to lock the doors behind him were clear in her mind, and she knew that she had done just that. She tapped Bella's head to warn her not to rush ahead, and she edged towards the door.

Tap … tap … tap.

Bunch paused a few paces from the door. Venturing outside would be lunacy. Relocking the door, however, seemed the highest priority.

"Sit," she hissed to Bella. "Stay."

The dog whined gently but lowered her haunches to the floor and watched Bunch intently as she inched forward to push the door closed.

"Wait."

Bunch swung the Webley towards the voice.

"Steady on, Rose. It's only me."

"Henry?"

The door swung wide enough for Marsham to slip inside.

"Dear God, did you have to make such an entrance? I could have killed you."

"Fortunately you didn't."

"Bella woke me." Bunch looked him up and down and frowned. "What are you doing here? I thought you had to get back to Town."

"Cawston and I decided you might need some help, whatever you said."

"You discussed me with her?"

"Yeah, we go way back." He smirked at Bunch's expression. "Not important right now. One chap broke into your office and the other came to try this door." He waved to the door where dimples had been punched into the Georgian wired glass.

"Your girls over in the flat must have heard the cars and got up to investigate. They shouted out a challenge and our visitors took to their heels."

"Oh heavens. I should go and check on them."

"They are fine. I told them to lock the doors and sit tight. I know what you said about Ralph, and I do understand that you have some kind of feud going on, but If I don't organise protection of some kind your father will have my guts for garters."

"Perhaps—"

"I shall call Botting and have a constable here to keep an eye on you. Then I really must go. I need to catch the 8.20 train. I shall be back before Friday, in any case."

"What's happening on Friday?"

"Wait and see. It's good, I promise."

Friday 2nd January 1942

Lying in bed, drinking tea and hearing Lizzie running her bath, Bunch felt life was almost back to normal. So much so that, being a Friday, she briefly entertained a trip to Storrington market. A lack of suitable stock to sell and an even bigger lack of petrol squashed that plan. The rest that she had expected to enjoy over the holidays had not happened and she longed for a diversion that didn't involve war work. In past years a holiday to St Moritz might have been in order – followed by a few days seeking the sun on the Cote d'Azur. "*La Belle* France," she murmured. "One day…"

"Shall I lay out your working clothes, Miss?"

The daydream bubble imploded and she set her cup aside. "Yes please, Lizzie." Recalling her assertion to Cawston, Bunch felt guilty that Lizzie had even offered. "You really don't have to wait on me, you know. I am quite capable of grabbing some moleskins and a jumper out of the clothes press."

"I know Miss. It's no trouble, though."

"Well thank you anyway, but in future I can manage."

Lizzie had gone when she came out of the bathroom; the promised uniform was laid out on the neatly made bed and Bunch felt a little guilty all over again. Plainly the desire for change needed to come from all sides. She dressed quickly and ran lightly down the stairs to breakfast and found Beatrice and Alice already at the table.

"You're up and about early today, Granny. Doing something special?"

"WVS regional board meeting," Beatrice replied.

"Ooh, rather you than me." Bunch pulled a face and went to the sideboard and sighed for a time when there would have been a half-dozen covered dishes to choose from. Today there were two. "Kippers or kedgeree," she muttered. "Fish might not be on ration – but really."

"It *is* Friday my dear," Beatrice said.

"In which case we have had Friday three days out of the last seven."

"The kippers are fresh down from Scotland and I have no intention of letting them go to waste. Stop complaining."

"Sorry Granny. Did I hear the telephone ringing?"

"It was Daphne. Poor dear is rather upset. It seems she had a visit from Maurice's Flight Commander to say that the boy hasn't come back as yet. She is a nervous wreck. I should go and visit her today if at all possible."

"If we are permitted by our jailors," Bunch replied.

Beatrice scowled and picked up the post from beside her plate. "And whose fault is that? Getting shot at by Italian gangsters! How long are we going to need these armed guards? Knapp tells me the poor post girl had a dreadful time getting past them. It is terribly inconvenient."

"Until these gunmen have been apprehended, I suppose," Bunch replied. "Or until we discover whatever it is they are searching for … or until they get bored with it all and go home."

"That is a lot of ifs." Beatrice replied.

"Henry Marsham ordered them here, not me," Bunch replied. Her grandmother's expression prompted a rapid change of tack. "It was early for Dodo to call, what did she say?"

"No earlier than Connie Fray. She telephoned me at the crack of dawn. Carrying on about an emergency parish council committee meeting. I told her I couldn't possibly get there today. She was rather snippy about it."

Bunch managed not to roll her eyes. Beatrice's friend and WVS cohort was never one to hold back an opinion and had an opinion on almost everything. She was a gold-plated gossip whose unerring ability to pick up every wisp from the local grapevine was legendary. *And all in her own inimitable style. The day Constance Frayn isn't snippy about something we shall hang out our banners and hire a band.* She had a notion that Beatrice would have been equally curt on being expected to answer the telephone before breakfast. "Did Connie say why?"

"The crux seemed to be that the parish council is convening ahead of the monthly meeting to discuss the hole left by Tallboys' demise. And that I should put a stop to your police nonsense because it sets the whole village in a tizz."

"The nerve of the woman. I've helped to solve a few crimes. And I very much doubt Connie would call you at some ungodly hour to lecture you on my choice of work. What did she really want?"

"She does have a point. If you were not involved in these cases we would not have had innocent people being pursued by manic gunmen at the hunt ball."

"I had nothing to do with that any more than an Italian POW being buried in the allotments. And Reggie Tallboys got himself murdered."

Beatrice huffed and pointed at her granddaughter with the paper knife. "I know you far too well, child, and there is seldom nothing accidental about what you do. You busied yourself with death and had that journalist sniffing around the place at your invitation."

"She invited herself. I'm sure William will have found her a safe place by now."

"Had she wanted it. I rather think that one enjoys the whole thing. As do you." The older woman's face softened. "I know it's hard to resist, and I suspect if I were almost thirty-two years old and unencumbered by a husband I would have been just as eager for the sheer adventure. It is rather harder as an old lady to watch her son's baby girl put herself in danger time after time. Take pity on my poor heart and try to stay out of trouble."

"Sorry Granny, I shall be more careful."

"Why do I doubt that?" Beatrice replied.

"I shall try. I promise. Now you were saying something about the parish council. What prompted Connie to pester you with this emergency moot? It can't just be Reggie Tallboys' sudden demise."

"As we haven't got round to replacing poor Reginald as its chairperson, the Reverend Day thought there was some urgent need to elect a new one, and decisions need to be made. Besides, somebody broke into the village hall during the night."

"Indeed? Was anything stolen?"

"Not that anyone could see but I gather they made an awful mess. These villains went in the church as well, but the fire wardens disturbed them. There would be very lean pickings, in any case. The vicar has been quite adamant we shouldn't lock the church in these troubled times but he does have the sense to keep the church plate at the vicarage. He's only left those tall candleholders by the chancel steps because they are silver-plated brass. They are terribly heavy and they found them under the choir stall. PC Botting was quite certain it had all the signs of a very thorough search."

"Has anything been arranged as yet?"

"Reverend Day and his staff will take on the general running for the hall for time being. There will have to be an election for the post of chair."

"Not you?"

"It should be your father but he's never here. I wonder if you would pop down there in my place. I am really not feeling up to it."

"Take your place? Just today?"

I imagine they want to co-opt you into Tallboys' place."

"No! Absolutely not. Granny, the very notion is quite ghastly. What about volunteering Barty? I know he's busy with the Home Guard but he does love a good committee."

"That is a splendid idea. I shall give him a call. He can start by organising a team to give the hall a clean-up."

"Tell Connie I shall go down this morning and see what's what."

"Is that wise if you want Barty to take over?"

"I think I must. Besides, I need to take Perry out for some exercise and it's a nice dry bright morning for a hack down to the village."

"That also may not be wise."

"It shall be perfectly fine. PC Botting will have things in hand by the time I arrive. I may even swing by to see Dodo if

I have time."

"The most sensible thing you have said this morning."

~~~

Bunch followed the headlands around fields that had been full of sugar beets and mangolds and finally came out on to the road that ran past the village hall, taking PC Botting by surprise.

He appeared at the double doors, his face grave. "Oi, you can't— Oh, it's you, Miss Courtney. Bit of a to do here."

"So I hear." She dismounted and tugged the quarter sheet over the pony's rump before tethering him to the bicycle racks. "Bella, sit," she told the dog. "Stay. Now then, Botting, what have you got to show me?"

"Quite a mess, Miss. I've taken photographs but there doesn't appear to be any sign of things missing."

"Vandals then?"

"The forced entry was a professional job. Not local hooligans, I imagine."

"And you say nothing missing, as far as can be ascertained?"

"Until we get people to sift through the debris it is rather hard to say for sure but there's nothing much to take, Miss. Ministry guidelines are quite clear on leaving anything that could be of use to the enemy. Besides which, everyone uses the place. WI, Girl Guides, WVS, us ARP, and the fire wardens. Plus the parish council, Victory Gardens committee… Just about everything except the Home Guard. They use the school now."

"Who are the keyholders?"

"The Reverend Day and the verger. He's just inside. Sid," he called into the hall. "Miss Courtney is here."

Sid West came into view, his rolling gait making him seem to take up far more space than his slight frame required. "Mornin' Miss Courtney."

"Good morning, West. Botting tells me only you and Mr Day have keys for the hall. Didn't Reggie Tallboys have a copy?"

"No Miss," West snapped. "He asked no end o' times but

articles of association says quite plain, no more'n three key holders."

"You didn't like him?"

"Bain't that, Miss Courtney. Like I says, rules is rules."

"Who is the third holder?"

"Why, Her Ladyship, Miss."

"Granny? Did she indeed." *Good for Granny.* "I trust you will get the door secured for tonight. Now, to business." Bunch went in to survey the long room with its white walls studded with windows, and its battered chairs and folding trestles all spilled in a heap at one end. The planked floor was strewn with papers and boxes. She looked through the open door into the hall's office. "It's a total mess. Fingerprints, Botting?"

"I've asked for help. Not much point though, Miss. Like Sid says, the world and his uncle comes in and out of here, and you know as well as I do, no burglar worth the name is going to break in without gloves."

"True enough." She looked around her at the carnage. "There just isn't anything worth stealing, so why did it happened, that is the question."

"Church bain't much better," said West.

"Botting, do we know which was broken into first?"

"By rights, the church wasn't strictly broken into since it wasn't locked," he said.

"I think I should have a peek. I take it the church is still unlocked. West, be so good as to watch Perry and the dog for a few minutes."

West nodded. "As you will, Miss Courtney."

"Come along then, Botting."

The Reverend Day emerged from the vestry as they entered the church and came striding down the aisle to meet them. "Miss Courtney. I can hardly believe what has happened! I cannot tell you how angry I am."

"I rather thought belief was your bailiwick, Vicar." Bunch touched his arm to take the sting from her poor humour. "It seems remarkably tidy for the scene of a burglary."

"Yes. I expect you will need to speak with Mrs Watson. She had begun to tidy it up before I arrived for Matins."

"That would be eight o'clock this morning?"

"Yes, but the combined powers of blackout and daylight rather dictate our services in these times. The fire warden arrived at a little after four o'clock on his rounds, I gather. They are so shorthanded now we decided they only need be here overnight when the sirens have sounded, which is still often enough. He came straight to the vicarage to tell me. I came and had a brief look but we decided to leave it until daybreak, and it never occurred to me that Mrs Watson would just set to before we could report the break-in to the police, and without saying a word."

"A very determined woman."

"She is indeed."

"Why didn't you call Botting right away?"

"Because, sadly, it's not the first time we have disturbances."

"The church was vandalised before?"

"No," he conceded. "We have had people sleeping here during raids, and naturally it's hard to turn people away when in need, but we don't encourage it generally, because of the fire risk."

"Has there been this kind of damage before?"

"Oh gosh, let me think. It was some time ago now. Early in the summer, I think. June. Or July."

"Really? I wasn't aware. What happened?"

"The font lid had been knocked down. Quite a chunk knocked off one corner. I have the piece in safe keeping in the hope that we can find a carpenter to make a repair. Didn't your grandmother mention it?"

"Possibly, but... What can you tell me about today?"

"The church was empty and no fire wardens stayed overnight as we've had no air raids. The home guard checked the place on their rounds and disturbed two intruders. Hymn books had been thrown around and the mess in the vestry was all over the place. Mr Ferris insists the organ had been tampered with. Thankfully, it looks as if our intruders hadn't discovered the doors to the under croft. Black as pitch down in the crypt."

"Thank you, Vicar. We shan't keep you any longer." She turned back to Botting. "Have you conducted a thorough search of the area?"

"I'd rather we wait for the Inspector before I poke around too much, if it's all the same to you, Miss. Only he likes to get a feel for things before people…"

"In spite of Mrs Watson?" She laughed. "I am sure this wasn't a simple theft. It feels more like a search."

"Yes Miss, and all the more reason I'd rather leave it for Mr Wright before I start moving things about."

"Yes. However, we should have a little poke around. See what we can uncover, both here and in the hall."

"Sorry Miss, but there's a possible link to those murders and he'd have my warrant card, quick as you like."

"All right, if you must. In that case I shall get going. Can't leave Perry standing around, and I need to toddle over to Banyards."

"Should you be running around on your own Miss? After t'other night."

"I am reasonably certain I was not the target. I shall be quite safe."

~~~

Bunch retrieved Perry and started towards Banyard Manor at a leisurely pace, arriving just before lunch, which Barty always had unfashionably early.

"How is Dodo?" she asked as she was ushered into the library."

"Asleep. Doctor gave her a sedative."

"Bad news?"

"Not good, though not unexpected. Peter called by to say that Maurice had been officially listed as Missing in Action. As we feared, it's rather knocked her for six, poor child."

"No Emma?"

"She got called back to Town for some urgent flap. She said she would try to get back tomorrow. I called the Dower earlier but Beatrice said you'd been called down to the village hall. Something about hooligans tearing the place apart?"

"There's been some damage done to the doors but the hall

itself hasn't been damaged too much. Bit of mess inside. Whoever broke in was clearly searching for something. Did Granny mention the village hall management?"

"Yes, she did. I'd be happy to help out, at least until an official appointment. Now tell me what happened at the hall? Is it linked to your case?"

"Why do you say that?"

"Because you have that look in your eye. Like a good pointer on set."

"You always had a good eye when it came to dogs and horses." Bunch sank into a chair and took the cigarette Barty offered her. "We think we may be a little further forward."

"And the hall?"

"It's a mess, as I told you. The hall was awash with craftwork and the am dram props. Worst of all was the office. It's not that anything important is kept there, but the filing cabinets had been emptied out. It will take weeks to sort out."

"Good grief. Makes me rather glad we lost the toss on meeting places. The school is far better for the Home Guard, anyway. More direct access to stabling for our mounted patrols."

"Is that going well?"

"Splendid. We cover a lot of open grassland where the HG transport can't go."

"But you prefer the car."

"Yes. Had enough of horseback war in the old days. If a van gets blown up it doesn't suffer."

"Driving that night, when the Italian was dug up ... did you go back past the church?"

"Well yes."

"And the car was gone?"

"Yes."

"And last night?"

"Wasn't on manoeuvres last night."

"But did any of your men report seeing vehicles that do not belong here?"

"I haven't read all of the reports as yet."

"Do you have them?"

"I do as it happens. Come through to the den."

She followed him into his study and stood a little uncertainly on the threshold. She had only been in this room a few times and she was struck as always how it was Barty in a nutshell. A neat room in the military fashion, with a traditional mix of bookshelves and wood panel walls, and an almost obligatory array of regimental photographs along with the usual scatter of cricket and rugger teams from various eras in Barty's life. On his desk was a wedding photograph of Dodo and his son George, and another of Dodo with George's daughter Georgianna. She wondered briefly where those photos would be if Dodo accepted Maurice's proposal. *Assuming we ever lay eyes on the poor chap again*, she thought.

"Here we are." He shuffled through a small sheaf of paper. "I assume you only want the patrols around the hall and church."

"To start with."

"In that case," he extracted one sheet. "Arundel Section were on third watch in village. They patrolled the High Street down as far as the Lowther memorial and the minor streets to either side. Church Terrace and alike."

"They were on patrol the entire time?"

"Heavens no. Most of them have a full day's work to put in once the sun is up."

"Then how does it work?"

"We have quite a large company for a small village. Three platoons of twenty-four men. Arundel, Bramber and Chichester. Chichester is the mounted squad who patrol the rural areas. Arundel and Bramber have three patrols each. Four men per patrol, and they alternate in four week stretches to patrol the west and east side of the High Street and side streets."

"It was the Arundel team on the east side?"

"That's correct." He pulled a single sheet from the bundle and scanned it rapidly. "Ah, they did report a dark-coloured car parked in Church Terrace at around two hundred hours. No driver seen. It had gone when they came past again at three hundred and twenty-five."

"Half-past three?"

"Yes. Mr Waite reports seeing the vicar and one of the wardens near the church around that time but they were some way off and didn't speak with them." He grimaced. "Bit of a professional rivalry between our chaps and the ARP."

"And the hall?"

Barty scanned the rest of the page. "Nothing on that sweep but some activity at five hundred hours. Saw a dark car driving away. Not the same one apparently. Waite was quite clear on that."

"Two different vehicles? That is interesting. I don't suppose they noted models or number plates?"

"They should have. I shall have words with Waite this evening. I doubt they saw much of the second vehicle."

"Numbers would have been useful but being able to verify the timing is good solid information. Can you jot all that down and pass it on to Botting for me?"

"Of course. I say, I am being a terrible host. Would you like coffee? Lunch?"

She was hungry but this new information gave her things to do. "No, thanks Barty. I need to get back and call Wright, and I shouldn't leave poor Perry standing around too long. Give Dodo a hug when she wakes up and tell her I shall call tomorrow. I'll see myself out. Toodle pip."

~ ~ ~

A stiff wind was blowing from the south and the weak sun had vanished behind a dull skyline. Bunch gazed up and wondered if it might snow, except that the sky lacked that tell-tale yellow tint. Snow would be a complication all round and she didn't relish being snowed in as they had been in several previous Januarys. Despite the chill she kept to an easy pace because though Perry was fit and willing, he was well over twenty years old and could so easily go lame if she pushed him too hard. They ambled into an empty stable yard and Bunch had already unsaddled Perry when she heard a car drawing onto the concreted forecourt.

She paused for a moment, brushes poised against the Fell pony's flanks, wondering if she should make an appearance.

"Probably Granny. Gone to the WVS meeting after all. The lure of seeing what's happening at the village hall is so strong," she murmured. Perry snickered quietly as if agreeing with her, and Bunch carried on brushing. Stable duties were more than a pleasurable task for her. Where riding was her thinking time, when she could let imagination run riot, the task of grooming was a balm for when she was angry, sad, or as today, just plain confused.

She leaned against the pony to brush drying clay and chalk from feathers and fetlock and swore as Perry moved away, making her stagger a few paces. "Hey, steady, you daft old bugger. I know it tickles but if you don't want to go down with mud fever all this muck has got to go. Now stand, dammit." Bunch gave him a few pats and slid her hand down his leg and lifted the hoof. "Steady," she murmured again as she combed out the worst of the clag and picked out his hoof, and sighed as a draught of cold air took the peace of her refuge.

She released Perry's foot and straightened up intending to greet the interloper with a few well-chosen words. "Daddy...?"

"Rose-bunch." Edward Courtney moved rapidly to envelop his eldest daughter in a hug.

"Daddy, you're crushing me."

"I'm sorry." He loosened his hold. "I came home as quickly as I could."

"Why? I should have thought Winnie needed you now of all times."

"Never a truer word." Edward leaned back against the stall door and scrubbed at his face with both hands. "It's been the usual chaos. He's been leading us all a merry dance and I couldn't leave until we'd finally made him rest."

"Rest? Him?"

"He was ... unwell." Edward fluttered his fingers over his heart.

"He had a—?"

A finger to his lips silenced her. "Not even here," he whispered.

"Is he all, right?"

"Fine. For now."

"Thank God. But if he ... if that was the case, why did you rush back?"

"My source said that you were being, well for want of a better word, stalked."

"Me? Who by?"

"Never mind who. Enemy aliens, I understand."

"I have had a few run ins. Italians we believe, but as you can see, I am perfectly fine. Reggie Tallboys fared rather less well."

"I heard about Tallboys. What has he to do with you?"

"Wright and I were looking into a POW and he's turned up dead. Tallboys that is. Letham's report said it was a professional execution."

"It was what? Oh, for Christ's sake, Rose. This detective thing is not some jolly jape! It has to stop."

"I am only doing my bit."

"You did your bit getting blown up in France. By some miracle you survived skirmishes with villainy but you are not invincible. These latest incidents ... they sound like dangerous people. Killers."

"Hardly in short supply of late. There is a war on you know—"

"Enough!" He guided her out of the stall and bolted it behind them. "The first report I had was that you were dead. Can you imagine how I felt?" He hugged her close. "This trip has been absolute hell. What a year we've had. Not just the war but losing your mother. Both of your brothers died young, and yes that was a long time ago. I am simply not sure I could stand losing anyone else just now, so enough. Please."

"I am not a child, Daddy." She disentangled herself and kissed him soundly on the cheek.

"You're 'my' child."

"Who can look after herself. Look, I know it has been a bloody year but I am still in one piece and as safe as anyone else is right now."

"You were shot at. Again. Ye gods, child. I sometimes wonder if I haven't raised some latter-day Boadicea charging into battle at every opportunity."

"I don't. Truly. Or at least I don't do it on purpose. Anyway, nobody was shooting at me. They were aiming at Marion Cawston."

"And that is meant to make me feel better?"

"Yes, no, I mean—"

"Shall we go indoors? Mother has tea in the offing. I'll tell you all there is to know over tea and cake."

In the drawing room Bunch briefed Edward on the case in as few words as possible. "It really isn't my fault. Wright asked me to look into some stolen root vegetables and it somehow escalated into multiple murder. Tallboys wasn't our sort, but Pammie was a friend at one time and I could hardly turn my back on her now."

"And this Marion Cawston? She's a journalist."

"Yes. Is that a crime?"

"I can't decide if you are being naïve or deliberately obtuse. I am as close to the war bunker as it's possible to get. A reporter, and a foreign one at that, trying to get close to my family raises automatic suspicion."

"Marion Cawston has a British passport."

"She has several nationalities."

"She told me that herself. You've had her looked into? Henry said he knew her."

"He does."

"Then I am curious. Is she a spy?"

"If you mean an enemy agent, then no."

"Then what is all the stink about? And come to that, why did you look into her background? Who told you about her? Was it you, Granny?"

"Why should I know about spies?" Beatrice replied.

"Dodo then?"

"No."

"Then it has to be Emma. The little sneak!"

"Not Emma," Edward said. "Though she has been a huge help."

"Everett Ralph! I might have known." Her father's smile made her pause. "No? Then who?"

"I am not playing twenty questions with you, Rose. And it

hardly matters."

"I would beg to differ. It's not fair for you to know and not me. If she isn't what she claims then shouldn't she be arrested?"

"Marion Cawston is Marion Cawston. Nothing illegal there. But I would advise you not to get too involved."

"I can't see her staying in Wyncombe once this case is wrapped up, if that concerns you. She strikes me a bit of a wanderer."

Edward grunted went to pour himself a drink. "Never mind the tea. I think we all have earned this today. Malt?"

"Please. And don't worry."

"I can't help but worry, Rose-bunch. We Courtneys are getting thin on the ground."

"We are. Changing the subject – and I realise you can't say too much – but is Winnie home now?"

"Not yet. He was going down from Ottawa to Florida for a few more days' rest."

"I can understand that. Was the trip *really* worth it?"

"If all goes well the first troop ships should be leaving Nova Scotia in a week or so. They will be here officially by the end of the month."

"Really?"

"I don't need to tell you…"

"I know." Bunch realised there was far more about the forthcoming arrivals but also knew better than to ask. "Has Winnie been very ill?"

"Most people would have keeled over but the old man is indestructible. Or he thinks he is. Rather like someone else sitting not too far away." He turned to the opening door. "Yes, Sutton?"

"Excuse me, Sir, Miss Rose, there is an Inspector Wright here to see you."

"Is there, by Jove? Then you'd better show him in."

"And then take the rest of the day," Edward added.

"I still have your luggage to unpack, Sir."

Edward waved a hand. "That can wait. We've both earned some rest. Take off the weekend. I have no intention of going anywhere. Have a good evening, Sutton."

"Thank you, Sir."

"Home for the whole weekend?" Beatrice drawled as she entered the room. "We are honoured. Hello dear." She presented her cheek and Edward kissed it dutifully.

"I think Sutton and I have earned that much, Mother," Edward replied. "And I think Rose will need some assistance. Ah … Wright. Good to see you."

"And you, Sir." Wright crossed to shake Edward's hand. "Rose… I have come into possession of some more information about the incident at the New Year ball."

"Oh excellent. Do sit down, William. It's not a little early to offer you a drink, is it? Single malt perhaps?"

"That would be good." He settled back in a chair and took the glass that Bunch handed him. "Witnesses have come forward. Or one witness at least."

"Weren't they all interviewed at the time?"

"The witness has made changes to his statement and for a variety of reasons it seemed sensible to visit him in person. Seems the young couple were out in the nut-walk when the gunmen opened fire. They saw two men take a shot at you and Miss Cawston before leaving via the kitchen garden and escaping into the side road where an associate was waiting in a parked vehicle."

"Who is this witness?"

"He wishes to remain unidentified if at all possible."

"Does he?" Bunch let out a raucous hoot of amusement. "Oh my. Canoodling by moonlight. I bet he was with Binky Farnham. She was making sheep's eyes at Larry Parrish all evening."

"Isn't she engaged to one of the Sanderson boys?" Beatrice said.

"Exactly so." Bunch exaggerated, pulling her face into calm. "Sorry, William, do go on. What did this person have to say?"

"Well yes, it was Mr Parrish who called me. He still had my number after the supper club case. I suspect he would have been even more reluctant, otherwise."

"He called you instead of me. The cheeky blighter. He only lives two miles away. You just wait until I see him next."

"He was being discreet, Rose," Edward interrupted. "He has come forward so do allow him some grace."

"I suppose I must. Well spit it out old chap. What did Larry have to say?"

"He gave as good a description of two gunmen at night as you could expect, and said he followed them – at a discreet distance. He says the car was a sporty dark saloon."

"Ho ho, our dark-coloured saloon. Or one of them." Bunch paused. "I do not understand why they ran off so quickly. Marion and I … hit the deck is the term, I think. They were frighteningly close and they could have fired off a few more shots. But they didn't."

"Mr Parrish said that somebody opened the French doors leading from the ballroom out to the terrace and that the sudden blast of noise sent them scuttling away. He seemed quite convinced that had the noise not distracted them the intruders would have fired again."

"Another of the nine lives lost. Wonder how many I have left?"

"Your brushes with death are not remotely amusing, Rose." Beatrice fixed her granddaughter with an icy stare.

"They are exhausting, "Wright agreed. "I'm not sure how many more I can survive."

"I didn't know you cared."

"Of course I – we – all care!" Wright snapped.

She shook her head. "That's very sweet of you but I am a big girl now. I can take care of myself. Now what else did Larry say?"

"Very little. We are still trying to identify the car."

"There can't be many vehicles like that on the road in these parts. Practically everyone I know has mothballed their haymaker motors. Rotor arms out and chocked up on blocks, as per the regulations."

"We are casting the net wider than the county. There's a general alert out for any vehicles matching the description but frankly I don't think it will yield any results. It's not difficult to cross this county using B and C or even D roads. I'd like a word with Miss Cawston if she's around."

"She's not here."

"We told you both to stay here – for your own safety."

"She said she had business up in Town and she'd be back tomorrow."

"Damn her!"

"Is that why you really came here?"

"Not entirely. I have an appointment at the vicarage."

"With Reverend Day? What would you need to speak with him about?"

"I am following up on the statement that Botting was given today by the verger."

"Vandals in the village hall and in the church are a bit below you, aren't they?"

"I heard about that but I'm here about an alleged sighting of Vito Pavessi."

"Who is that?" Edward asked.

"An escaped POW. His links to Nario Costa have come to light."

"This was the corpse on the playing fields?" Edward said.

"The Victory Gardens, yes," Bunch said. "And you know about Tallboys and his Italian connections."

"I never had much time for him but it was a nasty way to go. Why would this Pavessi chap hang around?" Edward said.

"We have a few theories. Nothing we can verify although Botting seems to think it's worth my talking with this person."

"I believe that these incidents are all linked."

"We are coming to the same conclusion."

Bunch gave Wright a quick rundown of the basics, ending with the sighting of the cars. "I do believe it's cars – plural."

"Perhaps they – whoever they are – are certain Costa had something of value and as this is the place he ended up, it must still be in the vicinity. They'll keep returning until they find whatever it is."

"And we still have no idea what this Costa person had?" Beatrice asked.

"That is what Cawston said she intended to find out."

Bunch glanced at her father, aware that he was watching both her and Wright minutely. She half-expected him to ask questions and his silence was unnerving.

Wright, however, seemed oblivious. "We need to proceed with caution," he said. "Please call the station if you get any hint of what this missing contraband is. Now I must leave. Thank you for the drink, Sir. Good afternoon to you all."

"Will you come by later?" Bunch said.

"Not today. I have to get back to Brighton once I've spoken with the witnesses. An arrest in another case. I shall see myself out."

"You shouldn't toy with him," Beatrice murmured as the door close behind Wright. "Henry at least is used to your jokes but poor William doesn't know where he is."

Saturday 3rd January

"Marion, hello. Back from Town already?" Bunch dug her fork into the muck heap before pulling her cigarette case and lighter from her pocket. "Gasper?"

"Thank you." Cawston took one and leaned in for a light, letting the smoke rise between them, helping to mask the smell, before she added, "I got what I needed and as it started to snow I thought I should get back while the trains were still running."

"Not too bad as yet…" Bunch glanced around at the small windswept scatterings in the corners of the yard "…although it wouldn't be the first time we've been cut off completely. I gather we may expect heavy falls in the next few days."

"You have a weather station around here?"

"God no. The local sages are far more reliable than the BBC. They might be using pinecones and seaweed or chicken entrails for all I know, but it is uncanny how accurate they are. Shall we get out of this wind?" She led Cawston across the yard to the stables. "Always warmer in here. Hello you greedy creatures." She fished a couple of dried-out apples from a box on top of a feed bin and offered one to her father's hunter Robbo, who accepted with well-mannered delicacy for such a large animal. The piebald, Maggie, she approached with more caution, holding a few scraps of fruit in a well-flattened palm and drawing her hand back before the animal could sneak a nibble at her fingers. "Oh no you don't, you little monster," she chuckled and rubbed the animal's forehead affectionately. "Watch this one. At both ends. She'll bite or kick given half the chance." She paused in front of Perry and fed him a choice piece, letting him butt his head gently into her chest as he chomped. "What did you discover?" she said, keeping her voice light.

"Seems we're looking for documents." Cawston heaved herself up onto the feed bin and sat gazing around her. "Just a couple of sheets, and easily stowed."

"One would think papers of any kind would be confiscated immediately," Bunch said. "When he was dug up his clothes had been cut apart, presumably by those resurrectionists. Surely they must have the papers by now, whatever they are?"

"Possibly not. I might even go as far as *certainly* not. These people wouldn't still be hanging around if Costa's treasure had been retrieved."

"I see." Bunch pursed her lips, avoiding Cawston's expectant gaze. However much the journalist knew she was categorically fishing for more. "What do you think happened?" she said.

"Best guess is Costa knew he was being pursued by Pavessi and Favero. Maybe he was injured and knowing he had little time left hid the package somewhere in the vicinity."

"Why here?"

"My contacts suggest he was looking for Tallboys. He may even have arranged a rendezvous to hand them over to a business associate of his masters in New York."

"Tallboys was a spy? I knew it! Except Costa must have known about his links to OVRA?"

"Costa would have had no idea Tallboys was playing both teams. In all probability Tallboys himself may not have intended to place himself in that position. More a case of his past sins finding him out. A spot of blackmail perhaps. I have no doubt OVRA had some sort of evidence that could have had him arrested. Before '39 he was just another opportunist with a shady side, who thought he was far too clever to get caught. I doubt he ever imagined he'd be facing those former associates on home soil. We know he did business with Il Duce's private office up until late 1938. When he saw which way the wind was blowing, he cut back and was biding his time."

"And this other team searching the village hall, are they … Cosa Nostra? What on earth was so valuable that both sides would send out assassins?"

"I doubt they came with that explicit intention but from the moment Costa arrived in Wyncombe Tallboys was a dead man. He'd have fared no better with either side." Cawston grunted a wry amusement. "Neither are known for their goodwill for anything that smacks of betrayal. He gave them every good reason to want him dead."

"And you?" Bunch demanded.

"Did I want him dead? Why on earth would you think that?"

"I am trying to decide where you fit in all this."

Cawston emitted a second grunt. "A seeker of truth."

Bunch gave a wry smile. "Do you at least know what the papers are?"

"Legal documents," she replied. "All I know is they could cause Mussolini personal damage. Il Generalissimo is so full of himself that those papers might be anything from an execution order for the Pope to a bar bill from a house of ill repute."

"Colourful choices."

"I'm told he's a colourful man."

"He is." Bunch gave Perry's neck a final scritch and hoisted herself up beside Cawston. "I was visiting Daddy when he was at a consulate dinner in Rome. That would have been '36 perhaps? Or maybe '37?"

"What was he like?"

"Genial. On the surface at least. Very sure of himself. Surrounded by well-armed – shall we call them assistants? Not someone you'd want to cross."

"So pretty much your everyday dictator."

"And the Mafia?"

"Costa was a blood relative to one of the New York dons. If Tallboys had betrayed them, even unknowingly, they'd likely kill him without question."

"You seem to know an awful lot about these people."

"I have good contacts."

"It would seem so." Bunch took a long pull at her cigarette while she considered how much she could or should trust this woman. Her instinct was to run with it, that as odd as Cawston might be she was telling the truth. Perhaps not all of it but enough. "And now you're telling me. Should I be honoured?"

"We're working for the same side," Cawston replied. "I think we can close this case between us. I can see you still don't exactly trust me and I don't blame you, but we really don't have much time. Call Marsham if you must. He can vouch for me."

"He said you'd met."

"We have shared interests."

Looking at Cawston for a long moment Bunch reached a decision. "What do we do now?"

"We search."

"Uh-huh." Bunch ground her cigarette out carefully on a metal scoop and stepped down to Perry's stall, feeding the pony a scrap of hay and nestling her head against his. Her instinct was that she should trust Cawston, yet logic was screaming at her to keep the journalist at arm's length. The woman could be an agent with a half-dozen sources. Bringing Henry into the equation could well be a ploy. "Where?" she said. "Those chaps at least knew what they were looking for but we have no idea."

"Costa was in unfamiliar territory and would not have had the time or the wherewithal to be too creative. He was buried in a hurry in the gardens where we have to assume he was killed. That's backed up by the village hall being torn apart. We should also assume they found nothing and moved on to the church, where they were disturbed. I am going to go out on a limb and say we start there."

Voices out in the yard held Bunch silent. Everything Cawston had told her made sense. Finding Costa's documents, whatever they might be, would bring the case to a close, she thought. And if something had remained hidden in that church all that time it had to be somewhere obscure that only a local might know. "Come up to the house." She strode out into the yard and called out for Burse to get the MG ready.

When she emerged from her room, minus the smell of stables, Edward had returned from his walk across to Perringham House.

"Hello my dear." Edward put his hands gently to either side of her face and dropped a light kiss on her forehead. "Everett sends his regards by the way."

"How nice."

"I can't imagine what Ralph ever did to offend you but I do wish it would stop. It's so— Oh—" He flushed as he realised his daughter was not alone. "Hello there. You're Marion Cawston, I take it?"

"I am." Cawston held out her hand. "Good to meet you, Sir Edward."

"Emma Tinsley tells me you also go by the name of Mary Cason."

"You two know each other?" said Bunch. "And … Cason?"

"My husband was Bennin Cason. He worked for the ministry." She raised her shoulders and smiled at Bunch. "I thought it wise not to mention it before."

Edward looked her up and down, his face unreadable. "I was rather surprised to find you here," he said at last. "In my home."

"I'm sorry for that, Sir Edward. Events at the ball rather forced my hand. I thought it the best way to protect your daughter."

"Hmm. There are times of late when I think she could use a bodyguard. Possibly one armed with a Crusader tank or two."

"Yes Sir."

"Look, Daddy, it's splendid to see you but we were just off."

"Where to?"

"Church," Bunch replied. "Quite safe I assure you. If Wright calls perhaps you can tell him where we'll be." Bunch stood on tiptoe to kiss Edward's cheek and hustled Cawston out into the drive.

"Rose, Rose come back—"

"See you later, Daddy. Toodle pip." She hustled Cawston to the MG. "A rapid exit is required before he lays down the law," she muttered. "Hop in."

~~~

As the little green MG pulled up close to the Lychgate it had begun to snow once more. Not a heavy fall but persistent on a brisk wind. Gritty white particles skittered into the gullies, camouflaging the kerbs and steps like talc on a bathroom floor. West had cleared the main path earlier in the day but already a uniform layer of snow had accumulated.

Cawston paused to examine recent boot prints that crossed the path. She glanced about her. Eyes narrowed against the brightness. "Two men," she said. "In the last few minutes."

Bunch looked around the churchyard but could see no one close by. Nor any vehicles that might give her a clue. She shrugged. "People come and go here all the time. Could be anyone. Let's get in out of this wind." She grabbed the heavy iron ring of the latch and pushed one leaf of the doors open. The clatter of the cast iron door handles was echoing around the empty church as the women stepped inside.

It was almost as cold inside as it was outside and their breath was clearly visible in roiling clouds. Bunch closed the doors behind them and paused in the narthex to take in the scent of furniture wax and damp stone, and that something else that made it indefinably churchlike. The font was in line with the central aisle and protruded slightly from its recess next to the bell ringer's room. In former days it would be bathed in coloured light from a towering stained-glass window but with the main panels covered by protective boarding the sandstone bulk was a more muted yellow under a carved wooden lid.

"Where do we start?" Cawston murmured. "Here?" She waved to their left at the neat rows of books shelved spines up for ease of taking, slightly battered hymnals and copies of Common Prayer. On the other side of the space was a table with a collecting box and a handful of neatly stacked leaflets.

"According to the vicar, Mrs Watson complained that they were all over the floor, so someone had been through them already. And surely Costa would have known that a hymnal was a risky hiding spot. Any member of the congregation could have found it, whatever 'it' is." Bunch sighed. "It would really help to know exactly what we are looking for."

"Papers of some kind. I can't imagine there'll be too many Italian documents stashed away in an English parish church."

"All right then. Let's put ourselves in the shoes of a courier for an Italian gangster trying to stow something valuable in a hurry. They are not concerned about leaving any markers for others to identify because they fully intend to return in person." Bunch looked around, her fists held clenched at her sides. "A plague on Martha Watson for being so bloody efficient. Not so much as a scuff mark to hint at where they searched."

"We should approach this from the beginning. It would have been high summer when Costa hid these things. A good sixteen or seventeen hours of daylight for him to have a long look around for the best spot. Is there a crypt?"

"Yes, a small one. It doesn't stretch the whole length of the building because it dates from the earliest phase. It's generally unlocked because the vicar felt it should be available as an air raid shelter. The main entrance is on the outside, but there's a narrow stairwell hidden away at the back of the organ loft leading down into a niche at the far end. Not easy to find unless you know it."

"Leave that for now then. What about the chapels at each end of the transept?"

"Not much to see in the north chapel. A brace of tombs with effigies — otherwise empty. Oh, there are two confessional boxes. I always forget those. They aren't used a great deal because Reverend Day isn't especially High Anglican, any more than his congregation is, and I suspect most people would be rather wary of telling him their deep dark secrets. He likes the bar of the Seven Stars far too much." She mimed drinking from a bottle. "As a widower he has too much time on his hands."

"Delightful," Cawston drawled. "And getting us nowhere."

"Then I suggest we gainsay Mr Holmes and don't eliminate anything at all. Start with a poke around in the pews and work our way along. The good ladies of the parish will have polished any obvious clues into oblivion, but if we take alternate rows we'll get through the pews in a few minutes."

They moved off to search beneath the benches, unhooking each lovingly needlepointed hassock in turn to check for split seams, sneezing at the dust they disturbed, and finishing with the three box pews at the head of the south aisle. Bunch sat back in her customary seat in the Courtney box and dusted her hands. "Martha Watson's team loses a house point. The corners of this box haven't been cleaned in months. I'm surprised Granny hasn't noticed."

Cawston looked to their right and left. "What now? Or possibly where now?"

"Let's assume Costa hid it somewhere easily accessed. Which rules out the vestry because that and the belfry are the only places kept locked. We should search the chancel next. The altar is cleaned weekly, but there are no end of niches and nooks around the choir stalls."

They spent ten minutes ferreting through the crevices of the choristers' box and another fruitless fifteen minutes kneeling at the side of a large chest sorting through mounds of music.

"Nothing." Cawston sat back on her heels. "I take it that tiny door leads to the organ loft. It looks like something from *Alice in Wonderland*."

"That one leads to the crypt. The loft is this way." Bunch ducked behind a panel at the back of the pulpit which obscured a narrow stairwell of bare wood risers and started up them in an awkward, crablike fashion, hanging onto a thick rope that was threaded through iron rings fixed into the stonework. Each step creaked in turn under her booted feet as she twisted out of Cawston's view. "Watch your step," she called as she emerged at the top. I have lost count of the times I've seen people slip on these things. Miss Hatcher has taken to using the long route around the gallery."

"Who?"

"The organist." Bunch stood to one side to allow Cawston into the loft, which was more of a recessed landing. The organ's gleaming console crouched there like some mahogany walrus king, displaying three key manuals of yellowing teeth and faded black stumps, with rows of draw-knobs and stops bristling from either side like stubby whiskers. And above it all was a fan of dully gleaming organ pipes.

To their left was a half-height pierced oak screen that

shielded the organist from the congregation but allowed an open view down to the choir stalls. Cawston peered through the screen to the nave stretching to the font. "I thought you said it was a small gallery. It runs the whole way round."

"Barely two feet wide on this side so strictly speaking only a walkway. I suppose somebody thought it added symmetry."

"Can you walk the gallery all the way round?"

"This side ends over the north door and begins again at the bell tower over the narthex and back along the south side as far as the vestry."

"Narth what?"

Bunch grinned. "The area behind the pews at the north end. There's the door into the belfry but that's always locked when it's not in use so I think we can view that as highly improbable. The south gallery has stairs at either side." She pointed at a cupboard to the left of the console. "Do you want to rummage through these stacks of sheet music? Or poke about between the pipes?"

"I'll take the papers."

"Have fun." Bunch turned to the organ and surveyed it carefully. Kneeling, she peered between the foot pedals. There seemed sufficient space but she was sure Costa would not have risked his precious pieces to potential damage in the organ's moving parts. She searched the console, moving anything that could be moved, lifting flaps and opening doors before moving to the pipes. Most of those were out of reach, metal tubes rising high above her.

Bunch grabbed a folding beechwood chair and stretched over the console to reach the pipes and though she was taller than many of her friends she could only just touch the metal tubes. She had a moment of hesitation before she put one foot on the polished side of the upper manual, wondering what the organist would say. "What the eye doesn't see," she murmured as she transferred her weight onto the mahogany frame. It gave her enough of a reach to put her fingers into the narrow mouth of the central pipe and realised immediately that there was no way anything more than a cigarette card-sized document could fit inside without blocking the airway, which would have set both choir master and organist investigating the duff notes in their beloved instrument. There didn't seem to be any way that something could be hidden inside a pipe. She felt into the gaps between the organ pipes, sneezing as she dislodged a shower of dust of cobwebs and mouse turds. "Errch, it stinks."

"You found something?" Cawston shuffled across to peer over Bunch's shoulder.

"Possibly." Bunch tugged at the edge of something soft and pliable – like leather yet not. She scrabbled for a hold on one of the pipes and wiggled the package back and forth, slowly easing it from the narrow triangle of space between two pipes. She dragged a folded wad of oilcloth into the light.

"What is it?"

"I'm not sure." She climbed down to unfold her find. "A waterproofed wallet. We had similar issued to us in the ATS but this is a lot thinner. A vulcanised linen, perhaps?" She prised open two press studs with her thumbnail and unfolded the end flap. Wedged tightly inside were two yellowed and slightly dog-eared sheets of paper which she grasped between forefinger and thumb and eased out. "It's in Italian," she muttered, "which is hopeful. Let's see, *Certificato di Matrimonio*. Dated 1914. Ida Irene Dalser and…" she whistled quietly "…Benito Amilcare Andrea Mussolini." She lowered the page to peer at Cawston. "Did you expect this?"

"No. Rumours about a first wife surface every now and then."

"First wife? Would a divorce be that damaging to him, assuming the church permitted it? Although Catholic divorces are pretty unusual."

"I think someone like Il Duce could make it happen if he wanted. May I?" Cawston took the papers and held them gently. "This is a copy of Ida's death certificate. And this is a hand-written affidavit dated a few weeks after her death. It's the most appalling handwriting so we shall need some time to translate it all." Cawston peered a little more closely. "From what I can work out, Ida was still contesting the divorce and had sent documents to the Vatican."

"Which would put his current marriage in doubt. That

wouldn't go down well."

"The divorce is an inconvenience. Bumping off Ida Dalser would be the easiest answer."

"He had her killed?"

"That would be a solution and proving he was behind it will always be the hard part."

They both swivelled towards the balcony rail at the barely audible yet unmistakable rattle of the church door and the softer clunk as it closed once more.

Bunch took the papers and folded them back into the wallet. "Probably the vicar." She peered over the rail. "Or perhaps not," she breathed. The two men stood a few paces into the central aisle gazing around them. One of the men was slender and athletic, the other more stocky, and both clad in dark overcoats and wide-brimmed felt hats. "Do you recognise them?" she whispered.

"No." Cawston pulled her into the shelter of the screen. "I would hazard a guess at enemy aliens."

"Here?" Bunch clapped a hand over her mouth as the vaulted ceiling's infamous acoustics tossed her words back and forth. Both men look upward, searching for movement along the gallery, their faces showing dull white in the gloom.

The slimmer of the two slipped his right hand inside his open coat and Bunch saw a glint of metal. She had no doubt the other was also armed. One or both of those men had already taken pot-shots at them in another place and she didn't imagine they would have any doubts about their trying again, even here inside a church. Nor would they make any distinction between her and Cawston. Her head began to swim a little in the effort of breathing slow and shallow so that the vapours could not be seen in the cold air. She felt as if she were back at school playing Grandmother's Footsteps, waiting for *It* to shout "you moved" and send her slinking back to the start. As seconds ticked past her muscles were pinging with the effort of standing absolutely still.

The men beneath exchanged a few unidentifiable words in hushed tones and the weapon was returned to the depths of a pocket. Bunch closed her eyes for a moment, bowing her head before daring a look at Cawston, who nodded and smiled and waggled a Browning HP automatic that Bunch had not seen her draw.

"Time to leave," Cawston mouthed.

Bunch stared at the compact, square-nosed little pistol in Cawston's fist and wished she had brought her father's Webley. But the idea of bringing a gun into a church had been unthinkable. She puffed her cheeks and looked over her shoulder at the stair head, listening intently for the scuff of boots on wooden steps, and allowed herself licence to lean forward an inch or two and peek through the carved lattice at the space below. She could see the stockier of the men moving along the south aisle, peering at the pews and moving hassocks, in a carbon copy of her own search.

The other, Bunch assumed, was somewhere below on the north side. In a few moments the searchers would reach the transept. Which way they would go from there Bunch could only guess. They might mount the chancel step and discover the stairway up to the loft or peel off in opposite directions to explore the side chapels. Either way, she and Cawston needed to be making for an exit and the only unlocked doors were either to the crypt, accessible via the chancel, or the way they had entered through the north porch. She pointed along the gallery and Cawston nodded, gesturing for her to go first. They started along the walkway, crouching low, trying to move silently across the bare boards suspended above the gunmen's heads.

The walkway was in shadow and Bunch didn't spot the warden's stock of fire buckets neatly stacked on the turn. Four empty buckets along with their stirrup pumps clattered over, one bouncing off each riser of the gallery stairs before hitting the church's stone floor.

"Run," Cawston shouted before the vessel had reached the floor.

"I am running!" Bunch lengthened her stride to take the stairs two at a time, skittering around the corner once she reached ground level and diving for the door and wrenching it open.

A barked order, *"Fermata ora!"* followed them into the porch.

"Stop be damned. Run!" Bunch felt Cawston's hand on her back, propelling her through the doors. They were yards from the lychgate when Bunch tugged at Cawston's coat and swung her around into the maze of gravestones and monuments.

"What did you do that for?"

"Because they've boxed my car in and there's a goon standing right by it." Bunch glanced behind them at the open church door. "Is that why they haven't chased us out?"

"Because they don't want witnesses?" Cawston looked all around, her eyes narrowed against the gritty snow gathering pace on a stiffening wind. "And because a chap like him is not going to be alone," she muttered, nodding towards the cars.

Bunch peered between the headstones and over the low churchyard wall. The soft top of her MG could just be seen over the coping stones, bookended now by black saloon cars. The man was leaning on the MG's bonnet. She could see that he was bulky even under his thick coat. His fedora was wider brimmed than Wright's and had accumulated a light scatter of snow. The wind carried the pungency of smoke towards the women from the fat cigar he drew on every few moments. He appeared at ease but Bunch was aware of a feline intensity in the way his gaze roamed constantly around him. "You don't think he's with those two in the church?"

"I'm certain. And his friends are plainly looking for the men who own the other car."

"I'm not sure I understand. If we were searching in the church then they calculated that we must know something. But what about that second car? Who are they, where did it come from?"

Cawston had relaxed visibly and let an exasperated smile appear at something beyond Bunch's shoulder. "Hello Joe. What brings you here, as if I didn't know."

Bunch turned awkwardly, almost toppling from her crouched posture. The man was slim and athletic, and handsome in that David Niven fashion.

"Cawston, hi. We seem to meet in the darndest places."

"Not always entirely by accident. Rose, meet Joe Scherino." Cawston eyed the newcomer up and down, chin up, head tilted. "Last I heard, you were in New York. What are you doing here, Joe?"

"Nario Costa was my cousin Isabella's husband," Scherino growled. "This is a *faida*. A family feud. Papa never leaves New York so it's down to me. You ladies should skedaddle cuz there's no nice way this'll end."

"I have my own score to settle," Cawston replied. "I will leave when I'm ready."

"Scherino?" Bunch said. "That was the family Pamela Tallboys talked about."

"*La bella Signora Tallboys*?" He sighed heavily. "Don Arturo was very sad to learn that her husband was doing business with Il Duce's *teppisti*."

Thugs? thought Bunch. *Takes one to know one.* "We don't know that he was."

"Tallboys was Nario's contact." He shrugged. "What he didn't know was Pavessi was aware of that and headed him off."

"You seem certain. You have proof of all of that?"

Scherino barred his teeth in a grin. "From, as you Brits would say, the horse's mouth. Eventually."

"Where's Pavessi now?"

"You ain't gotta worry about him no longer." He gestured towards the church. "Me and Terzo've been tailing those guys."

"You saw them come in after us?"

He shrugged and waved at the church once more. "No. We pulled up by that little toy car of yours and saw their saloon. We guessed they didn't know you'd be here. Just their good luck – and your bad."

"You didn't go in after them?"

"Start a gun fight in a church? Nah. Not my style."

"I never suspected you chaps had such scruples."

"You see too much of the movies. We got three things nobody messes with. Family, fidelity and faith." He counted each down with a gloved finger. "These're things Mussolini don't have. With those papers we can prove it.'"

Bunch patted her pocket and felt her pulse lurch. She checked her other pocket and felt all around her body where no pockets existed. "Oh hell. It's gone. I must have dropped it."

"You can't have."

"It's not here." Bunch turned her pockets out with an increasing sense of panic. "It must be up on the gallery."

"Shit," Cawston muttered.

"How in hell do we get it back?"

Cawston peered round. "All right then. Rose, you said there was a way in through the crypt?"

"Preferably by a back way," Scherino added.

"Of course."

"Great." He gave a low whistle and a few hand signals to Fiore, who nodded and ducked behind the wall.

"Follow me." Keeping low Bunch led them onto the path to the vicarage. Once they had a clear line of sight to the entrance there was a dull crack and the slamming of the church doors.

Scherino paused and looked back. "Dammit," he muttered. "I wanted them outside. Now they'll hole up in there."

"He shot at them?"

"Yeah. I knew it. I told Papa I shoulda brought Arty. Fiore's a good man but he's dumb as an ox."

"We should get a wiggle on," Bunch said. "While they're distracted."

"Wiggle away, sweetheart, I'm right behind you."

"Manners…" she snapped "…maketh a man."

"Sorry. I guess I'm not used to speaking with real ladies."

"*Get* used to it," Bunch hissed over her shoulder and dived off the main path to a recess between buttresses, and to four steps that led down to an oak-planked door. She turned the doorknob and pushed the door open, pausing at the shushing of dead leaves caught beneath the sill. She opened it wide enough to slip in. The meagre light slanting in from the outside showed very little. As Bunch had intimated, it was not a large space, half the size of the church above. The ceiling was low and arched, supported by stone pillars. The niches that had contained burials had been bricked up. There were blankets on chairs and benches flanking a couple of wooden trestles.

She moved to light one of the lamps left in readiness for those escaping air raids but Cawston tugged her arm, shaking her head and pointing to the ceiling. Bunch nodded and led them across to the far side, becoming more sure-footed as she gained her night-sight. She halted by the steps that curled up to the door behind the choir stall.

"Only one way up?" Scherino breathed in her ear.

"And a door at top." She set one foot on the bottom step. "On the other side that door is hard to see unless you're standing right in front of it. Follow me." Scherino's lips parted to protest and knowing he was going to tell her to stay behind Bunch stepped forward to make a stealthy assault on the stairs.

Reaching the top she laid her ear to the door and listened. Scherino and Cawston stood a little below her, wary, with weapons drawn. *And I left the Webley in my room.* Another listen at the door before she lifted the Suffolk latch, wincing at the unavoidable click of cast iron, and eased the door open an inch or two and stopped. Voices, whispers, echoed around the arched ceilings, and she heard a muffled crump from outside the building. She glanced at Cawston who held the muzzle of her gun and mimed firing it. *Ah, silencers? Terzo is keeping them occupied.*

Pushing the door open wide enough to slip through on hands and knees, she moved rapidly along the stall. Cawston let the door behind her close as far as it could without latching and signalled to Scherino to make for the organ loft. He pointed to his chest and then a walking motion, using two fingers, towards the south side, pointed to the two women and upwards.

Bunch slipped into the stairwell and crept into the organ loft, her steps masked by the loud noises coming from the south transept. She glanced down at the gunmen; they had left the porch and were barging at the locked vestry door. *Presumably on the assumption that because it's locked it must be important,* she thought, *or more likely an escape route.* There was a way out through the vestry, it was true, a door used only by the vicar and church wardens. But the door was a stout one, reinforced long ago and hinged with steel plates after an attempt to steal the church valuables. The men's attempts to barge and kick their way in had come to nothing. It would not take them long to realise they could not gain entry and start a fresh look around the building for another way out.

She ducked back to join Cawston on her hands and knees searching the floor around the console and the foot-pedals. Cawston shook her head and signalled along the walkway. "Buckets," she hissed. "Where you tripped."

Bunch scuttled the length of the gallery and crouched beside the scatter of red buckets and tangled stirrup pumps. She felt among the debris for the oily feel of the waxed package. Cawston knelt beside her, raising her head to peer over the panel. One of them knocked a metal pail and Bunch felt its metallic clang as it tumbled down the stairs, like a cracked bell tolling a summons.

"There!" Cawston lunged forward and snatched up the slender package.

Bunch drew back from the top of the stair well as a shot rang out. A searing pain in her left calf made her scream and pull her knee up to her chest. She clasped at her leg that was oozing blood.

"Bad?" Cawston hissed.

"Bad enough to put making another run for the door rather out of the question." She could hear a rapid exchange between Scherino and the opposition. Angry exchanges were shouted out in machine-gun bursts, belligerent, and for the most part so explicitly biological that it defied her Italian language skills, or would have done had she been able to take it in. What was uppermost in her mind was that the leg she had injured in '39, as a driver in France, the leg that had taken a full year to recover, to be walked on without pain, had been torn apart a second time.

"We have to move, Rose. We have to move."

"Where to?"

"Back the way we came. Scherino's got those chaps pinned

down over on the other side."

"It's not going to happen. You—" She cocked her head at a distant, frantic clanging of a bell. "Police car," she said. "I left a message for Wright. We can sit this one out now."

Cawston held her hand up for quiet. The bell had come to a ragged halt somewhere outside and the arguments in the church ceased. Cawston peered over the top rail. From outside came a shout. "Police. Lay down your weapons and come out with hands behind your heads."

The call was answered by a volley of gunfire.

"This could take a while," Cawston murmured. She pulled out a penknife and cut the worsted material of Bunch's slacks away to expose an ugly wound seared across the calf. "Bit of a mess," she said. "But I don't think there's a bullet left in. Just chewed up the muscle. Not for the first time either. Where'd you get those scars?"

"Accident," Bunch snapped. She wasn't sure why she was reluctant to say more but felt there was judgement in Cawston's gaze.

"Okay. None of my business." She pulled off her scarf and wrapped it tightly around the wound. "Apply pressure," she growled.

"I know."

"I forgot. You were a nurse." She grabbed her gun at a scuffling at the loft end of the gallery and lowered it as she saw Scherino. He beckoned and when Cawston shook her head scurried along to join them.

"Inside the church. This is the police. You are surrounded and there is no escape. Give yourself up."

The megaphone made his voice sound tinny but Bunch could not mistake Wright's steady tenor intoning the stock phrases that she had heard a dozen times in a dozen films. There was silence inside the church and out and she stifled a laugh in spite of her pain. "Wright is having fun," she whispered.

"Perhaps, but he won't risk letting this become a siege."

"Nor will those guys," Scherino added. "And it'll be kinda hard to surround a place this size on his own."

"What?"

Scherino held up a forefinger. "One police bell. One car. One officer – two if he's lucky." He nodded towards the church below. "If I noticed it, you can bet your ass ... pardon the language, ladies ... you can bet those guys will've. And they won't stick around for the cavalry to show up."

"What then?"

"You'll be safe enough once they see us leave. Here." Scherino reached inside his coat and handed her a snubbed Beretta pistol. "You can shoot?

"Yes."

"Good. Then we draw them outside."

"Will you be okay for a bit? With the leg?" Cawston asked.

"Hurts like the devil, but yes."

"I feel terrible about leaving you to—"

"Just go." Bunch eased herself onto her good knee. "If they see you leave they won't imagine there's anybody left up here."

"You hope."

From outside came the sounds of more shouting from Wright, demanding those in the church to give themselves up.

Bunch watched Cawston and Scherino scurry along the gallery and vanish behind the loft screens. A few seconds later they appeared briefly in the choir stalls and the sound of the door opening and closing came clearly across the aisles.

Wright was calling again from outside.

In the church below there was silence and she raised herself a little higher to look down from the gallery. For a few seconds she saw nobody and then a shadow slanted through the open door. Bunch checked the safety was off on the pistol and hitched up a little higher, stifling a grunt as the movement sent a slice of pain from the wound up to her thigh.

The shadow solidified into Wright's familiar figure moving cautiously into view. A scuffle from somewhere beneath the southern arm of the gallery caused Wright to duck into the rear pews.

Someone flitted between pillars, crossing the transept and into the box pews.

"Halt. Halt or I shall open fire." Wright slipped from his

position to the first stanchion on the south aisle. "Lay down your weapons."

Bunch could see Wright peering around the pillar. To her left she saw a second man cross to the choir stalls on the north side and out of her view.

Wright raised his arm taking aim as the crypt door opened, just as a glint of metal in the choir stall caught Bunch's attention. "William! Get down!"

A single shot ricocheted off the stone pillar and Wright fell back into the nearest pew and out of sight. The crypt door clattered shut and silence returned.

"William! William! Are you hurt?"

"No."

She lowered the gun and closed her eyes as relief washed over her. "Bully for you," she called back at last. "Because I bloody well am. Who's outside?"

"They've gone, dammit. Just Glossop in the car, and she isn't armed. I sent her for the cavalry."

Bunch inched herself a little higher against the panel for an unobstructed view. *Terzo must have made himself scarce when William arrived. Interesting but unsurprising.* She heard a car start up and left, followed by a second. "Your gunmen have just left."

"Dammit!" Wright said again as he struggled to his feet and raced to the end of the aisle. "Dammit!"

His expletive echoed around an empty space and Bunch felt an urge to laugh at the incongruity of it all. "Language," she called. "This is a church."

"And firing live rounds willy-nilly is perfectly acceptable?" he snapped. "Cawston? Where is she?"

"God knows." Bunch grunted and clasped at her leg. "I do know she has what Costa and Tallboys were killed for. Bloody hell!" She slid to the floor; the Beretta pistol clattered down the stairs and bounced around the stone floor.

"Rose? Are you all right?"

"Not really."

Wright stormed up the steps, shouting her name. The world was shifting by ninety degrees and the floor under her cheek was gritty with spilled sand from some of the buckets, but she was no longer conscious to notice.

Epilogue

Bunch eased herself into a wing-backed chair and set her crutches aside. Getting around was becoming easier and she couldn't argue with Edward and Beatrice's insistence of a period of convalescence after two weeks in hospital. She had refused The Red House rest home with its pastel-coloured walls synonymous with her mother's death.

Edward had been astonished at his very modern daughter's choice.

The Straithglen had a reputation for serving those who required comfort as well as privacy, perhaps even secrecy, as they were nursed back to health – for a price. It was close enough to Edinburgh to be accessible while at the same time being escapable when residents felt they had been cosseted long enough. It was a long-established bolt hole, and just the ticket.

Bunch had visited an old friend here ten years previously and remembered it fondly for its slightly shabby gentility, its dark carved oak doors and primal Arts and Crafts wallpaper and drapes, its dark red leather chairs and strategic lamplight. It was a warm cave-like refuge for wounded bears to hide away. "Because one doesn't want harsh light when feeling like death," she told herself.

While she contemplated the person seated on the other side of the fireplace, an elderly waiter served whisky and water.

"Will you be needing anything else, Miss Courtney?" he asked.

"No, thank you."

"Very good Miss."

She took a sip of whisky and tilted her head to examine Emma Tinsley's angular features. "Lovely to see you Emm, but I can't help feeling you've made the trip for a reason. So out with it. To what do I owe the pleasure?"

"Your father asked me to give you a little catch-up on events."

"You mean, take away any excuses I have not to do damn all except convalesce?"

"Something like that." Emma took an envelope from her bag and handed it across. "I also have a little missive from Daphne."

"Oh yes. Dodo said she was going to write." Bunch noted both the unfranked stamp and slight wrinkle to the sealed edge, and frowned. "Censored?"

"Lord no. Your father only wanted a quick look to make sure Daphne wasn't giving you excuses to tear back home."

"Why would he assume that?"

"Daphne wouldn't alarm you on purpose but we thought I should bring it in person in case you needed some additional details."

"Do I take it that she's in a state over something. Is she all right?"

"She's perfectly spiffing. Far tougher than your father or mine give her credit for."

"I know that but you haven't answered my question."

"It's all in the letter. Read the damn thing out loud and then I shall answer it."

"Aloud?"

"Yes, then I may save us all time by filling you in on the stuff she's not aware of."

Bunch frowned at Emma and wondered if she was already aware of what the letter contained. If she did then it was hard not to feel a sense of betrayal. She slit open the envelope flap with her nail and took out two sheets of paper.

> Dear Bunch,
>
> Sorry not to have written sooner. Absolutely run off my feet with all kinds of stuff. There was such a kerfuffle over your fight in the church. Goodness me! The village is divided between Lady Rose the patriotic fighter and Rose Courtney defiler of holy ground.

Bunch lowered the paper to stare at Emma. "Are people really blaming me?"

"Not at all," Emma replied. "Well … except for the usual suspects looking for an excuse to raise their own pet peeves."

"I can imagine." Bunch turned her attention back to Dodo's missive.

> You asked me to bring you up to date with all the news that Granny and Daddy don't want you to hear about and to be honest I am not sure I know anything that you don't. Emma is being terribly secretive about these Italian chaps. People are saying they killed Reggie Tallboys because he would not sell them the deeds to the club. Granny on the other hand claims to have it on good authority that Reggie was a gangster. Imagine! Barty says it's all nonsense. But when has that ever got in the way of a good rumour! He did say there is still at least one prisoner on the loose because his mounted brigade have been given orders to comb the Downs for a hint of him.

"I take it that is Pavessi?"

"There is, as a matter of fact, some good news on that front." Emma gave Bunch wry grin. "Pavessi was arrested trying to board a ship bound for Venezuela. He denies murder, of course. Iain thinks it doubtful that any case can really be proven against him, which is a bit of a blow, but the general consensus is that Tallboys was murdered by whoever shot you and Favero was done in by an as yet unidentified prisoner. Costa we may never know. The odds are on Pavessi, but it could as easily have been Tallboys. If Reggie didn't actually deal the fatal blow he was a part of the event. Henry still feels there is a good case for Pavessi being an enemy agent rather than simply military, which would bring the same penalty."

"He'd hang?

"If he's found guilty then yes."

"And the thugs in the church?"

Emma frowned. "Gone to ground."

"What? All of them?"

"Your policeman chum Wright is absolutely spitting feathers because it naturally makes his investigations look a poor show. There are quite a few people who would gladly join you up here in the glens to keep out of his way."

"Poor William." Bunch looked back at her letter and continued reading.

> It's Pamela Tallboys I feel sorry for. Not only lost her husband but found out he was a wrong 'un in the same blow.

"Except that she knew," Bunch observed. "Pamela knew exactly what he was."

"That he was a villain?"

"Not that he was on the wrong side of the law perhaps, but she knew he wasn't good. I dread to think what went on behind those doors. Here, Dodo mentions it."

> There were a lot of rumours going around that Pamela would close the club. Perhaps even sell the place. I never thought that. Pam will do anything to save Westmere. She surprised everyone when the first thing she did was to sack the committee and rip up the rules on female members. She lost some existing members but once the better weather comes I think she will make a go of it. She has the small holding to fall back on and from what I have heard, Reggie had quite the portfolio.
>
> You may have heard that Marion Cawston has vanished. Done a moonlight flit leaving the Brices a bundle of bank notes on the table and no forwarding address.

"Do you know what's happened to Cawston? And that American chap she left with? I would bet you a crisp white fiver of my own that she'll turn up again."

"Cawston was last seen entering the US Embassy."

"With the documents that Costa was killed for?"

"We are not sure."

"Perhaps the US secret service has them now."

Emma shrugged. "We don't know. Scherino has gone to ground. He's a known hoodlum back in America. If there is any possibility he took possession of those documents they've all been smuggled back to his bosses."

"Do you think they'll be of any use?"

"That will depend on which way the war goes. What else does Daphne have to say?"

"Oh, let's see. Georgi has a cold … poor mite. Um … WVS beetle drive … dah dee dah … oh, listen here to this."

> I've had some news about Maurice at long last. He's alive! His CO came to tell me that his name has turned up on the Red Cross lists. Seems his plane was brought down over enemy territory and he was picked up by a German patrol. He had a spell in hospital and has ended up in a POW camp. I will let you have the address as soon as I have it. Awful to think he's locked up but at least he isn't MIA. I should be glad of that at least. I still feel dreadful about how we parted company that last night. He asked me to marry him and I sent him off with a flea in his ear.

"Oh, good heavens." Bunch set the pages on the table beside her. "Is Dodo in an awful fug over him?"

"Somewhat. We keep telling her it was a very dangerous mission, which he knew perfectly well, and being taken prisoner is far better than drowning in the North Sea. Barty has no idea how to cope with her guilt. I have to be in Town more often so I'm trusting your grandmother to put her straight."

"Granny to the rescue, as always." She tucked the sheets back into the envelope and lifted her glass. "Shame about Maurice. I did well by comparison."

"Other than the small matter of a bullet in the leg?"

"The case was solved," Bunch replied. "Mission

accomplished. Not that you'd know it with how some people seem to react."

"Wright still hasn't been in touch?"

"No." Bunch took an angry mouthful of single malt and grimaced as she swallowed it down. "I did have a visit from Uncle Walter. He came up from London especially to see me and suggested that 'in view of my injuries I step back as a Police Consultant, just for the time being.' Time being, presumably, to be equated with however long this war lasts. He can be such a pompous ass."

"He's dispensed with your services? I can't say I'm surprised."

"Not as such. Did you know he gave Wright an unofficial reprimand? Endangering a civilian. And it was Uncle Walter handed me the job in the first place."

"That would explain why Wright has kept away. He's been warned off."

"I suppose so. Given that nearly all of my cases have come through William I can assume future consultations will slow to a trickle. Plus, Daddy has been rather forthright on the subject too."

"You can't blame Sir Edward for wanting to protect you," Emma drawled. "You have an unfortunate knack of finding yourself in the line of fire." Emma held a hand up. "Not your fault. It never is. Have you thought there might be other things you could do?"

"Such as?" Bunch narrowed her eyes. "You plainly have some other plan in mind."

"Plans? No." Emma pointed at Bunch's damaged leg stretched out across a footstool. "Get back on your feet before you start searching out bigger windmills to tilt at."

"Indeed." Bunch raised the glass above her head. "A toast, then. To good health and better luck."

Glossary

ATS – Auxiliary Territorial Service

BEF - British Expeditionary Force

RAMC – Royal Army Medical Corp

Cat D – lowest fitness level of military medical. Medically unfit

Fante – Infantryman (Italian)

Il maiale – Pig (Italian)

ITMA – It's That Man Again – a popular radio show from 1939 to 1949

Min Ag – Ministry of Agriculture and Fisheries

Min Food – Ministry of Food

Min Works – Ministry of Works

OVRA - O*rganizzazione per la Vigilanza e la Repressione dell'Antifascismo* (The Organization for Vigilance and Repression of Anti-Fascism)

WAAF – Women's Auxiliary Air Force

WI – Women's Institute

WLA – Women's Land Army

WRNS – Women's Royal Navy Service

WVS – Women's Voluntary Service

Wyncombe CC – Wyncombe cricket club

We do hope you enjoyed reading *Deadly Plot*. If you did then why not leave a review with your bookseller; or spread the word to friends and acquaintances via your own blog – and don't forget to send us those links! For further information on the other Bunch Courtney Investigations books visit
https://janedwardsblog.wordpress.com/

Sign up for our newsletter to receive the latest information at
https://janedwardsblog.wordpress.com/contact/

Jan Edwards is available for interviews and events.
Contact Penkhull Press at
https://thepenkhullpress.wordpress.com/

All the Bunch books are available in print and as Kindle editions. Signed print copies can be obtained directly from the author via the above links.

Author's Note

Finally: This is a work of fiction. Wyncombe is a fictitious Sussex village that I envisage nestling in the South Downs some 18 miles north-by-northwest of Brighton, but I have tried to be accurate with all other geographical landmarks. Wyncombe's residents are likewise products of my fevered imagination. Historical figures such as Winston Churchill are referenced for verisimilitude.

Milton Keynes UK
Ingram Content Group UK Ltd.
UKHW040628180124
436246UK00001B/8

9 781916 286573